NOVELS BY MAUREEN McCOY

Summertime
Walking After Midnight

DIVINING

BLOOD

Maureen McCoy

Poseidon Press

New York London Toronto Sydney Tokyo Singapore

POSEIDON PRESS

Simon & Schuster Building
Rockefeller Center
1230 Avenue of the Americas
New York, New York 10020

This book is a work of fiction. Names, characters, places and
incidents are either products of the author's imagination or are used
fictitiously. Any resemblance to actual events or locales or persons,
living or dead, is entirely coincidental.

POSEIDON PRESS is a registered trademark
of Simon & Schuster Inc.

POSEIDON PRESS colophon is a trademark
of Simon & Schuster Inc.

Designed by Chris Welch
Manufactured in the United States of America

1 3 5 7 9 10 8 6 4 2

Library of Congress Cataloging-in-Publication Data
McCoy, Maureen.
Divining blood / Maureen McCoy.
p.   cm.
I. Title.
PS3563.C352D58   1992
813'.54—dc20   91-40164
                              CIP
ISBN: 0-671-75065-8

*I am grateful to Toni Morrison
for the special encouragement and support
granted me as an Albert Schweitzer Fellow
in the Humanities at the State University
of New York at Albany.*

FOR PAUL

AND THERE ARE THREE THAT BEAR WITNESS
ON EARTH: THE SPIRIT AND THE WATER AND
THE BLOOD; AND THESE THREE ARE ONE.
—1 JOHN 5: 8

PART

ONE

THE SILVER SMILE, New Orleans, ringed all around them now that the tug was pushing mid-river. Out in front, six rust-red barges cruised steady and low as crocodiles. The *Pat Furey* plowed through frisky, suspect water: down here the Mississippi ran wild with salt as it muscled on into ocean, and river crews heading north, a little confused, as if whisked back from the finish line at the moment of jubilation, craved final flings and serious acts of bravado.

With the city at a gracious distance and the gulls drifting high, Captain Cheramie broke the rules of safety and convention. He raised an open champagne bottle against the September sky. He nodded at deckhands. "Everybody joins me." And men galumphed in their boots, grinned at the bottle and at the city with its muffled sounds and pea-sized perils, and at Delana Mae Walsh, who stood among them with a sleeping baby wrapped across her front in a sling. She chewed Black Jack gum with her mouth wide open.

"To Del Mae," Cheramie told the crew. His hand, like a root, held the sparkly bottle. More bottles lined the deck. "Now, at the end of her run, we can reminisce. Admit that in the beginning we thought we'd die from her pot pies. All we'd known were old women with plenty of cooking time, never any girl cook or TV dinners. Then," Cheramie said, making sure of the perfect attention around him, "she caught on to fixing biscuits and gravy, bless her, only to desert the galley completely. She took on the wheelhouse, didn't she. Girl *pilot* shamed people twice her size, locking us through smooth as a lie." He raised a glass. "I trained her right. Here's to my mate, Del Mae."

Cheramie paused to take a big drink. His voice rasped on against blue autumn air, harmonizing with the diesel engines below. Underneath, the river was shooting like rapids over sand, no rocks or natural barriers to stop it from rushing on down to flood and laze over his native bayou country.

"Let us not forget her pot pies," Cheramie called. His hair was wild as the river's dream: shocked-out fuzz, yellow-silver-brown, brushed straight back and still capering all over his scalp. "That first dinner, which we feared as death itself."

"She brought us through the worst electrical storm," a deckhand rejoined. "I'll remember that."

"Hey," men agreed, "she's been with us." They were a full double crew, eight deckhands and a sub each for captain and engineer. Used to twelve-hour shifts, everyone was awake for the sendoff and beaming as one.

A little hum preceded Delana's response: "I'm going out like the eels. Seven years on the river and all the eels rush home." She switched her long black hair, held at her neck by a piece of leather with a stick running through it. The ends waved over her shoulder blades. She fluttered her lashes but could not get a slithery effect from the periwinkle eyes. The newborn, an unmistakable girl, slept.

"Forget that eel talk," said Cheramie. "Seven is a gambler's number. A good luck number," he stressed with a sweep of the champagne bottle.

"It's the seven-year itch," she said, "when eels go off to mate."

"Well, that's been done," Cheramie said, and men laughed

and shuffled around, all but one: a big, redheaded, slouch-bodied man smitten from the start. Delana gave him the eye.

She said, "Johnny Red's a father." His moon face was as famously open as always, those blue prize-marble eyes on her, the mouth way, way too red inside, forming its little "o"—everything an impression of roundness, smoothed down and worked over as if by the river itself. His head sat squat, with nothing at all of a neck to support it; squat like a vase, and she had not cared to remark on this oddity during seven years up and down the Mississippi River—over two thousand miles long—traveling New Orleans to St. Paul day in and day out; thirty days on, thirty days off; nor had she asked for photos of relations; nor had she ever said, "Are there any true albinos in your clan?" And in the beginning she had requested only that he please put some suffering to the pronunciation of her name: go long and slow on the middle: "Say *aye*," she had sung, then told a blank-faced Johnny, "The religious version of my name is Magdalena."

She held the baby tight. A girl with no neck, now that could be a fatality, a very sad thing for a girl baby who already had half a chance of growing up too freckled for sun; who had struggled into being on a hot still day in a shotgun shack in Baywater, New Orleans, as Delana lay alone, the blaze of chartreuse walls so intense as to spill and fracture color. She went through the birthing, the whole howling buck of production, alone, clinging to the vision of yellow-green sequins dazzling the walls and bedsheets and even the darkness behind her eyes. A lone girl birthing a baby, it was from the shimmer of color that she divined a hope of survival. Sequins lavish only the living. You are not given sequins to look at in your final moments. You will not be flooded in disco light right before the end. She lost consciousness, strength and reason, but vowed a circus of protection for her girl, whose minnow body followed with a whoosh once her battering, bloody head made its way out into light. She had meant to have weeks more pregnancy ahead, ages of pregnancy, giving Johnny time to finish his run and get off the barge to come up home. Instead, she lay there alone, reading the sequins' ouija, hearing some kind of tremendous humming, and she passed out. Revived later by the medical team, she heard "Congratulations." And "Nixon just resigned."

Now here stood Johnny, faithful as the sun was harmful to him.

Delana was going off the river. Motherhood was putting her off the river. "And that's good," Captain Cheramie contended. "Twenty-four years old and you're already done with one whole epoch. You came on a runaway and turned into a cook. You went on to piloting. Now look at yourself: the mother of a fine baby girl."

So she was to pack up the years concerned with tonnage and the judging of currents, nighttime steerings and calculations that let you miss piers and every kind of submerged object. From somewhere on shore she would keep track of the river, not that you could call that distanced lulled interest keeping track. On shore, only by reading the river journal's news, printed weekly since Mark Twain days, would she learn, for instance, the outcome of the latest bizarre scheme: the mauling of paddlefish in order to make caviar. Paddlefish had sucked along the bottom of the river since the time of dinosaurs, and now this ugly trend: people splitting paddlefish guts to make caviar. In the river's long history this was just man's latest low dream.

"Del Mae," said Cheramie, "you're starting out your last run. Give us some kind of toast for the occasion."

Her sleek hair switching back and forth, she turned from Cheramie to the redheaded engineer. She said, "Goodbye, adios, Johnny." Everyone groaned.

"Something good!" Cheramie insisted.

She handed the sleeping baby to stout Opal, one of those old worn-out Memphis women known to cook up and down the river. She took Johnny's hand, which was smooth and did not show veins, and the two walked out on the main deck. They paused there, smiling, talking, and then Delana led Johnny up the stairs, her hair waving black over her shoulder blades, led him up to where guest quarters were housing them like a regular family of

Caribbean cruisers. Above that, the all-glass wheelhouse drew down the sun, and popcorn clouds tumbled the skies. And everyone followed out on deck to watch, as always with fascination and guilt, the business of a couple, their resident tugboating couple, still a pretty marvelous phenomenon in 1974. Old crewmen like Cheramie remembered the days of communal bunks. You *lived* with your crew. Late sixties, someone might have seen it coming: separate cabins, hello girls.

A low sun pricked at skin. People shielded their eyes, glassed from champagne, and smiled high at the couple, Johnny taking such slow bashful steps, his head nodding like that of a mechanical toy. The clacking of feet on metal, going up and up, lulled the crew. New Orleans lay behind them, just a low ring of glinting teeth now, and some of the gulls had fallen away. The tow was sleek, and long as a football field, and sculpted like a fancy white cake, each ascending tier set back, smaller than the one below. The winking-glass wheelhouse was a topknot ornament. On the second deck, Delana stood with one leg on the rail, looking down to the water. A slim, mid-height woman, she wore a pair of Johnny's pants hitched at the waist and rolled at the hem, and with the sun blotting everything from behind, she was a dark unrecognizable shape. Johnny was simply big. Delana's arms waving against the sky looked unusually long. Her hands with the fingers spread, each one outlined against that sky, held a funny rigid nervous appeal. Johnny, for no good reason, climbed on the rail—sat on it—and followed Delana's gaze. He nodded, maybe prayed, at that water so coyly dimpled. If anyone had looked at Opal he would have noticed the cook slightly extending her arms, offering that baby up to whatever conscience rode the high deck, in a flash of premonition miming, "Here's what counts. Look here."

Then that baby howled.

Suddenly Delana's arms flew forward and Johnny was sitting on air, and despite his size and weight, he fell through blue space light as a feather, and just as slow; falling and falling; and his body did not jerk or cringe or clutch or twist. He fell through the air in that sitting-on-the-rail position, the body sure that it deserved to sit; it would sit again. His hands held his knees, and his head jetted down.

"No, no!" people yelled as Johnny fell through space, the little horizon town of teeth unable to offer a grip. He hit the water with a tremendous smack. He went under and the brown water grew still. People stared at bubbles and rings. Then men scrambled after ropes and life jackets and the lowering of a raft. Opal clutched the baby and looked up. Delana was leaning over that rail, her hair snaking in the breeze, and she peered intently as anyone else at the water. She might have spoken to it as she stood there and looked just long enough to see Johnny Red bob to the surface. The father of her baby, a seven-year love, and she had thrown him off the tow. She looked up to watch a plane go by. And chewed that gum.

Johnny broke surface, good, but with a look on his face that drove an engine up men's spines: a wet fixed look of serenity. And waves rippled out from there. The men hauled him on board and whipped him with towels and threw dry pants at him, swearing, "Man, a gar could've bitten you in half!" His face made them crazy, that look more naked than a fish.

The men said saltwater had saved him, brought Johnny back up to surface. You have this happen in the upper river and he'd be dead. "Dead, man, you hear what we're saying?"

"She loves me," Johnny said.

Some kind of thanks.

"Opal, bring me the baby?" Delana called from her high perch.

"For what?" shrieked the older woman. "Nincompoop, for what?"

"Just bring her on up."

Opal scurried forward with the baby, her bad hip jerking.

"You threw Johnny over."

"Love makes me drastic," Delana told her, taking the baby. "Tell me how else was I going to leave him? How else, Opal, but give him to the river?" She bent to kiss her baby.

"Don't you put that ugly mouth on your child. It's all black from your gum." Opal clanged down the metal steps. Indignation shook her plump arms. Her apron flew.

She told people, "She's got a long way to go."

"Go to jail," someone called loud, for Delana's ears.

Opal crossed her arms on a low-riding bosom and stepped back from the men. "The hormones will drive a new mother. Believe me, they will drive her."

"Ummm," said Captain Cheramie. He had worn his shirt with epaulets for this occasion but looked just as helpless as the other men considering Opal's decree.

At dinnertime Delana came back on deck. She was wearing the baggy pants (why?), with a great red sash holding them up. She came to the mess hall with the baby, and Opal (in cahoots, that was clear) served her an enormous platter of food. Breakfast food!

Delana chowed down.

What the hell? men said with their eyes. Opal stood behind the ravenous Delana, mouthing, "Postpartum."

If after all the other business there could be a worse thing, it was Delana's appetite. Unholy appetite that the old cook was stoking with glee. What had come over this woman wearing men's pants and eating with her elbows out, insisting on breakfast food at six P.M.? She devoured buttermilk pancakes and was sopping up egg, puncturing yolks, which was bad enough, but the spearing of link sausage you could definitely do without. It made men sick. Someone grumbled that he'd like sausage *patties* for a change. Opal's cackle shut him right up.

Delana finished eating and went over into a blank stare, the keen clear stare of a pilot watching dawn break. Men tried to sip their coffee quietly. When the baby sent up a cry, Delana answered, "That's right. Thunder at me." And then—insult beyond redemption, fight you could not call—she popped free the breast. Men lowered their goo-goo eyes just as fast as anything, but who could manage the dread that ran in their veins? The minute that breast popped out they were no longer men to her, just posts, dull nothings, and the shame and surprise of that fact sank them: men who had been tattooed at length without flinching; men back from bombing the green earth of Asia; big guys who, late at night, at the tense and boring end of a run, while feeling the fear that men feel on knowing they will be hitting shore now and thirty days with a woman lies ahead or thirty days of nothing special, admitted they had done some bad things to women. With shore rushing up blue-black, a guy would turn to a buddy, be full of panic and shame and the excitement of shore life too, then just go ahead and admit to having lived like a TV show, where at the conclusion of the story you're sorry as Jesus but glad you got that drama in first. Belts and kitchen knives had sung. *I know it.* Hell, things have happened. *To me too.*

The point was, you get on the river to stay clear of certain things: mowing lawns and Saturday shopping for kids' shoes. You don't get hooked into women's orders and sorrows. You are here to stay free of the traps. But now the *Pat Furey* had baby smell blown all through it. The tow was blown through with talcum and sweet oil and the skin fragrance of a baby. Zingy light filled the crew's minds. Talcum and velvet skin and mother's milk were staggering aromas.

And in high times like these, Cheramie goes pure Cajun on you. His voice has already hushed down to tell about places in this world where the little lost babies gather, places in the dark woods filled with dead-baby spirit—there's nowhere else for them to be—and you do not go into the dark woods there, the little *duennes* with their tiny turned-in feet, howling, died without baptisms, and they howl in the woods where the spirit lies thick in warm night air all year round. Used to be some in the bayou, he said, down Bayou LaFourche, but there's been too much plowing up of the land, and anyway, it's more an island thing. You bet the *duennes* call "Sister" to the new unclaimed soul. She calls right back to the other side, which she has no reason yet to fear.

Baloney.

But still you make a pact: don't let the baby trance you with
that howl. Go on and shave, trying not to look too closely at your
face or you're liable to see your original pinkness, and who needs
it? Well, in a few days they would put Delana off exactly where
she came on in the first place.

Best to remember the good times.

After the early cooking frights she had run the *Pat Furey* up
and down the river, locking in fine under all conditions. They
had loved her that tough. Little girl could keep on, her eyes lit
with the thrill. And they had even loved her melon look in pregnancy. Remember the slow syrup in her voice, her absorption in
listening. Her hair grew streaks red as Johnny's. They celebrated
her changes in those last months even as Johnny Red went
around with that doomed dreamy look of a man tarred over by
love. Damn if he didn't start walking slow, and did his belly grow,
poor fool? Now men were reminded: John Melody has lost his
tune. Girl working the tow, it had finally come to grief.

JOHNNY CAME FROM the bathroom wearing boxer shorts.

"You're so fresh and strong," Delana cried. "You had no idea, dumpling. You're invincible."

"I could have died," he said.

"I did you a favor," she swore. "You can feel your own strength. It's more than you thought."

"Next time you want to see strength, give me barbells."

"I'm worn out too. The revelation killed me."

You could not convince a man that, together, his newborn and woman had tossed him to the river for his own good, in a kind of helpless fit of understanding and resolve. In the baby's scream Delana had heard a *yes*. Give Johnny the river wholly and absolutely. Give him his heart. Let him know strength. So came the glorious push.

Flopped down, unable to budge, she wiggled her toes to make sure something worked. Splitting up, she and Johnny needed faith, but what it was and how you got it, she wasn't sure, knowing only that drama figured. Baby Robin had arrived just like the miracle of television and dreams: an unasked-for wildness, a surprise; and just as with early TVs and the least-formed dreams, the baby transmitted only in black and white. Of all that the doctor said, this is what struck Delana mad: The baby sees only in black and white. She must grow into the wild Crayola hues: the burnt siennas, brick reds, and blue-violets of dream and desire. So Delana festooned the cabin to hurry her along. The room looked nothing like the same dark-paneled cell where an inspector rode two weeks a year. She had tacked up pinwheels and streamers, things that would move gently in the breeze of an open window. Baby Robin lay sleeping on the bed, her face a perfect pearl, and her marbly arms poked from a sheaf of red felt. Silver edging gave away its former use as a Christmas tree skirt.

Johnny pulled on his jeans. His amazing whiteness of chest, the carroty little forest of hair, caused Delana to hide a smile. His pure ballast, even if his chest pooched in a way that gave his nipples a sad, downcast gaze, was such a fine thing on a man. Soft and sturdy all at once, that was Johnny. Considering the whole field of nearly invisible hair that covered his great slab back, and Johnny's light but confused movements, she wanted to believe he *was* his favorite constellation, the bear come down from dark, like magic, not quite earthbound. His feet had never touched mud. In his long river life, Johnny's feet had never touched mud.

"I can't move, I'm exhausted," she said. "It's a good thing I'm on the water, or I wouldn't move at all."

"Could have died," Johnny muttered at his zipper.

His splashdown had scared some eels, that was all. She had seen streaks of silver flip up to the side of him. Eels looked up toward light and dimly saw a man hurtling toward their den. Oh, if only they had teeth, that's what they were thinking. They wanted to bite and bite, sex raging on their minds. "Imagine," she said, caressing Robin's bald head, "losing your baby teeth and no new ones come in. It's crazy for eels. It's backward."

"Nuts," Johnny said, swatting a T-shirt through the air. "Both of us."

Delana ran her teeth over the back of her hand. Any baby eels around, they would have bitten him. Then what? All the stronger he would be. Johnny had outraged some toothless eels, big deal. "If you'd come up and just swam away toward shore instead of facing the boat, forget it," she said. "I'd never speak to you again."

"I'm taking you to your father without a fight."

"That's right. I'll show him this baby," she said. "I'll hand him a baby."

"A good husband takes you home with a baby. What else am I supposed to do to convince you? Marry me."

Come home, Daddy wrote after hearing the baby news. Two words on lined lavender paper. With this baby, guilt and shame were completely bled out of her, completely, Delana thought; seven years of silence is over. It's why I'm so woozy, so extra woozy.

"Hitting the water nearly ripped my face off."

Johnny was in no mood to quit, but his eyes were all over that baby with questions and love. You could not ask a riverman to leave his domain. With help, though, he might figure out a way.

Streaking bold colors from the pinwheels at the window filled the room, and Johnny loomed in and out of view, taking up the tiny cabin with the extremes of love and fear. And dropping into Delana's mind was a great picture of eels. What is sleeker and uglier than a toothless eel? "A single female eel lays twenty thousand colorless eggs. How does she feel? I wonder. How worn out is she?"

"Eels," Johnny said through his very definite teeth. "They're nothing." But such facts awed him; such information Johnny had always been eager to share with her. He looked out the window, trying to keep those teeth clenched, a man who goes weak on river lore.

Now, in fall, eels and more eels were mowing their way south out of the brown flood, going home. Delana could imagine them underneath this boatload of men, swimming like mad. Grown up, turned toothless, seven years old, suddenly they stop eating. They stop and gather, and in those murky water canyons they spend hours blinking and mourning in a gossipy group, trying to think what comes next. What is missing? they wonder. Then passion sears their eel brains. They fly through river water to the sea, every one of them female, these river eels, and at the sea they find the man eels of their same generation, who have been, typically, drifting off the edge of the continent. The man eels' eyes have doubled in size, they want mating so bad. Big eyes. That's all they can show for love. Until the females attack. And Johnny's eyes were big and blue as the sea itself.

"Could have died," he kept up.

Her voice snapped. "You'd die going off the river, remember. That's the point. That's the common belief."

"Honey, marry me," Johnny said, flailing the T-shirt. "And look at me, please, Delana, when I say it. They'll think I'm a prick up there in Illinois, bringing home an unwed mother. Say yes. We can get off the water anywhere along the way."

He went dreamy with possibilities. Why not stop at Memphis or Cairo? he wondered. Or they could choose a funky town, an unknown, the way they liked to do, and go scouting for a ring, a big rock ring for her, something so encrusted with fake jewels the true heart of the matter would shout through and shame anyone who gawked or teased. For himself, Johnny vowed to wear a crimson tie. The plan would be this: dock and hang out until a very late, desperate hour. Very, very late, he insisted, holding Delana's shoulders now. Real late, they would thread past the hubbub of taprooms, shoeshines, photo booths, bail bond hawkers, and the appreciative crowd that goes with, to raise the justice of the peace with some hell's-loose kind of knocking.

"Seeing the baby, he'll marry us, no questions asked," Johnny claimed.

And did he have a witness lined up too? Delana teased lazily.

Would a sound-asleep baby pass for a witness, or would the blood relation—she liked saying it and repeated "*our* blood relation" —be asked to leave, pretend still to be unborn?

He said, "His wife will be in hair curlers, ugly and furious. She'll give you dragon looks before, during, and after. I'll mention a honeymoon bash and completely turn her stomach."

Here was Johnny begging for the right romance of it. His favorite picture of them was taken in a mid-size southern town, up the street from the port in front of a pawnshop with the most extraordinary display of hanging guitars, their laminated speckles catching light: guitars shaped, colored, and posed as if to define sexual attraction once and for all. Above their heads the window was lit in neon: UNREDEEMED BARGAINS. Together and smiling, she and Johnny stood, taunting land life.

"Dumpling, I've already done the most romantic thing, and it's just worn me out." Her head fell back on the mound of pillows, leaving her blank throat cocked toward Johnny's ruminating eyes. Her heavy eyes fluttered and closed, then fixed as slits on Johnny. He trundled this way and that, a figure from a child's book: the gentle bull who would suffer the bee sting; the mother bear surprised to find a child with a pail of blueberries following behind her; all the stories her own mother, Dovie, had read. Neither Johnny nor Delana had said the words for nine months: *What next?* It was too much to think of, life beyond baby Robin's arrival. Now she was here. Baby Robin is here: mottled, smush-faced baby with surprise lungs. And life is spinning, breaking up, and Johnny does not comprehend. She wanted him on his knee, yes, but to babble of fantastic change: "The current flows north!" To effect it. Instead, that life of river-watching had taught him to keep on the watch. It looked to all the world as if she were leaving Johnny, when in fact he, suffering the superstitions all rivermen have of a dead life on land—the air there knits itself around you, chokes off rational thought and action; the trees are too tall, blocking out light, making observations like *That's an easterly wind* meaningless; the dust and cement underfoot wear away the spirit's movement—he, Johnny, would do the deserting. Nobody says, "Johnny, you could leave the river." The words to form that thought are knocked so far back in the head, in the history, the life, Johnny's response could only be stupefaction.

Her eyes closed heavily now. Imagine the man who will surely swear fidelity on the grave of a mother he never knew, then he runs off for one entire journey of the moon. A month passes and he shows up again, all rustly with river smell, suspicious and claiming things he has no right to claim. "Where did that chair come from?" he'll wonder. "You say company sits in it? What company?" Imagine a wretched month of teething; now comes Johnny, and all he sees is the gleam of tooth. Thirty days on, thirty days off, was the river schedule. Love's typical bad arithmetic.

"Married men come back on board crazy," she reminded Johnny. "They slip in their own mop buckets; they run the barge aground."

Johnny's chest was glow-in-the-dark white, strong, just soft enough: the finest pillow she had ever known, a comfort on dark river nights when love threatens to cross over into panic. But the baby was even whiter. Little moon, its whiteness and tugging mouth dimmed all other light; dazed her; made it easy to say, remarkably easy—sweet and *toothy*—to say, despite the sidelong beckoning look of his chest, "You go on, Johnny. You'll just go on."

"She's my baby too."

"And she knows it. We didn't make a dumb baby. She's three weeks old and her body is like a brainy sponge. Touch her anywhere and she knows it's you. And by the time we get her up to Illinois she's going to know more about this river—in baby code, some deep baby code—than we can imagine." This had to be true.

Johnny could not help but go soft. He had taught her to recognize the fragrance of green corn a mile before you saw it and the glug sound of a deer slipping in for a midnight swim. "You think so? In her little head maybe she hears fish voices?"

he asked cautiously. He rubbed at his clipped red beard, thick and fine, not a single gray hair. When he paled for deep thinking, freckles came out like the stars. His dreamer heart could not resist such lore: the sounding between innocents, why not? "I guess a baby could be like those tiny whales, the little pilot whales with radar in their heads. Honey, that soft spot on her head bothers me. I notice how it moves when she eats."

Low sun in the cabin had settled on Johnny, raising his chest hairs to burnished gold. She drew back from the little girl dolled up in felt. "Watch her," she told Johnny. She went to her desk drawer and took out a box of brilliant paper stars. She came back licking a pink one, then pressed it to the baby's forehead.

"Honey?" said Johnny.

"Just between us. Just for now." She stood back. Before Johnny knew what, licked little stars of all colors were being pasted to his chest. He was ticklish like all people in love, and he tried to hug himself and turn away, but Delana, so sluggish moments earlier, was swift. Leaving her, her man must look like no other. He must look like a holiday, or neither would survive.

"I look crazy," Johnny said, grinning, and he went sunset red in the face. She finished him off by lifting her blouse and starring her breast emerald green.

Now her eyes were closing back down. Johnny sat carefully on the bed and leaned over her, touching her shoulders, then her arms, lightly. Where do I touch now, anyway? she sensed he was asking.

Right off, she had gone for this man who was twice her size, roly-poly big, twenty-four to her willow-boned seventeen, the black night pressing them together. But waking near dawn that first morning with him, Johnny already gone, she remembered his whispering night chant: "I love you." And before cracking three dozen eggs for omelets, she ran down to the engine room and caught him loving his engines: hand bracing one's chugging rump; the other engine receiving a luxuriant chamois massage. His shirt was out, betraying the whiteness of a redhead's back. A cloud separated his upper and lower self, showing off the pure and insubstantial nature of love. She cried, "You're so white you're ugly. You're too big. You're as old as my sister." Though Marcia, she remembered, was already twenty-five. She warned, "Stay there," as Johnny turned. He said, "I'm the same by day as I was last night. I'm the same." She accused him of making this up out of a magazine. "But I love you," he said. In front, his shirt had stayed tucked. In a flash she thought: A redheaded man on the river knows more than all the rest. He's going to feed my heart.

Now he searched her face for guidance. "You're going on shift," she said. She brought Johnny's head low on her neck, down farther to the star. He looked up, questioningly, that one indent on his forehead passing for a worry line. His eyes bugged out like a bachelor eel's.

"A taste," she said, which she felt, upon its commencement, actually did touch her heart's blood.

Then he was leaving, paused in the doorway, bursting with a looming helplessness that had nothing at all to do with being the *Pat Furey*'s chief engineer. He was confused and wildly gratified, but self-rebuking—a man with pasted stars on his chest.

"You still live with a runaway's heart," he blustered. "I've expected us to last. And," he added, "I could have died."

With Johnny gone, she lay still and sought out the river's mood. On such a large vessel, a triple screw with ten thousand horsepower, capable of hauling seventeen tons of coal, everything was so steadied that it took a near capsizing to actually feel the rolling of water beneath. Fifty feet of water they were slicing through. Lie there still, and even the most experienced river rat—deckhand or pilot—might miss the current's thought, its nasty plan to rush you into a flood bank or, as now, the clear channel beeping that was sweetly urging, Relax, move along. And beneath that, maybe, a giggle. The slightest giggle came from way down below.

She raised up and looked out the window on the last lights of

New Orleans. In early September, by sunset, the waterskiers and fishermen let their craft list toward shore. Wide low marshes shelter ducks, and muskrats plunk down off the levees. The ugly eel, Anguilla, races in dark water. In the upper river, leaves are breaking out in color. Driving on the river was a small nothing compared with touching its mud heart. The baby drew her on up home. There she would douse her hot new-mother hands.

She lay back down and pulled the yellow shades. Even from a thousand miles away she could feel her father sitting right there on the sweep of Illinois yard that rolled up to delirious heights: her daddy, Dr. Skylar Walsh. Whenever the *Pat Furey* sawed up and down the river past that stretch, she knew he felt its glide. He would be unable to spot her way out there in the channel as he lifted his head from bush-trimming, or his bees, to see way down that roll of lawn what looked like a bathtub toy pushing barges the length of a riverside town before it; yet he saw her. Whenever she got close, got past Cairo, came up on Hannibal, smelled Keokuk, something like cottonwood fluff blew through her. Her mother was dead six years, and her daddy was taken care of by his second wife. Doctor marries his nurse: it is an old story made new to the individual lives affected, and of course that was none of her business, not one bit, she said. Here's my baby; I'm bringing a baby girl off this water. He said, *Come home*. She clamped Robin to her breast, where no daddy belonged in dream life or memory, and they would fall asleep together. Sleep seemed like the mind's innocent vacation, an act of faith purer even than sending Johnny off that rail. Oh, her hands tingled, though: they loved to touch love; but she knew best its hot backside. Like now, she just had to resurrect the tongue of Daddy when—look—it was only little Robin there, sucking sweet.

She pictures them, Johnny and all the men, how they mutter and curse, wonder and scratch. Then see how easily they give that up to sleep. And letting go of the day, they cannot know that in the night the baby will be a stunned emergency, an inflammation in her mind. In the morning, she will barely remember how she rocked her baby in the night, diapered her, set her down again, a black guiding fear all around. Exhaustion is total. Of course a mother's first deep fear comes in the night: your utter fear, your complete helpless terror. In the night a new mother drifts on a planet of nerved doom (Mars red, Delana determines from the vapors swirling her mind), while Johnny's chest rises and falls in the wavelike rhythms that guide all normal sleeping hearts, and he twinkles from those stars pasted to him. Even in sleep the man is all blazoning hope, his breathing a gigantic release. He is a naked redhead incapable of tricks.

She will float away into sleep, feeling her heart beating beyond, over there: baby in the cradle. She will not call it two hearts yet, not in the night anyway. (Say moon, if anything. You are my moon, baby girl.) She is sweaty, not dreaming, and she drifts in a sleep of swords in which a baby cry or a snuffle rings out red. The night runs on, a deep blank question down the river. She is learning why the earth itself ranges round in flood and fire and volcanic heavings. Mother mother to all, it gets so tired of use.

It is time, always time, to feed the baby, and on the planet of nerved doom Delana will stir in faint memory of her own parents, think how it might have been that her own unwanted newborn voice froze them. They laid her down, and they just walked away. She believes she has this crib memory, when the air was scented a charming vanilla. There, baby. Bye, baby. Sleep.

She moves to the window with Robin. Midnight is Baton Rouge's most wondrously ugly hour. The sky is raving and men below are in conniptions. They call this stretch Cancer Alley, where plumes of red-yellow poison crush beautifully against black sky. All around, land is squat with luminous silos, armatures of hideous proportions, and from great high spouts and spigots bloom tremendous flowers: torrid roses and lily tongues of such length the men below roar their love. A night passage under this wild, chemical sky has always meant the luck of long life. Men swear it. Let the sleeping baby reap that. Delana steps out, gives

the baby a brief shot of raw air. Cheramie, below, has gone tour
guide for the men: "Ummm, benzene—we love it. Right over
there, a million plastic forks are being made, how nice. And
armrests for your car, ain't you glad? We love benzene."

Her heart beats outside herself and surely her own mother's
did too. (Did your nipples hurt so, Mother? Did the orange poop
shock you?) The benzene sky touches hard and waters the eyes.
Young vets glitter under it, and one named Hank has told her,
This is the closest you come to being an angel. He had floated
over blistering Asian earth, surely an act deserving his induction
into the permanent divinity of the unharmed. Here's God talking
big, he has said at Cancer Alley. Make a wish, man. Fast now,
spit above your head and make a wish.

I N FOURTH GRADE Delana had started wondering, What about Sally? At school the chair across from her remained empty. A boy had died. *Meningitis* was written on the board. The teacher stressed the funeral's privacy, that the class would not attend. Looking at that empty seat, Delana could see exactly where the boy's shoulders had rested against that little chair: his blue plaid collar, his red hollyhock ears. Little sister Sally, who died before Delana's birth, was never recovered from the river, and it seemed as likely that they had buried in her place a bony little chair.

When her sister came home for a weekend, Delana asked, "What about Sally's funeral? What was it like?"

Marcia was holding a gown to her front. It was shiny blue and made a noise like wrapping paper. She flounced on her bed. "Sally's funeral was very . . . pure," she decided.

The sisters shared a room upstairs; really it was half the house, with walls knocked down. This was an arrangement, an addition their mother had overseen practically the minute Delana could walk. Here was a place for sisters to be, with their eyes trained on each other even in the dark, never mind that one lived away most of the year. The girls had their own bathroom, and the wood walls were left exposed, smelling sharply green, unlike the rest of the plushy house. The old river captain's home rose up from the central Illinois banks of the Mississippi River on a lawn as high-breasted as a holiday turkey. The family lived shaded by oaks and catalpas, and Delana in summer would perch in the mulberry tree with its squishy buglike fruit and watch the water below.

Because she had grown skittery after that day on the boat, Marcia was sent to the special attention of the Nauvoo nuns, downriver thirty miles, where she remained for all her school years, never mind the family's vague Protestant history. St. Agnes Academy for Girls enjoyed no corresponding boys' Catholic school. That's how serious the nuns were about girls.

At home this Saturday, Marcia had spent hours sorting nail polishes and jeweled barrettes, forbidden fruits at St. Agnes. The year was 1960, and she wore her beatnik clothes, head-to-toe black, and it was impossible to know that soon she would be married. Right out of high school she would be married and thickened at her waist and calling, "Jack, Ja-a-a-ck, will you listen?"

A wide stretch headband brought her face forward all the more, with her brush-bubble hair pushed up and away. When she laughed she became all teeth and eyes, and her light freckles matched her hair. A senior at the Catholic school, she was philosophical.

"Remember, there was nothing to look at, Delana. Sally's coffin held nothing. They weighted it with flowers all over the top, but you knew that it was empty. They had six pallbearers anyway, and they suffered on their red faces for the lack of weight. I didn't know then what was wrong, but their faces—their pretending—is what made me cry. I remember Mother whispering, 'Picture her happy in her favorite blue velvet dress.' And I squealed, 'Not in summer, Mama!' And Mother had to throw a hankie over her face."

Marcia threw up her hands. "Afterwards we came home and ate like pigs. Whole cakes, slabs of ham. Pure salt and sugar. That's what we needed." She looked around the room. She grabbed up her evening gown again. "Luckily we don't have to be children forever. Oh, poor Delanie, you're so young." Then she was twirling and twirling with that dress held to her front, twirling as only a big girl could do. Meanwhile, a boy sat downstairs waiting, with his waxed animal hair pushing a sharp smell into the cushions.

"I'm responsible, Delanie. No one else around here *talks*. You're older than Sally ever got to be, remember, and I have to teach you everything." Marcia pulled out a drawer and grabbed a whole collection of brassieres. She threw them—live things—onto her bed and giggled. She held up a red lace one, and Delana was startled to realize where the idea of valentines came from. The bra had no straps, so all along the edges you traced the rise and fall of a wave.

"Hey, Marcia, we're just like the Beaver Cleaver family except with girls. The same ages. Hi, Wally. Say it, say I'm the Beaver."

"Oh?" Marcia's laugh was quick, adult. "Well, yes, sure, Beaver. Hi. Four of them, four of us. But Ward and June are such idiots."

They heard their mother climbing the stairs. At home Dovie did not wear her nylons; she wore anklets with strapped-on shoes of a kind that kept something penitential in the walk: high heels pushed her twiggy body back away from you. Delana wondered if at a certain age you just said, "Now I prefer to be totally uncomfortable."

"Knock, knock," Dovie called out, getting near the top. "Marcia, honey, your date is waiting."

Marcia ran to the stairwell waving an open lipstick, which satisfied Dovie into a clip-clopping retreat. From downstairs came the sounds of Sky's toy train in operation. It ran throughout the house. Tracks shook, bells clanged. Everyone leaned to the sound of the train making its way through the kitchen and the long hallway.

A funny-pitched voice said, "That's a coal car."

Marcia puffed up her cheeks full of air and then popped them loudly. "Ding-dong, Jack Rose calling."

Marcia claimed that the bug-eyed look their mother wore, as if her eyes were weird indestructible goggles protecting the real thing, had not always been so. "I remember how she used to look, before she saw the one thing that no mother can bear to see, Delanie. Her child just—poof—disappeared. It's like the river took her eyes. No, she never used to look like a poison bug from a movie. Huh-uh, she never did before."

Marcia quickly applied the lipstick at hand. "I'll do your hair," she said, shrugging dramatically toward the downstairs. She pulled free the ribbons and had to hold Delana's head tight under one palm in order to brush through the long thick hair that lay, unbanded, like a pair of shiny dog ears. "Let me wet the brush."

Marcia continued the story—oh, the story! The only story that Delana prayed to hear end, "They danced by the light of the moon, the moon, the moon. They danced by the light of the moon."

Sally was four years old when they lost her, Marcia seven, and despite the many codes and secret exchanges that went on every day between them, despite their Woody Woodpecker finger-printing kits that had arrived in the mail just that morning, eight weeks after cereal boxtops had been sent in, on that family boat Marcia had remained as helpless as an adult.

"Of course Mother blames him for everything," Marcia said, brushing. She sat cross-legged on her bed. She had lit little incense cones that turned the room smoky and foreign. "The only man on the boat, a doctor, no less, and he couldn't save his little girl from the Mississippi River." Not that he didn't try, she conceded. Marcia swore she saw Sky take four steps on the water "*in his thongs*" before flubbering down, and that a scary politeness seized Dovie. "Sky. Now, Sky," she had called in her tiniest warbler's voice.

"Dovie and Sky," Marcia concluded, "they're hopeless!"

She said anyone could tell by their parents' names that they were only semi-earthlings, skimming their toes in real life, and it was standard knowledge along this stretch of river that Dovie lived on a cloud and that Sky couldn't keep the peace with his stethoscope, so he took up silly hobbies.

"Beekeeping, and playing with a puppet! And by the way," she said, "thank our doctor father for never letting us have a decent Fourth of July, not once."

True, every single Independence Day the wounded came up the hill, right off the river, with fingers burned from firecrackers or the blood of a drunk running out a bare toe; skins were blistered by the sun suddenly chilling folks to death at dusk in their motorboats. They would come on, holding stomachs explosive with spice, dessert, and beer. Or a wife might appear, kneading her arms, having just broken down over marshmallow-roasting or because of "The Star-Spangled Banner," desperate to confess that it was on these blue-sky days, with everyone waving a flag and the tuba going, that she realized what a terrible thing loneliness was and how much of it she'd got and how her family was strictly from Mars. Dr. Skylar Walsh would give such a woman salt pills and turn the full sense of his looming green eyes on her. Skylar Walsh—Doctor Sky to the kids—would put down his own barbecue mitt for any one of his neighbors and tend a hurt on the spot, then send him off to revel some more. Or, if he needed to take a person into his office in town, fine; there he would strap an old-fashioned lamp to his forehead and look very much like a concerned Captain Kangaroo.

"He just loves penance," Marcia charged, loving the word with her mouth. "He does all this stuff for people, but he lost Sally. The only man on the boat that day, her father—Lord Jesus, a doctor!—and he couldn't save Sally from the Mississippi River."

She said Sally's disappearance just confirmed the old notion that the Mississippi River, unlike all others, will not permit a drowned person's body to rise. And that's what the mourning doves are all about. She said, "Call it the River of St. Jude. I'm surprised the explorer Jesuits didn't."

They kept the pictures taken on that day: Sally in a swimsuit that tied up around her neck and ruffled over her bottom like a young duck's growth, a frill that could not save her. There were large polka dots all over that suit, shouting dots. "White on navy," said Marcia, who had sat on the boat touching knees with Sally. She was born three years before Sally and could remember when they brought her home, a baby, from the hospital, and how her head was acutely pointed. *Soft head, scary.* That worked itself out, but of course, Marcia said, Sally had been marked. That day on the boat, why had Sky done it, why, why had he mentioned his Miss Steinbach? *Two curse words: Miss Steinbach.* Why on a boat would you mention your nurse's upcoming salary raise? "Celery, yuck," cried Sally. Stumped by phonetic mystery, she spoke a child's last words. "What would Miss Steinbach want with a bigger celery?" Then she stood and made great propellers of her arms. She flipped over the side of the boat and was gone, gone down. "She went down to God, which," Marcia said, "is not the natural direction. She hit something instantly. You didn't even see a hand flutter.

"But it was an ascension," she affirmed with the boarding-school gleam in her eye. When she had been new to St. Agnes, a nun found Marcia parading alone with a crown of wild rose bramble on her head. She hadn't bothered to remove the buds, and some bees were swarming the air. There she was, a child revealing the wonder and pain and faith in being. She could be heard calling, "Where are you, Jesus? Hello, Mother of God?" honeybees fluttering gold above her head. The lurking nun called Dovie. She swore, "I have just spied a vocation."

"Sally's reaction was . . . I think it was inspired. She was only four years old but ready to die. It was awful to see, but just think of the good part, Delanie. She ascended. Sally ascended into heaven." Marcia shuddered and clenched the bedspread they sat on, gorgeous, but to Delana it felt rough and dry, like cotton balls. "Look at yourself, Delanie, so solemn."

"Go on," Delana said, not wanting to stop the story, in love with the way Marcia's turtleneck came right up and cupped her face. The stem, the flower . . . Marcia closed her eyes for a long time, owing to the difficulty of continuing.

No ghost story could compare to what Marcia knew, Marcia with her brown eyes and brown hair spiked gold with belief. The way she would curl up and move her face to the words, her freckles offering unfathomable clues. For ages after, incense would seem to Delana like the major ingredient of understanding, the illumination drug. Her breathing was stuffy and her eyes teary. Marcia did not need darkness for effect. When she paused with the brush held high, Delana's heart slammed her chest.

"Stretch time," Marcia said, springing off the bed.

Delana was made to go to the window and look down to the blank river. Depending on the mood, there it was, pocky or in a bluster, but never still, and it gave cause to the life all around it, allowed the land to be particularly alive with insect life and small swift snakes who would not know of their ability to frighten humans; it banked a legion of bullfrogs, who gained in their lovelorn valor after dark, just like anyone, calling, "Jug of rum, jug of rum." An alligator of a barge was gliding along in the far channel.

"Marcia, you really think Sally knew what she was doing?"

"In a way," Marcia said. "Yes."

Below, that barge was gliding by, and a frog seemed trapped in Delana's heart. "She sacrificed herself. Is Sally a saint?" she asked her big sister. Sometimes now Marcia left behind her religious books and movie magazines rich in bust cream ads.

Delana might have been a boyfriend, judging from the gleam on Marcia's face, the new harshness in her voice. "Exactly right. That's perfect. We'll call sister Sally a *virgin martyr*." Marcia hugged herself and pushed her broad headband back farther, making a heart of her face. She slapped on bottled holy water, which Delana was disallowed, the parents keeping her as unchurched as they strictly pushed Marcia to it.

In Marcia's books Delana had read that the virgin martyrs were the bravest, bloodiest, most spectacular lovely girls in church history, girls with the courage to stab themselves through the heart or gouge out their own eyes: "Die, die, pretty ones. Die rather than *succumb*," Marcia had said with the glitter of her own wildness rushing from her lips to spangle the vast woody room. Delana looked at Marcia's wall, which displayed felt pennants, their tails up like dolphins'.

"Will you tell the nuns?" she wanted to know.

Marcia frowned and ran her tongue over her lips, licking off the color. "Hmmm. That's a good question."

"It'd be neat if Sally got added to the saints' book."

"Well, of course, Delanie . . . let me think. . . . You see, it takes proof of three miracles. That drags on forever. People come forth with vicious protests. . . ." Marcia shook her head. "No, we'll live with the secret of her bravery, baby." She suddenly made apparent her full-breastedness, hugging Delana from behind. "This secret knowledge will bind us as sisters. I'm telling you, it was a rapturing farewell.

"But imagine." Marcia hissed in the sweet-smelling room, moving to sit in front of Delana. "The only man on the boat, a doctor, no less, and he couldn't save his little girl from the Mississippi River. Of course Mother blames him."

Marcia sat so still now, her black velveteen Capri pants banded tight on her white calves. Delana followed her example. She breathed in and out with great exaggeration, pushing forward her flat chest. The incense required this. She kept her eyes flutteringly closed, so she could still glimpse Marcia but do right by the incense. She kept inside her straining chest the awfulness of the frog frenzy, the dark clanging question that kicked in her heart: Who do you like best, Marcia? Me or Sally? Who is your real sister, Marcia? I'm only here because Sally is not, right? I was born because Sally died.

Marcia sprang off the bed and gathered up the dress. It rattled and shone. "I'm off to the dance," she said, "but first I'm going with Jack to the drive-in, and tonight's movie," she said, positively smacking her lips, "is censored by the Church."

. . .

Marcia came home for the summer.

"Take me out there," Delana asked immediately. "Take me out to where she drowned, please."

"No, baby," said Marcia, "we're all through with that. You couldn't force me on that river. Ugh. Jack Rose could not get me on that water." Marcia had foam all over her legs. A faint bubbling noise signified the killing of hair. She wiped away the dead hair with squares of tissue.

"Describe the spot, Marcia. It's past the chorus line willows but not so far as the witch cypress, right?"

"Ummm, yeah. It's around there."

She would find it by herself, then. Delana had hung around the Lanier boys, Dillworth and Waldeen, to get the knack of ripping life from an outboard motor, and she would go anywhere she pleased on that river. The two-tone boat looked the same as from the old photographs. It had been perfectly preserved since that day. The family had brought it home hitched to the car as always, because what else would you do after a drowning, just jump out of your own boat and run, leave it there to knock around and be a worse kind of ghost? Skylar Walsh drove himself and Dovie and Marcia home, turned the car backward in the circle drive as he would after any event, backed the boat into its garage, slammed the door on the killer, and that was that.

So there was Delana ten years later, after all that, boat thoroughly greased and gone over. Dovie and Sky, with their fans and picture books out, operated on the assumption that lightning never strikes the same place twice; they were calm, nearly joyous. Whenever the only waterborne Walsh came home windburned and walking with her hips gone wide, their smiles were explosions of pride.

"You named me for the Magdalene Mary," Delana announced with a ten-year-old's flourish. "I found my patron saint in Marcia's book. Mary Magdalene's her name, and her birthday's coming up July twenty-second. I want a cake for her with candy hearts set in white frosting."

"Now, catkin." Sky's little name for her. "Marcia is a special case, and Mary Magdalene had her own problems."

"I've named the boat M&M."

Smiling and smiling. They could not stop loving the evidence: see the girl who will not drown. She cannot. They didn't notice how miniature she was, a girl with legs like pulled taffy.

"You might want to learn water-skiing," Sky even suggested, up and pacing with his hands in his pockets. His hair had been silver-dollar rich ever since Delana could remember. "I wish I could teach you the ropes, Delanie. Say, get those Lanier boys to give you a whirl. Those river rats know what they're doing."

And though it wasn't absolutely unheard of at her age, the sight was uncommon enough: a girl just out of fourth grade driving her own boat up and down the Mississippi River, standing up to steer, a browned tube of girl with her braids racing back. It was the kind of innocent audacity of spirit that made the adults turn away. But no one would have dreamed of saying, "Dr. Walsh, what's going on? She's awfully young. . . ."

Sky would have been crushed and disbelieving. If Delana Mae weren't full-fledged, why would he have given her a little bee-keeper's outfit to wear alongside of him whenever the hives needed scraping?

And so Dovie and Skylar Walsh, with only the tiniest aggravation from whiskey in their blood, and being secure in a living room filled with African violets and a lavish toy train system, could time and again wave goodbye. Goodbye, Delana! Have a great day on the river, dear!

She went down the hill carrying Dovie's jellyroll sandwiches and a thermos of lemonade she had fixed herself, two comic books, and paper and pencil, thinking she might send notes in bottles. Her one free arm ran back and forth like an extra propeller. Dovie and Sky watched and smiled from the bay windows.

Delana kept the boat moored at a sagging old dock. She waded into the mud, hopped aboard, and in moments cut loose and sped across the water full throttle. She beat out a grain barge and created waves for a couple of fools floating on inner tubes, then went straight on for Dillworth Lanier and his LIVE BAIT sign. He was two years older than her and had just finished gassing up a man's Chris-craft.

"What do you want, DeeDee?"

Delana stared at him. She would not answer to that nickname.

"Delana, need gas?" He put one hand on his bare belly, which was all sucked back. He walked in ripples, exactly as if he were swimming. He could have been wearing the frogman flippers too: he lifted his feet with such strange care, something only a boy would do.

"You ought to fish," Dillworth said, more kindly. "Don't you know how, or what? Get some good channel cat to take home."

"I'm just out riding," Delana said. She remembered the dime-store sunglasses she had bought, and now put them on. And she was glad suddenly for the T-shirt over her suit.

"Doctor Sky would know how to gut them and salt them." It sounded vaguely insulting, but Dillworth Lanier was smiling.

"I'm going down a ways," Delana said. "To some backwater spots." Her eyes felt lazy with lies and hidden heavy excitement.

Dillworth squinted at the clouds. "You won't get rain, anyway."

Just a girl carrying Dovie's little wrapped-in-wax-paper sandwiches, the only waterborne Walsh, Delana was still hearing her parents' "Goodbye! Have fun!" as she stood and made the boat go fast. She loved the sensation of being lifted by the armpits, and the way air cut behind her knees. As far as she knew, driving a boat was no more complicated than dredging leaves from rainwater.

From Dillworth she zoomed away and cut the motor once the crippled cypress came into view. Marcia had loosely described the area: "Get past the four willows and then go out around the cattail thicket. Look to where the oaks are more bush than tree." She drifted, and when the air swept back and forth on her brow and hummed on its own, she knew she was hitting the Sally spot. Water slapped the boat's sides. She sat low, felt a few more waves lick and nudge the boat, and she lazed for some time in the pool that marked sister Sally's home. Her eyes nearly dropped shut. She picked up a scent, a jumbly smell you would not catch speeding by with a skier in tow. You needed to fall into a slow drift, and then it could catch you. Here the water was hot on her hands, but she threw it on her face as if it would cool her anyway. She ate her sandwiches, which now smelled like river too; and they tasted richer and took twice as much chewing to get down. She had crossed some border and now languished in a perfumy place that held only—and mightily—the presence of Sally. She thought she was in an area, a kind of circle about the size of a garden. The boat lapped around, shifting course, nosing like an old family pet. And lazing there, she came to know Sally's whitey-blond hair and the voice that shot out in clear sharp accusation.

"Hi, Sally," she said down to the water. "You've never met me. I'm your sister too. I'm your big sister now."

She came back the next day. Same thing; good. News for Marcia.

Who went white on Delana's entering the room. She was standing at the mirror with a pillow under her sweater. "A baby growing would look like this," she told Delana, who then blurted her news. Marcia's face grew great plum splotches. She squeezed the pillow. "Take me there," she said. "Hurry and take me there."

So Marcia came, wearing a sleeveless turtleneck meant to cover the vital parts (heart, throat), a chiffon scarf tied over her poufed hair, with silver clips set to make sure that it would stay in place; Marcia, wearing Bermudas that showed knees the size of jar lids, got in the boat, made the sign of the cross, and looked firmly ahead. It would not have occurred to her how odd the sight was of a beanpole kid steering her into the river, that it should be reversed; if anything, the older should be guiding. And Dillworth Lanier said nothing as he gassed them up, either out of deference to Marcia's vast advantage of age (he being twelve, she seventeen), or maybe the sight of an avowed landlubber Walsh afloat stopped his words. He and his brother had once gone to Dr. Walsh against their own father's wishes and asked if they might buy his old boat. Their father had been the one to fish the Walshes out of the water that day, so they knew all about it, how the doctor streamed water, having jumped in the river, how Mrs. Walsh sat staring at the blank river, so full of yellow. She might have been observing a total eclipse of the sun, the way her eyes burned and died. Their father swore he saw one thousand fissures seam Dovie's eyes. Freeze-dried is how the brothers thought of it. Dr. Walsh had listened to their cash offer from behind his screendoor. "No," he told them, in the tone of a cop.

"I wonder if you've found the real spot," was all Marcia would say as they headed off from Dillworth. Of course the river had done some high-banking switches since her days on it, had eaten away big mouthfuls of the land here and there and sprung whole forests of saplings and sturdier brush off its banks. In places, shadows were thrown halfway across the brown water. Marcia held on tight and looked around blankly. Delana, steering, could not believe how young her teenage sister looked.

She drew the oars awhile, and then she got the feeling of the wave passing through her, the silent webby feeling; a moist clutch and then the cool churning aromas that whorled out from a heated place. She cut the motor and folded herself down in the boat. Marcia sat up stiff, blinking in her new contact lenses; that's what was different about her: the small glass disks put her eyes to half size and made her look so much younger. The boat, its own creature, drifted and poked through water.

"I sure smell tea," Delana said.

"That's the willows," Marcia protested. "That dark-tea smell is just the willows. Oh, rats, Delanie. That's all? Just tea-smelling willows?" But the swoon and tickle had come on Delana. Her eyes felt pushed down by the sun, yet her whole body was breathing in, feeling so light and lifting.

"Violets," she began. "I smell roses, too, and something like a new pine door. Maybe modeling clay." She switched her braids.

"Lemons . . . rusty nails . . . acorns." A carousel of fragrance. And this time Marcia, squinting, listened to her every word, syllable, even the pauses. She took in long drafts of air. Her spine was impossibly straight.

For the first time in her girl's life, Delana knew more than her big sister. She knew more about Sally than anyone else on earth did.

"Black Jack gum," she said. Her voice was thicker, darker with assurance.

"No." Marcia jerked forward. "I'm chewing cinnamon. You smell cinnamon. Here, smell it up close." She took out her gum and thrust it at Delana.

Delana shook her head. "But I smell Black Jack."

"That's what she chewed." Marcia rocked around excitedly. "She chewed black gum. She loved the light-blue wrapper. Daddy would slip her half a piece. I've never told you that. I never have!

"Jesus Christ," Marcia said, in prayer more than exclamation. "I know what this is. I'm in the presence of celestial perfume even if I can't smell it. I am here in the presence of a documented Catholic miracle." She rose with a jerk, and the boat rocked. "Oh," she cried, and sat down again. She made a little steeple of her hands and prayed, "Jesus, Mary, and Joseph."

Delana remained sluggish and overcome here, as before. Even the high cat cry of a speedboat acting stupid, causing water to slosh and roil, did not take away this indelible fragrance. Sally, Sally, she called from her heart. Look at us all, sisters on the river.

"I want to chew some Black Jack gum too," Delana said.

Marcia came up slowly out of a fixed stare. "There's this great stigmatic priest from Sicily. People smelled it on his hands, on his stationery, in the air around him, something so powerful and evocative, a sort of trancing fragrance. I am sure that women kissed his hands to get at it. Kissed his palms and licked his fingers. Delanie, you're smelling celestial perfume. That's what it's officially called, the scent of heaven on earth." She looked at the riverbank. "If you were a bishop or someone great from another century, you'd point over there and declare that spot for a church. It would get built."

And the way Marcia looked at her! She was full of astonishment, wary, haloed in the soft envy due an older sister at the dawning of dethronement. She had suddenly recognized the young heart's purity, glimpsed the ugliness of aging along with its privilege.

"You'll grow out of this, Delanie," she said softly. "You'll lose the ability like you did your baby teeth. Don't ever forget. We won't forget this. We have all the evidence we need."

"For the Book of Saints?" The Black Jack scent made Delana's jaws move in rhythm. It was the strongest smell of all. Her mouth watered.

"Evidence of the truth. Of what is, *of what is*," Marcia cried. "A spiritual experience."

And Delana wondered aloud if maybe the river didn't send up such consolation and soothing out of every spot where someone went down, only no one much bothered to return to the site of a drowning. It wasn't the same as relatives visiting grave sites, laying on wreaths. No one came back like this, looking, straining; no one ever stopped right there and let himself try to sniff and feel and connect. All the celestial perfume out there went unsmelled. River barges rolled right over it, mowed it down. Maybe the whole two-thousand-mile-long river was just boiling with memory, ran sweet and wild with it. It was memory the river lugged all up and down itself, and it was too much to be still and tame in that kind of memory. Under the leather lily pads and their creamy flowers, the celestial perfume beaded up and danced. But you had to be there looking and sniffing in order to catch it.

"No," Marcia said. "You're wrong." She was the big sister again, the girl firm in logic. The power came from Sally's acute and sudden perception of truth and lies. Just like Hiroshima and all those bodies melted to shadows on the pavement—surely

Delana had seen those films in school by now, hadn't she?—Sally had left behind the proof, the truth of perfect sacrifice.

"Let's not forget who she is," Marcia said, and the sisters chorused, Marcia loudly, Delana as if in a dream: Little virgin martyr.

"Throughout the ages they have been God's favorites," Marcia said, twirling the ends of her pink scarf.

T HAT'S A TOGA you've got on her." Johnny was
wild in abrupt wakefulness. "She's in a costume.
She doesn't look like a real baby."

Johnny's was a thrilling pain. Delana told him, "She's fine."

She had left one tiny shoulder bare; the other featured a
rhinestone brooch securing a magnificent fringed scarf of mul-
ticolored threads. The baby's bottom was enormously padded,
round and white as the fading morning moon, and her rubber
legs poked out from fringe as if they were the real adult thing,
with something to show. If she could have found one lick of hair
on that glare-white bald head, Delana would have wet and pasted
it into a curl. She would have managed to attach a bow. In fact,
she had penciled on brows. The baby looked satisfactorily intent
even in sleep.

Since the dunking, Johnny's face had retained a red glow, the
beautiful stain of anger, anger so red and new and fascinating,
a warrior's beaming color, Delana had to caution herself against
pushing it to full glory. Its heat radiated the question: Who are
we? Who are we now?

She said, "A costumed baby looks wanted, so she'll feel wanted."

Johnny smacked his thigh.

She crossed the room and opened the cabin door. Johnny had better just keep cool, better tamp it, hose it, give his new anger plenty of air. What had sounded like a low grinding noise was now revealed as music blasting up from the lower deck.

"What's going on?" Johnny called. "It's six A.M."

Delana stepped out on deck and looked down. Everyone was stomping in steel-toed boots. They had gone goofy to Creedence Clearwater blasting on the four-speaker stereo from Taiwan. ". . . rolling, rolling, rolling on the river." One deckhand was flipping his mop around. A dance partner, the mop was tossed against the man's left arm, then dipped way down and brought up spinning. It was whirled overhead on an open palm like a mindless idea of desire. Men whooped and yelled things at the mop-girl. They stomped their boots. And catching sight of Delana watching, deckhands roared louder. They looked up to her as if to say, You can't touch us with this game. This game is ours. This is the opposite of your breast.

With sunup, red flags on the barge pointed sharply into the glassy light over Arkansas. Now the air is salt-free; good, she thought. The river was running gold past slick-chocolate mudbanks, nature's morning light begging you to strictly admire her beauty. See all the shore work and machinery as ornament for that light. The sounds of work floated harmonic and pure off the polished buildings and boats. The great arm of a grain elevator—in sections pulled down from a height—zigzagged and fastened to a docked barge. The tiniest taste of metal, a nail's worth, like a lick of blood, tinged the air. As the record was being changed, there came a faint hum that was the rush, rush of grain, tons of grain being vacuumed down the chute, tumbling down to fill the capacious barge: white rice hard and translucent as teeth. Arkansas is rice king. Inside that great bin fleets of rats would be dancing in surprise as their glut of food suddenly rises up, a funnel, and the roaring commences from outside, shaking

the silo. Once in a while August heat brings on an elevator explosion, and the whole thing goes: grain catches fire, rats are
tossed to heaven, workers are blown apart. Five miles away
windows quiver and burst, and way out in the fields, cradled
on the soybean leaf, fingers have been found basted black. Siloed
grain, Delana considered, beats just like a heart, and it is more
volatile than any white product known. You feel its pulsing heat
from an extraordinary distance. She went back inside to red
Johnny.

"Aren't you confusing her?" he worried. "Last night you had
her in that stiff bell thing. Her head stuck out like a light bulb."

"That was glen plaid, so she'd know practicality," she told him.
"New babies change by the hour. Time-lapse photography would
point this up, I'm sure. I refuse to neglect her stages of growth."

"But babies are supposed to look fuzzy. You know, Delana?
Opal gave us some things."

"We're bonding," she told him.

Johnny hulked around the room still shirtless and came back,
morning light flashing and flaming on his hair. He was combing
it down with his fingers, but no way, said a million frisky red
hairs; they thrived on direct sunlight, and in his chest hairs all
those stars winked. He had woken mumbly from a dream of an
Illinois sky. "Black and orange were the only colors, but I smelled
ripe apples dropping. They were so ripe I couldn't unpucker my
mouth. I couldn't speak at all. It was your dad's place, I'm sure.
I tell myself it's OK I'm taking you up there. I'm escorting you
to this *guy*."

She felt adult enough to go.

Sky had written two words on a piece of lined paper torn from
a small legal pad. The argument's effect was in the color of the
paper, a convincing lavender, as near to the color of her eyes as
any paper could hope to be, if a paler hue. A man who has not
embraced his daughter in seven years needs a special way to call
her home. *Come home*, coaxed the lavender softly, sincerely, and
(Delana swore) aromatically. She smelled the flowers of home:
the dark purple Kool-Aid whiff of iris.

Johnny was looking at her as if to say, How could love become the enemy? You tell me that. How?

Because of its strength, she thought. Like siloed grain, like anger. Because of the shock of its absence. The saddest thing of all would be to go through life denied the privilege to taste another's salt, man's or child's. She tasted her child's hand, little fingernails already dirty—how? Like a trick, these little rims of dirt, beyond comprehension; as if in her sleep Robin went digging in sandboxes, here was some baby-dream manifestation of her pure, sly otherness, something spooky Cheramie would look at and say, "Uh-huh," that she'd been to the island, digging with the lost and lonely girls, the unbaptized dead: she's so new to this life she's still just visiting. From a little vial Delana daubed water on her own face and then on the baby's. For balance. To anchor that baby. "It's river water," she explained. "On land you never leave it completely behind."

Below, Jimi Hendrix music scalded the air. She peered out to see the dancing man, his mop transformed into a hip-riding guitar. Another crazy male thing, fake guitar-playing, faces contorted in dreams of achievement. Music flashers. This act had no female equivalent. A woman's needs are not so fractured. The baby put Delana farther away from the shenanigans of men, their fake guitaring and their helpless dancing mops. The baby prepared her to let Johnny go.

Johnny looked glumly out through the open door on the deckhands' parading, but his ears flamed, listening to her with the baby. She gathered up some trinkets, the dime-store things she had snatched out of Woolworth's last minute, on their way to the dock in New Orleans.

"Hear that sound?" She hunched over Robin. "Those are good-luck pennies in a Chinese purse. And when you get bigger and find pennies on the street, you don't dare touch them unless they're heads up. Don't ask me why. Some kinds of wisdom get passed down. Here's a music box shaped like a grand piano. Of course it plays 'Dark Eyes.' This tiny corsage on black velvet means that someday you'll dance." Johnny snorted and stamped in the doorway. He was a big man light on his feet, but he had never danced; Johnny didn't move that way.

"Baby," she went on, "most people resemble an animal. Cheramie says I have whirligig beetle eyes, but he's also called me an eel. Your aunt Marcia is an obvious spaniel, even with her hair curled like a poodle's. Your grandpa is an elephant. Now, your grandmother Walsh, who's dead, was the ostrich, thin and—"

"She's not all Walsh," Johnny protested. He moved in close.

Heat can be a toxin. Once, Sky had demonstrated this with washrags and lighter fluid, but still she had yearned to bury her face in the sweet, hollow fumes, never mind danger. Aroma was her weakness. She could nestle in the bread smell of Johnny's armpits for hours. In childhood she had been so staggered by the gasoline smell at the pumps, no amount of urging, no matter how long the trip, could get her to use the rest room, not while the gasoline was pumping. She would sit in the car against her parents' chidings, too weak and loving to move.

Her body was streaming sweat, Johnny's anguish was so great in its lack of solution. She would not explain that her costumed baby covered for her fear and exhaustion in days of helplessness, helpless giving. She could scream and shatter everything with, "You take her. I don't know how to be." Someone must be in charge. The mother must be. Or had she inherited Dovie and Sky's lacking? No, tend the baby; make her into a rose, a bunny, the world, and she will thrive. She told Robin, "I was just getting to the paternal part. That's where you get a solar-system look. Sun and moon come out as red hair and pale skin on your daddy, and the stars that don't wash off we call freckles."

Johnny lit up like Christmas.

"Robin, see Daddy," she said. "His face shows the red of his heart."

The first time she had seen Johnny, he stopped in the galley doorway, saying, "I'm elected to get you started." He had found her standing over a pot of salted water in which dead onion had risen; she was hoping to stare it into soup. "Chop this celery," he told her. "And what you want is Bermuda onion." She had never eaten celery, she told him. There was never any celery at home, ever. "And you're going to cook?" She took the celery and chomped down. She had to spit out its bitterness, all water and strings. She laid the bunch on its side and whacked it to pieces. Johnny moved back slightly, saying, "Good." What else? she'd wondered. "Get some meat in that water, a bone, will you?"

But who was he? "Engineer. John Melody. You'll hear them call me Johnny Red." Melody, she'd said. What kind of a name is Melody? "Actually, Irish," Johnny told her. "Isn't yours too?" They are different, completely different names, she swore. Melody! Her leaden forearms could not help but relax. How did he get on the river? she demanded to know. The engineer looked out the window to yellow-brown water, checkered from a little breeze, and as he spoke, one extraordinary white palm winged away like a dove. "It's my natural territory." He said he had come on young, with Cheramie, having been raised and then deserted in death by his father, Cheramie's buddy from back in the war. The *Pat Furey* was named after a grandfather who had taken both men in after V-E Day. "By now I know the smell of limestone in the dark, and I like things like that. I know the stars by season. I love engines. I watch things. Is that enough?"

Was he a pacifist? she asked. *Named Melody. Where else could a big man go, named Melody?* He spluttered and showed dimples. "OK, say that too. My heart tells me I won't be called. Anyway, they're after teenagers."

His skin was incandescent, his face round and ready to blush. And his eyes were lucky blue marbles fringed by lashes too light to reveal themselves when you looked straight on. Freckles, she was sure, were extra salty. He was not a man for war, a redhead, so unnaturally clean, his cheeks tinged milk blue. *Melody.* Trust him or nothing. Accept the most invisible man.

The baby's face became a terrible plum and she howled.

Johnny threw his hands over her. "Is she normal?" he anguished. "It's so sudden and piercing. Maybe the crazy clothes are hurting her." His big hands covered the baby's entire front.

"She's not totally used to living is all, and she protests."

This information sank Johnny heavily onto the bed. His demanding voice was soft, though. "That toga shrinks her. She's an ant wearing a toga."

Delana began reciting: "The owl and the pussycat went to sea in a beautiful pea-green boat."

The rhythm relaxed Johnny.

". . . They sailed away for a year and a day to the land where the Bong tree grows."

Now he took the baby's arms and swayed them in time. He made her little hands do pattycake. His hands were so smeared with freckles they were brown; the terribly white palms were like some creature's brave belly flashing itself to show off love, tender love, its endless maneuverings and varieties, all real, some startling, some hideous or fine, or mute—relentless, rolling-over love—and Delana squinched her eyes (not fast enough) against the tricky wild variations flashing at her: father love and beggar's love; an oak's affair with soil, the preciousness of two ants laboring a bread crumb into tall grass. No, thanks. Don't show off the whole crazy infinity, please. New-mother love took all she had to give. She upped her volume: ". . . They dined on mince and slices of quince which they ate with a runcible spoon. And hand in hand, on the edge of the sand, they danced by the light of the moon, the moon, the moon. They danced by the light of the moon."

Johnny sat on the bed smiling, bare ornamented chest slightly drooped, the roundness of his stomach emphasized. His ear was cocked toward the engines below. Already he'd forgotten contention, a man who chooses water over land. That is *why* a man chooses water over land, Delana reminded herself. In the galley that first time, Johnny had announced, "I know why *I'm* here." Big eyes had opened wide, asking for her story, one indent alone in the forehead giving away his thoughts as troubled. A sign of hope is what Delana read through the pucker. A man's hope. At home the day before, she had just learned to read such a look cold. She had read it on a boy's face wanting sex, then it had flamed on Daddy, later, in the very same room, as he thrilled and raged at her luminous calm. After chopping the celery to please this guy Johnny, she had sliced up the red onion. "Ta-da!" she cried, raising the knife. "You love me." Johnny's face went sunset red. She told him, "You're called Johnny Red because of your face, not just your hair." She moved toward him. Softly, surprised, she exclaimed that he had no secrets. "You're a ballsy chick," said the red man.

Now he wondered dreamily, "What's that word? What kind of spoon is that, honey?"

"Ridged." And she demonstrated, leaning over him and scraping her teeth along Johnny's shoulder, back and forth across delicious land. A red star came off on her tongue. "The owl and the pussycat demanded a grapefruit spoon."

"Marry me," Johnny whispered.

She squeezed his hand. "Seven years is common-law. We're there. Come out on deck."

Johnny scratched an armpit, frowned, but he followed once again.

A cadre of whirligig beetles, flashing metallic in the sun, making a black patch on the water, seemed to know, like everyone coming downriver—every skiff and waterskier and fishing party bound to see red flags on the *Pat Furey*—that the barge carried oil, so give wide berth; and they lazed nearer and nearer to shore. But let even one fly drop from a tree and the whole whirligig tribe would go after it, bloodthirsty and quick. Johnny had told her, "It's like they have four eyes. They see above and below water at the same time." New girl cook, she had pictured all the hungry chewing that went on beneath surface, the creation of waves being nothing more than upheaval caused by the call of the hunt.

Then Johnny had shown her something more violent: tadpole skins floating among a school of the living. Floating skins meant the life had been sucked out by a predator. The skins, with nowhere to go on that thick water, floated among the living and frenzied them. "They sense their fate," Johnny explained, strictly botanical. "They swim with the dead anyway." She was standing with him off the galley deck. Her hands smelled of lemon butter. She wiped them on her apron, turned to him, and announced, "So do I. My sister Sally went down before I was ever born." "Jesus," Johnny swore, "your surprises always have a pain in them." Then out came her longest knife yet: "She died an accident, and I was born one, but the opposite of what you might imagine. I think all the big stuff is the opposite of what we imagine. Even the worst stuff, like with rape and stuff," she had said, wiping and wiping those hands to get past the grease of the butter, get down to the tang of lemon. "Do you know what I mean?" Johnny stepped away and gagged over the rail; luckily they were on the lower deck, and even so deckhands peeped out to imitate and mock him, assuming, of course, that his wretchedness was a hideous manifestation of being in love. "Just what I've feared," she cried. "You can't take the truth. Someday you'll have to face it. You'll have to ask questions." Johnny had shaken his bowed head no. Tadpole skins floated and floated on green water.

Now rumbling came from below. From the middle deck they looked over the rail starboard to see men in bandannas and boots, a mop being bashed against rail and deck as the Jimi Hendrix chords blew crazy, somewhere in California Jimi Hendrix bashing his guitar to smoke and wire. That's what they saw in the mop: love claimed and surrendered. That's what men cheered on.

Heads turned up to where Johnny and Delana stood. On light holiday air, the murmur rose fast: "Stars?" Men who were made demon by rock 'n' roll crowed, "Now she's got him wearing stars?"

With a cry, Johnny remembered himself and spun back into the cabin. Too late, he would hide away the chest that had been glinting red and blue and green and gold for all the world to see.

"Damn you, Delana." He swatted wildly at his chest, and she joined in, pretending, too, that the stars were nasty as bee stings. She pushed aside his arms and used her slight fingers, then her teeth. She nipped sharply at the awful stars.

"Now I'm a real fool. I'm completely unmanned. I could just tie you up or something." Johnny's arms fell heavy with the impossibility. "You owe me, Delana. Honestly, you owe me something."

"What, Johnny? What do I owe you?"

His fluster was severe. "Well, at least . . . blush fines."

"Blush fines? Is this some river law?"

"No, it's ancient, from my family." Already he was breathing easier, gone to some other view of life, anything but the straight-ahead. "The old Celts had you pay *up* when you insulted someone."

A law in favor of blushes! A law to protect redheads!

"Oh, dumpling," she said, "you're always going to blush. I can't do a thing about your blushes. Cover them up. Get sunburned. In winter use a heat lamp. But you're bound to blush."

That day with the tadpole skins, she remembered, the river had resembled green silk stretched over a larger, rippling sensuality that would split the seams of its own flesh in order to carry you on farther, much farther than you had been. It was dusk, and the water had laughed at her, mocking her alarm and hesitation. It was really the voice of the drum, the huge old river fish that at nightfall sends up a muttering so strong it is understood to be the river's true voice. That drum could shame and silence even the deckhands who, right this minute, were bellowing along with the tone-deaf Fugs, singing, "Monday nothing. Tuesday nothing. Wednesday a little more nothing."

I N   B A Y W A T E R, New Orleans, west of the French
Quarter, south of Magazine Street, she and Johnny
kept a shotgun shack and rotated its use freely with some local
fishermen Johnny knew. Once in a while the schedule fell off
and they would return to find a guy who smelled purely of salt
and snails flopped on the couch.

Simple, how hilariously simple life had been. Delana stretched
out alongside Robin, tiny in her pink wicker cradle, remembering.

Simple. Until her baby came to life as pure, raving, bullhorn
emotion. Mother and baby had fought each other for who knows
how long, those chartreuse walls raining down their color. And
Delana could not say when the face of salvation happened by.
The woman at the window appeared featureless dark—sun
smack behind her—leaning way in on the sill of the wide-open
window that lacked a screen; bringing relief like a cooling breeze,
and something better: her soft voice was just like touch. "Oh,
my. Look what we've got." And then the humming began. It

presided over the body's war, jacking up volume and range, claiming more and more of the paltry air as Delana struggled on; it leeched out resistance. The song of the strange woman's voice became immense as a scream of deliverance tore from Delana. Bones slicked out of her. "That's right," soothed the helper-face at the window. "You've got yourself a girl." Delana understood: the howl of girlhood had ripped her apart. Years of silent girlhood snapped with her spine. How extraordinary and fine, girlhood, she thought, in the moment that her own girlhood finally ended. She passed out trying to laugh along with that woman whose hum was a madrigal. Done with duty, the stranger walked on. A starched nurse with the medical team roused her, saying they were alerted by pay phone, a local operator assisting, the caller claiming to be without a dime. A few days later a big pink cradle appeared on the doorstep, wicker so thick with paint it must have been done over a hundred times fresh for a hundred Baywater babies. It was shaped like a seashell. Delana had inhaled the new-paint smell and felt a hum rush through her ears, someone humming about this baby's going to be so fine.

Simple, simple adventuring, before. That's how she and Johnny had lived, and on their thirty-day leaves it had never failed, the way marauding love overtook them. Oh, their runs through money had been thrilling. They directly ate a sumptuous meal wherever they landed, then took top-floor lodgings in downtown brick hotels and tumbled the sheets limp, while way down below old men dreamed on the porch, content to think they *allowed* the younger man to burn himself up with a woman. At local music fests Johnny sometimes took the stage with his harmonica, looking lost and easy in the rhythm. They cruised everywhere in hundred-dollar cars, mostly old black Valiants. They watched the crowning of the King of the Hoboes in Britt, Iowa, and went over the river to Elmwood, Wisconsin, for UFO Days, where nearly one-half the townspeople had seen or communicated with the beyond. Guernsey farmers in striped overalls

who had formerly dreamed only of weather breaks now swore
on the UFO. Along Main Street low hedges were sheared to look
like saucers and evergreens were barbered to a significant fairy-
tale point.

Neither one had ever cared for liquor, staying instinctively
alert to its spirit-killing qualities, so they took in every last detail:
remembered how summer corn gives the land a nice crew-cut
look; agreed that the smaller the town, the better its Fourth of
July, the more honest-tasting its barbecue.

Just as much, they loved to get back home. In Baywater, toy
trees and vacant lots buzzed with the most private kind of life:
even weeds and cement took on more life out of sight of water,
and people strutted, knowing they were the most important
things moving through the day. Here you would see anybody,
all kinds of people out humming: blacks and whites, the glad
cool home-shruggers. The pure flaunts. The ones for whom a
home caused such pain as to trigger a major allergic reaction,
the only antidote known being flight. Home could be fatal, Delana fiercely believed. So it was good to live in a house whose
walls bucked with the hot sun or the rain. And let the wind blow
through. A house whose thin walls and humble square body did
not interfere with the earth's lines, and gave people that sense
of being out in the world when, in fact, they had stepped inside.
Nobody lost by going inside. Nothing disintegrated or hushed
up. This was not a house full of the barricades from her growing
up: plush divans and high-gloss staircases, obstacles to natural
ease, which is to say honesty. The Baywater home would not
incite anyone, and here Delana concentrated on her bone and
feather and rock collections. Scarves waved from the walls, alive
with secrets and news. Johnny was the one who bought the curtains (French frilly), so with the windows thrown open and free
of screens—there was nothing *to* screen—the curtains would
dance or slink. "Such great weather vanes," Johnny had observed.
Everywhere in the streets of Baywater radios played as if TV had
not even been invented. Curtains danced and people danced,

sometimes all wrapped up together. Great old radios rested on metal-tipped legs and slugged away at romantic melodies. Who could dance to TV?

And on the streets came freedom, all jewelry and charms worn in full view, tickets and luggage in hand—dreams laid out like a deck of cards. Lots of river rats moving along jaunty, looking far down the road. In their minds they gauged invisible tides. Men wore pants bright enough to get them killed outside the parish. Women laughed, resplendent in maroon. Delana wound a bright turban to her head, and her hair flew back in licorice whips. Out walking, people would call, "Hey, Swami." And she loved the knowledge that she fit. She loved the gassy exhaust of the Desire Street bus, which stopped at the corner, took coin and disgorged people all the same, as if passion had nothing at all to do with staying alive.

Limes fragranced the air. A full tree of them nuzzled the back wall. The flare of those curtains, the murmur of ripening limes. In all ways, she and Johnny had domesticated their buggy shack into a notion of French languor. And they painted everything inside soft and rosy, adding turquoise trim in the front room. The bedroom nook was completely chartreuse and smelled of limes.

After a honeymooners' week she had found the pink home of Mister Fats Domino. At her age, seventeen, Marcia had talked about this house in her knowing way. "It's a fact that Mister Fats Domino welcomes people. He publishes his address." A fact from one of her magazines, she stressed. "If I ever make it to New Orleans, I'll walk right up to his house." A pink house that the magazine went on to describe as a "bungalow." The exotic word sounded to Delana like everlasting love.

It was still pink, as if waiting for her discovery, she thought, finding it very nearby. Still pink, not fresh and hoppy, rather a secure, perseverant pink, and therefore truer than a bright, new pink. Lizard cars sunned in the drive and a brocade curtain spanned the picture window. She was seventeen and ripe for revelation. Surely this pink house told the story of being famous and free. Here was Mister Fats Domino's reward: a little house that sat there with the coy indifference of a fragrant sweet. What the world could be! Crickets bounded up from this paved stretch of walk, and when dinner forks clanged from within, her body swayed, nearly collapsed, to the music. Pink superseded any history of pain. It was the color of the moment, holding the sound of harmonious dinner forks (so intimate), softly sure this was all that mattered. She would tell Johnny that their weathered shack, too, needed a pink exterior. She grinned at her feet and moved on among crickets. There was suddenly nothing more adult than not knocking on Fats Domino's door.

She had come up from Port Sulphur heavily pregnant, leaving Johnny down where heaps of yellow sulphur cooled along the riverbanks. She had come home alone to the little house whose wood frame was, after all, so porous no paint would adhere.

On and off the barge she and Johnny had lain around incautiously from the start—people who did not plan for futures and therefore did not consider fortunes except in terms of mile markings, channel depth, and what a purple horizon would cost in travel time: the exhilaration of reaching grandly insignificant goals and triumphing over a host of small crises. Then pass on unperturbed, strain your eyes forward for the new drama. That's good river life. Real fugitive love. It let you cast your eyes on the water adoringly, as if camellias were raining down. Why ever look away?

Once, at a fair, Johnny spoke out about their utter disregard for lovemaking caution. He speculated that the river jiggled things wrong in a woman. "Like truckdrivers' kidneys. They're in a tango all day long and get messed up." He looked sorry.

"Are you saying you've been trying to get me pregnant?" she shot back.

They were standing on the sidelines of a Kentucky watermelon-seed-spitting contest. A voice honked through a bullhorn: "Twenty-eight inches."

"I didn't mean that." But Johnny's shoulders heading for his ribs showed that he did. The minute she said so he knew that he did. He had been hoping. "It's funny nothing's happened. I mean, I guess we're lucky," he ended lamely, and the big slouch-bodied man blinked his guileless blue eyes at her from above a pale fruit rind. His face matched the red melon juice. His rusty hair was a crucible for the sun.

"How far can you spit?" Delana challenged him.

They loaded their mouths with seeds and spat unspectacularly into the dust, and she knew that saying the impossible had now made it likely. Johnny carried her piggyback to the car, she felt so weak with a sense of future.

Still, the pregnancy astounded them. They were children caught eating the PTA cookies.

Out front of the clinic which had declared their future, they approached an old black Valiant, over which Johnny took an oath never to drive beyond thirty miles an hour with Delana and the unborn in it.

The unborn seemed such an apt reference to impending birth: it's not living here; it's away, unborn; act as if you don't care, hardly notice, really, to ensure its health and safe birth. *"Oh, dumpling, the unborn is kicking." "Hmmm, is that so?"*

"The unborn will debut in New Orleans, then," Delana decided, touching the black car's fin. "He'll be a little Mardi Gras king." A baby girl was as unlikely a notion as self-forgiveness, a need not yet formed in her mind, just a thing that pressed down on her lower left side whenever she thought of home.

"You want one, honey." Johnny spread his big arms, which suddenly looked made to balance crystal. "I'm so grateful. I'm just so happy." They drove away in the Valiant, Johnny tooting his horn.

In what were to be her final days pregnant in the Baywater shack, Delana made a batch of fudge, packed the small plaid suitcase, swept the linoleum floor, craved limes to the point of slicing them into her cool bath water—she could not get cool enough—and rubbed the fruit over her shoulders and knees and breasts, up her thighs, around the belly, then all through her hair. She played radio show tunes low while putting up a daisy chain of flowers picked from a vacant lot overgrown with wild beauty and ruptured cement slabs. She thought, standing in the little Baywater house, smelling her own long absence from it, that the earth provides everything we need if we will just let it; everything to chew on and enough places to lay down the head.

THE DAY MISS STEINBACH was all over town in a tango skirt, it was like an announcement for Delana that, yes, the nurse had been to Acapulco with Sky, and she didn't care who knew. The way she walked, hem flipping past, like "Cha-cha, everyone." He had taken her to a hepatitis conference, so there. But didn't her curves shame her by their obvious call for attention and harm? A full woman's body—what a thrill, what a horror.

And during that January thaw, even when she was perfectly alone, if Delana moved her head quickly away from the sun it seemed that red taffeta streaked by. She saw it flouncing in the clouds overhead, and the color of rickrack played off doorknobs and bathroom fixtures and even, today, off her candy striper's smock. Her thirteen-year-old body responded to every whistling breeze. Its heat threatened to mock Dovie's example of constraint. A feeling, the verve of red taffeta, swirled around her knees, so delicious and painful a feeling, such a xylophone she had become suddenly—play zinging up and down her; the feeling ran to her head and announced itself as her first true secret, a melody mad for the heart.

She thought of mayflies. On a summer night a thousand may-flies rise up from the Mississippi River, and you rush down the lawn to watch. They rise up and swarm the sky to mate and drop their eggs back into the water. Eggs sink into Mississippi mud. There they grow so slowly and in such darkness, you declare them dead. For a whole year you forget. A year of darkness in river sludge, and finally they rise up out of the water screaming of summer, and of course they mate immediately; they must do everything at once and know exactly what must be done, time being precious in their one-day lives. To feel death as strongly as air and love, they race to the nearest electrical light and burn themselves to ash. In the morning the river highway is brown. In her mind, Delana hears the sizzle of ecstatic death.

She was at the hospital, another Tuesday, done carrying Mrs. Oldsmith's urine cup back down to the nurses' station. Next, she would serve treats and keep an eye on the kids while her father, their Doctor Sky, performed with his dummy, Rex. As a little girl she had pressed Marcia on her weekends home to tell more, tell everything she knew as she was packing up the creams and jeweled barrettes forbidden at St. Agnes Academy for Girls. She had finally insisted, "What about Miss Steinbach?" Marcia had paused to say, "They've been adulterers since before you were born. They shack *up*, Delanie."

If her older sister had attended school at home, instead of kneeling with the nuns down in Nauvoo every day, would she ever have been conscripted as a candy striper? Hardly. No. De-lana, not Marcia, was the one slated for public service, the draftee daughter in a hair net. And at thirteen, full of belief in this self, she was suddenly thinking that she would not even mind war, a far adventure charmed with the sure thing of boys wanting the mercy of touch. The racing itch in her palms, temples, breasts, could be flamed and cooled in a jungle dream. Join the Red Cross.

"Come on, Annie," she said, tugging one of the little cowgirl's braids. Annie's pajamas, charged with ponies, were tucked up to the armpits. Her wrists were covered with wild bandanna pieces, part of the cowgirl act. Annie Oakley's real name was Ellen Bell, but with guns buckled on and the lip stuck out, you had better call her Annie if you wanted to move her down the hall.

"When I get out I want pet mice," Annie said.

Delana pointed to her slippers. "Put them on, Annie."

"I'm going to train a whole circus of mice. They'll wear shiny clothes. The girl mice will dress like Cinderella."

"White mice in puffy pink dresses," Delana said, shoving a foot into its slipper. "I like that."

"The boy mice will wear tall black hats full of magic tricks."

"What will they do for fun?" Delana urged.

Annie considered, hands on her guns. "After the circus ball they'll go on rides and stuff. They'll love the roller coaster, a whole mouse family in one seat." She was giggling. "And all in a row they'll eat the same hot dog. It'll have lots of stuff on it but no bun, just the wiener. And they'll bite whoever they hate. If I say, 'Bite,' they'll do it."

"Let's go, cowgirl."

Delana stepped to the door, holding Annie's hand, and here came her daddy down the hall, carrying the wide-eyed dummy Rex on his arm. Her heart hit the drums: Miss Steinbach came too. As his private-practice nurse, she belonged clear on the other side of the river, in a small office painted green, way, way over there on the Illinois bank. She had no business crossing the river, no business at all in the state of Iowa. For some reason the nurse wore her uniform mummy-tight. Her little cap managed to look clever; maybe clever thoughts kept it upright on the waves of brown hair. She had no business in the hospital, none. At home, Dovie would be fashioning gumdrop trees or floating some scarves off the ceiling, as if to ensure "Home is a holiday."

Delana stood by, impersonating one of Annie's white mice, who would play statue even while quivering inside. Her teeth wanted to bite. The length of hall sucked in its breath, the heating system's trick. You only realized it had been blasting and blasting once it shut off. The noise shut down just as Miss Steinbach passed by closer than Delana had ever let her get. Her mist of powder was some bathing treacherous sweetness that Hansel and Gretel could not help but follow.

Annie went, "Bang, bang!" too late, without unholstering her gun. The entertainers were safely long gone down the hall.

Delana followed to the nursery, where all the children who could had gathered. In their harness contraptions were those victims of broken collarbones—testimony to failed leaps from young maples and handstands done off bicycles. A blond boy held both arms out, two casts. Another's head was shaved blue. Leukemia gave the child saints' eyes; they looked way over to where the unseen lay, and rested there. In the corner someone recovering from eating furniture polish felt well enough to bully an impetigo case. One curly-haired girl was so small in a regular-sized wheelchair that she looked fake, propped up the same as Rex.

Rex had begun bowing and nodding at the kids in their robes and Christmas pajamas. Daddy and Miss Steinbach reclined, set apart in the shameful way that winter suntans mark people off. Accentuated by medical white and smiles and fresh knowledge from the hepatitis conference, they wanted to appear guileless. No children in the hospital suffered hepatitis, Delana had noted. In five years no one in all of rural Illinois's middle-river stretch had reported hepatitis, her heart declared. But just in case, Daddy glowed with new information. He owned it and the sun too. Miss Steinbach smiled, turning her head slowly—Rex Number Two—smiling above the children's heads. The hospital fun room smelled from clay projects set high on shelves, on newspaper, and its being overheated caused your throat to close right up.

Doctor Sky cleared *his* throat and began: "I almost got out of the house without Rex, but he said that all his fans were waiting for him. What do you think?"

"Yeah!" shouted the roomful. Then a little songbird voice rose. "Where is the fan?" He got laughed down.

"Does Rex want a girlfriend?" someone called out.

"Girlfriend," Rex exclaimed, without Sky's mouth opening: his cheeks twitched; small trapped birds beat, wanting out. Rex's whole body flopped around. His face was shiny, painted wood, resembling Howdy Doody. He wore a red bow tie and a dark pin-striped suit. Like a Disney character's, his hands were covered with white gloves. "Well, do you want to be my girlfriend? Can I walk home from school with you?"

Kids laughed and worked their shoulders. The one little voice rose again. "What's a girlfriend?" And someone yet tinier-sounding asked, "What's a Girl Scout?" The leukemia child scooched on his knees to relay the answer to his friend: "There are *Boy Scouts* for boys."

"Rex, I think the joke is on you," Doctor Sky told his dummy sternly. He shook Rex's head and winked at the kids.

"Jokes? I don't know any jokes," said the chicken-necked Rex.

"I have a joke," a kid called out.

And so began the routine. Rex called on a kid to come forward and tell him a joke. His head needed scratching in order to help him think of an answer. The audience cried out answers and warnings and new jokes out of turn. In all the uproar, Sky continued to smile. Rex sounded amazed; every day of his life he could enthusiastically swear he had no idea what you get when you put a car in the oven or why the moron threw the clock out the window. And Miss Steinbach nodded. There was all the time in the world in the hospital fun room. When little Annie Oakley faced off Rex with her gun, yelling, "Bang, bang! Bang, bang!" the dummy was prepared.

"What a cowgirl you are. Now listen, Annie," said Rex, "I can say something to you in a foreign language; it's meant only for you, Annie. In the Finnish language." His head bounced with each syllable, causing his eyes to go open and shut. "*Katsokaa lehmatyttoa*. That means 'Look at the cowgirl.'" Annie Oakley trained both guns on Rex while he taught the whole room to say it. Slowly: "Cockta ka leh hemma tittu. Cockta ka leh hemma tittu."

Delana sang out with the children. Words, provocative as war. Cockta ka leh hemma tittu. Words Sky owned. Oh, Daddy! Who couldn't adore Doctor Sky? What all didn't he know? Finnish! Where had he learned this? Cowgirl, no less. Not even cowboy. Sky's magic included a perfect call to a dwarf Annie Oakley.

Next Rex was singing: "I've been working on the railroad, all the livelong day," flapping his wood eyes and one arm, his mouth working open and shut.

"Can't you hear the whistle blowing, rise up so early in the morn, can't you hear the captain calling, 'Dinah, blow your horn.' "

And Sky's lips did not move. His head required a viselike rigidity when Rex sang. Shackled words lumped around in his mouth, but his lips did not move. He stayed still while Rex jerked about. "Dinah, won't you blow? Dinah, won't you blow? Dinah, won't you blow your hor-r-r-rn!" And the children were all singing and tossing their heads, loosing sound and rhythm and misery. Miss Steinbach provided the percussion by her slap-slap on the knees as she sang too. She kept her mouth dainty, her eyebrows high, and it was a fake sweatless working on the railroad that she sang of, a tin triumphant love she beamed into the room and sent out to prickle Delana's skin and raise a challenge. A current ran between them.

"Oh, someone's in the kitchen with Dinah, someone's in the kitchen I know-oh-oh-oh, someone's in the kitchen with Dinah, strumming on the old banjo . . . Keep singing."

Delana turned to snack duty. She filled one big pouch pocket of her smock with a stack of small plastic cups, the other with a tube of saltine crackers. She picked up the pitcher of grape juice and walked around the room, serving the children. Then it was Miss Steinbach's turn. Delana walked to her holding a plastic cup, which like the others, was sterile, the kind ordinarily used for taking urine specimens. She looked back at the singing children and saw a roomful of smudged, dark mouths; she saw hurt wild children in a hospital, singing and singing.

". . . Fee-fie-fiddly-ai-oh, strumming on the old banjo." And everyone was clapping, the cries going higher. The juice had instantly revved them up. Scuffles—some elbow-poking, braid-pulling—were breaking out. And when Delana went to Miss Steinbach, who was already indicating thirst and possibly grati-tude by the hand clasped on her throat, the racing swirl of red taffeta and all the heat of Acapulco itself scored Delana through the middle. Gravity was crushing and shifting everything about, willing her, forcing her down and bending her almost dizzy. What was it? I'm sick, but my daddy is a doctor, she was thinking. He'll take care of me. And she was leaning into Miss Steinbach as if she might kneel at her orthopedic-shod feet and beg, Please, go away, no tango skirt in town. And as she was holding the cup toward Miss Steinbach's face, willing that her request be noted, she poured grape juice directly onto the woman's lap. In Delana's other hand the unused glass flipped around and fell to the floor. A purple pool, fuzzed and frothy at the edges, formed in the white lap. Delana jerked back. "Forgive me," she whispered. And as if to show her equanimity, she continued to pour from the pitcher, continued spilling grape juice onto the floor and her own shoes.

Miss Steinbach, who, frozen, had watched the spreading stain, now shrieked. She reared back, away from her lap, a thing, it would seem, entirely distinct from her person.

"Oopsy daisy, Miss Steinbach," Rex told her.

Kids came leaping forward, pajamas billowing like sails. With their smeary mouths open, they circled the nurse and stared at the widening purple stain. "Yuck!" they cried, and instantly be-came airplanes, kangaroos, mad fish out of water, machine gun-ners. They all rushed away without touching her.

Dammit. But Delana kept her thoughts to herself. Who could have predicted the extent of the woman's upset, the horror and paralyzing grief on Miss Steinbach's face? She was a nurse, after all, used to gushing blood and bones stuck out at wrong angles, to flab and liver-spotted hands. And if the nurse ever found a hepatitis victim around here, she'd be looking at yellowed skin, something really gruesome. And hadn't she touched every kind of pus, all poisonous marks? What on earth was wrong with this damn Miss Steinbach? For Christ's sake, a nurse howling and refusing to fix herself. She knew how to strap people down and shoot penicillin in the butt, and look at her. The white perfect cap had slipped too.

"It's a stain, that's all," Delana cried out. "You're not hurt." She had retreated to the snack table but still held the sloshing pitcher. Her yell immediately shut up the children, and fascinated, they came to her slowly, waving their arms. And again the building was sucking its breath, so it reverberated all the more; the silence begged to be slashed, and out came Delana's hot words: "Buy another old uniform. It's not your Mexican skirt that's ruined."

Miss Steinbach was gasping, and a lifetime of airless silence passed by before Rex's jaws could get going. Still, they clacked without saying anything, this eerie clacking coming from Miss Steinbach's side.

The kids shrieked their delight, with Annie in the lead. "Bang, bang!"

Delana grabbed her head and pushed her palms against her ears. Killer, killer, our family killer. But her fist was stuffed in her mouth to trap the howling words.

Miss Steinbach hissed. "Spiteful, awful girl. What do you know?"

"Oopsy daisy, Miss Steinbach," Rex repeated, so loud, so harshly, it was Sky speaking, just barely disguised. Her daddy was winking at the kids again, the way he always did when Rex got too dumb. "We've had an accident," he said, pseudo Rex.

"Yes," Delana and Miss Steinbach cried out together.

The kids clapped and contorted and pointed all over again and pranced. How they loved to see it, a nurse, any nurse, with juice in her lap. It was nurses who made them eat peas and potatoes off their metal trays, these witches who did not understand that dessert is bartered. Little vegetable-haters, now they were up and squealing like baby pigs and raising all manner of deformed and strapped-up arms. And eyes sick with routine and confinement were shining toward the defeated Miss Steinbach and all the world that existed under awful indoor lights. A girl with a bush of hair ran off, yelling, "Wee, wee, wee, wee, all the way home." A boy imitated a fire engine racing through the party.

Dr. Skylar Walsh boomed, "It's time for our farewell parade. Rex, will you lead us?"

Then, Sky waved one arm like a baton. In Rex's voice he said, "Follow us." And they set off, Doctor Sky doing exaggerated high-stepping, his silver hair as good as a drum major's tall hat, some minor small-town Captain Kangaroo just shaking the money out of Rex. It razzed the funny bones of the little ones right now. They fell in singing with him: "The people on the bus go up and down all the livelong day."

Miss Steinbach finally stood and wrung out her skirt, which now featured a map of Texas, the closest state to Mexico. Delana swept up the crumbs from dozens of saltine crackers, and she couldn't think why the great Texas stain that had given her so much satisfaction now reminded her of death, brighter and nearer than she had ever wanted to see it.

She sang out too, high and loud to cover her portentous feelings that Miss Steinbach's horror was somehow justified, even with her hatefulness and the woman's mean shameless wearing of that tango skirt all over town. There was some adult reason she couldn't yet fathom, some reason to put yourself out like a mayfly. Delana had hot breasts pushing at her candy striper's smock, legs that hurt with growth, a woman's blood that sang. She knew real blood from fake and this smelled like real blood, this fit of Miss Steinbach's. The song of real blood tatted the air. And the children sang with Rex. They loved the verse that marked their kindergarten wisdom, broke the grip of a mother's lap. They were big boys and girls, singing, "The baby on the bus cries, "Wah, wah, wah," all the livelong day."

W ATER'S YEASTY TODAY," Opal called. She was smoking off the galley deck, and without looking at Cheramie approaching, she shot down the cigarette, slapped her slow hip into motion and went back inside. He had seen it too: river foaming elastic and dank, with crosscurrents sliding under one another. He followed Opal. He had just seen Johnny go aft with a handful of cookies. And silly, but he wished he'd been first to find the cookies. The aroma of baking chocolate was enough to unnerve a grown man. He followed after it.

The cook was scraping bake sheets in the sink. "Johnny doesn't have any business working this trip," he griped to her back. "He moons around when he should be sleeping."

"It's bad," Opal agreed. "I tell you I heard such a squalling earlier I went up to see for myself what the devil was happening next. They don't know anything. I found Delana forcing a rectal thermometer on that baby. The baby was naked except for a tiny mouse-ears hat."

"Ridiculous," Cheramie said, taking a cookie.

"I told her she needs land and women. Johnny's even worse. He went frantic from the baby's cries and begged her to do something. *He* was the one who'd grabbed for the thermometer. That cry just pierces him. A man hears only pain in a cry. A man's guilt runs so deep, about all he hears in a baby's voice— or a woman's, for that matter, Cheramie—is alarm and pain. He can't do much about either, but knows he's supposed to."

"Opal, that baby has to be loud to get the message across to them."

"Well, she stopped, the effort was so hard. She went black-purple without air, and Delana nearly fainted. I came in on this. Of course I blew on that baby's face to start the reflex. They thought I performed a miracle, they're both so blank. You breathe in a baby's face to start her up. What do they think wind *is?*"

Cheramie shook his head.

"Johnny went to his engines. He says an engine's running hard," Opal continued. "I asked him, 'Has one ever run soft?' "

"I see what's coming." Cheramie had managed only one bite, and chocolate was burning the roof of his mouth. He groped for water.

"Yup. Pushing him in the river means she wants him off it." This was not funny, but Opal began clucking, and Cheramie noticed the roosters printed on her apron upside down and all over, a big troop of them extending from the broad cook's neck down to her knees like that much more bossiness.

"What would she get? He's a man made for the one thing he knows. If Johnny goes off—"

"You lose him, Cheramie, and she gets a zoo animal. Hormones are talking. That baby takes up her world. Anything else is luggage. She's scared."

"Scared? Who'd know it? Man, the way she eats! What else do I smell, Opal? What's for dinner?"

Opal motioned a handful of spoons toward the oven. She was filling the big stainless-steel sink with water now. "Roast beef. I browned it on the stove. That's what you smell. We'll have twice-baked potatoes, and there's plenty of real horseradish."

"You counting horseradish now like it's some vegetable?"

"Don't be dumb," said the cook, straightening. She clapped her hands, in huge yellow gloves. "Horseradish clears away romantic notions. I'll slather the roast for Delana. Don't think I'm feeding her heaps of just anything."

He admitted, "I didn't know. . . . You're a good cook, Opal. I always said we've been lucky with you."

"It's what I do."

"Think if we'd got you when Myrtle gave out seven years back. Think how different this cruise would be."

"You got a girl, Cheramie. And she did not cook with horseradish." Annoyingly, this started Opal chuckling. "She survived right well."

"Knocked us flat."

"Goodness alive, did she, now? She fretted you that much?"

He managed to stuff a whole cookie in his mouth, so all he could do was gesture and frown. Sweet, damning fire of baking chocolate.

"Uh-huh," said Opal. She watched him eat. "What fresh-baked cookies do," she said, bagging some cookies and handing them over, "is dull fears and whatever else a man needs dulled. Better eat plenty."

In the wheelhouse he did not have to look at Opal's shrewd eyes. Just eat cookies and watch water. Look down on the burly heads of trees. Cane grew shorter and shorter along the banks, an indication they were heading north. Out of the canebrakes flashed wood ducks—fancy green-and-purple birds streaking onto the water, purely show-off. It was easy to think that light on the water is simply creation's business. On these sunny days you swear the river hosts an angels' dance. And just thinking of getting upriver, you can almost smell the honey of winter on the wind's tail. And sometimes, usually about the time you're heading for a leave, that water looks like a sea of nipples, but who are you going to tell it to?

Not Del Mae, coming along fanning herself with an envelope. He opened the wheelhouse door. "Mate, don't you sleep now? I'd think you'd be out cold with shock after your exertion." Getting no response, he went on, "Well, I was hoping for your company anyway."

"The baby's asleep. Johnny's got her and I needed air. Here. Marcia sent me this picture. She said she'd die if I came off the water and didn't recognize her standing there."

Cheramie saw a thirtyish woman in baggy shorts and curly light-brown hair. Something at the mouth recalled Del Mae. Some family resemblance, a question forming there on the puffed lips. They looked like bee-bitten lips. He grunted. "Women's supposed to be weak from having a baby. Not throw men around." He squinted out on the river in fifty directions but could not find some legitimate interest to fasten onto. He turned back to the little refrigerator and, banging the door a few times, said, "Look here. Opal bought pink juice. I always did like the surprise of what a cook orders."

Del Mae had found his cookies. She withdrew a big one from the bag. Her fingers looked sweet and narrow, without devilment.

"Damn, girl. You threw Johnny in. That was gruesome."

He drank from the bottle to hide his grin and rested a hand on Del Mae's shoulder. She was running her fingers over the bumps of the board lights, that fascinated glint in her eye he had seen on her the first time up here: girl cook come to fillet men's hearts. He couldn't have known that in no time he would be training her, girl cook in the pilot's seat, young guys being picked off by the army. She didn't so much as knock or ask permission; suddenly a teenage girl was standing where no woman had ever been. Girl cook, she had walked right into the wheelhouse, man-sized apron looped around her neck and cutting under *breasts*, hair net twirling on her finger. Eyes aflame, by Christ. When the girl tossed her long dark hair it flew slow and heavy, like smoke around her face. Baby hair grown long, never really been cut. It had that shine. A runaway girl liar, claiming to be eighteen, and Johnny moving toward her from the start. His own protégé moving on the girl so naturally, being so wholly gummed by love it made you blush to think that Johnny had been waiting for this girl, for the feather that would knock him flat.

He stopped glugging juice and looked at the label. Guava. "I'll remember this when I go off. I'll get me some pink guava juice." His hand lay on Del Mae, hot with the panic of goodbye that unfinished business festers. Right off, he'd had to cut down the music her name brought on him. He shortened it to Del Mae. About the time they came and required official licensing for crew work—1972 it was—five years' experience for piloting, there was Del Mae, trained and cool. They handed her a certificate: qualified first mate. *Waterways* wrote something up about her.

"Girl, you hexed us into needing you and now you split. We're going to be like guys at a mission home, lost and grumpy. We're going to forget to shave."

"There're plenty of girls around now," she reminded him, "if you just like the idea. But if you're talking about missing me, it's OK to say so. I'll miss you guys too."

"You'll go back to New Orleans and keep house for Johnny," he decided. "We'll all visit there."

"A woman needs a black dress and real big bosoms to look right blessing sailors. These nursing boobs are going to deflate. You know I'm done with New Orleans."

Damn, she could shut up a man. Her blouse had wet bull's-eyes down the front, and no matter where you looked that's what you saw, and you felt old and dry just looking, just knowing how damn fluid she was.

She nudged him from the high straight-backed captain's chair and seated herself. The wind was down to a coo, bringing up the fish-and-metal smell, the river's underside; and the glint of sun on water made cat-eyes. From up here the river showed its true width, an impossibility to see from shore: its channels and islands bunched with trees and the occasional hobo fire there. When you came alongside of boys banked in rowboats, they would be sure to stand and pee theatrically. As witness and pilot you were obliged to hit the horn every time, an acknowledgment that you, too, were caught out silly and free. Once he had spied lovers flashing in the willows. He had sighted a girl bent forward, yellow sundress flipped over her back. She held on to willow shoots way out in front of her—like ski poles gone out of control; her back was a tabletop (that flat and steady) while the man thumped from behind; those two young willows she held on to were the only things shaking on a still bank. The girl stood barefoot in mud; the man wore boots, as if boots would keep some distance on the disturbance he was creating, keep control there. Cheramie had understood and approved those boots. But the hem fluttering on the girl's back taunted him anyway.

He bleated at the willow-bending couple, and maybe the trees, which had commenced a fine waving, shook even harder, now he thought of it, but they did not signal surrender or mercy. What he saw was sass. Willows were rebuking the man; he was made foolish and lost before the smooth fearlessness of a woman. That girl was rooted in mud and she was joking him with the willows. His boots held mud, not power. His tiny shove was nothing next to the girl's wild love with trees. The buttercup woman shimmered in the light. She moved with the willows as if she were one of them, and she could last with them, last way beyond that man.

And looking down on that action, Cheramie had seen the bluff of five failed marriages. From now on, he vowed, just give me a side dish of woman. That'll be enough, he thought. Nothing more or less than the safety (and challenge) built into taking on another man's woman. He knew his reasoning was a cover. He wanted Del Mae.

Now chocolate filled his throat. He admitted, looking away from her, he was the same kind of fool as that guy who found his woman planted happily with trees. A carefree yellow hem or something else: there are so many ways that women's joy can take the dirt out of you, weaken you to beggary and shame.

"We got a nice mixed load going up," he announced, afraid

that Del Mae might be getting on to reading his thoughts here now. His voice was rough, needing water. Water, juice, liquor, new kisses to rearrange memory and fade it on out. "We got four empties, two holding scrap, and we took on petroleum down at Baton Rouge. You were sleeping."

"I saw the red flags. Ghost barges and explosives are riding with my baby." Her voice kept its new nonchalant pushiness, but he saw gold flashes of fear in Del Mae's sundown eyes.

"Doesn't mean dick. It's a working tow here. You're on a working tow as guest and demon. You got us all crazy. Here," he told her, "do like it's your first time steering."

She took deep breaths and nodded, relief for both of them. Cheramie moved to stand behind her and put his rooty hands over hers, now holding the levers. The gleam of metal and all the winking board lights; the low rasp coming from the speaker overhead; big, black, one-eyed radarscope, the river's only rival for her own burning eyes: all of it, Cheramie felt, calmed and thrilled her as in the beginning. The whole world—your chosen world—waited and wished for your touch in order to heave along. A great dark need had pumped her insecure heart. No wonder as a little runaway she had climbed straight up to the wheelhouse. And galled him as they rode high above barges, seeing land, sky and water at a three-hundred-sixty-degree sweep, a bird's-eye view, the sun strapping their backs. She had exclaimed, "Up here the sun feels like flesh itself." "Ummm, it's strong," he'd agreed, alert to a hunter's language. Skin and flesh. Skin was anything, flesh meant women and men. She said, "The river's heart beats really fast." His head swam with the vertigo thrill he knew she felt. He'd seen other first-timers seized by the hungry agitation that comes on those who can touch the river's pulse.

And when he stood behind her that first time, covered her hands and pointed the barge right at a concrete pier, the girl had cried out. Her hands were stuck under his; he felt them— little kittens—smelled pastry in her hair. She pushed back, trying to lift herself away. He took her straight on, leveling against the jerkings of her small, strong hands. "Watch," he said. "You just watch. A good captain acts right off his belly." Coffee breath hit the crown of her head and came right back to him. Chewing on her hair would have been supper enough. He could have done it, and more—licked her knees—and kept concentration on the river, his sap was so high. The current that had pointed them right at the pier worked, as it always does with the engines reversed, to angle the tow smoothly—long snout of barge shifting—to approach the passage clear as ever and exactly dead-on. There went Memphis. She called it a great musical instrument risen up on the horizon. Her soft girl voice said, "Too much."

After one year on board with the girl-cook-wanting-to-be-a-pilot, he burned up with thoughts of her, would be content to feel her hiss and slap. Blame a year of eating crazy food dressed up to look like clouds and confetti; the girl-filled air that kept him charged. Under a slice of moon, six years ago he went off shift at midnight and went to her door.

It happened at New Madrid, where the river gets ideas. It speeds free as a comet, hitting the deep water now, and wants to rush down, jump course, and leave New Orleans dry. The women of New Madrid have strong, raw voices that carry far onto the water, and one of them is always calling out. Cut the engines and you hear them calling out. The corn grows fast and the women call harshly. A long time ago an earthquake here turned the river north, and you could think that flood frenzy still commands every sort of behavior. If ever the river is evil— and evil does come down from the north, everyone in the bayou knows that—here is the spot. Blame that river, man. He had walked off shift and stood in the still night and smoked; moved deck to deck; smoked and looked out and hankered. He went after the girl cook.

Blame the river's free fall, the lowing voices of New Madrid, for that night six years ago when he fidgeted in the waiting black air, understanding that he craved attention, even the spitting kind. He knew Johnny Red would be down with his engines till dawn.

He went to the girl cook's cabin, with its lights full blaze. Knocking made the door swing open. He could look back and say that door had been propped, not shut. She had been waiting. And what a girl does in her room at one A.M., he saw, was play the radio and sit on her bed with paper and pencil. It had to be Dear Diary from the way she hugged the paper to her chest at the sight of him: secrets and girl dreams spelled out in curlicues and waves.

She put the pencil in her mouth first, before speaking. She made a point of creating a dagger around which she said, "Hello, Cheramie. What do you want?"

He stood there, inside now, the door shut and locked behind him, and he looked around. Where had she gotten all this stuff? The room was draped with scarves, gauzy and silky, tacked up in a way that erased the idea of four square walls. Some had lights shining from behind. You couldn't find a sharp edge, a piece of the paneling, anywhere. You got no impression whatsoever of regular four-sided walls, like a normal room, only this billowy look, some carnival trick. Well. He sucked in his breath. She lived in some kind of teenage idea of love, that was exactly the point. She was—what—nineteen now? She would claim to be nineteen. She let him look all around until there was nowhere to look but at her, the girl with teeth clamping a pencil.

Her legs were drawn up now, her jeans tight on her hips, the hems flared out so leg showed way up. She wore this white blouse you could see right through to skin. Short sleeves puffed out like caps over her arms, edged with designs, and bright-colored tassels dangled onto her arms. That pencil in her mouth spread her lips.

"You're scared," he blurted. "It's too steady with Johnny."

Out came the pencil. "You should know, the way you keep switching wives. I guess you think love's boring."

She'd thrown him off already. "That could be, girl. It does

rearrange you." Shoots down the roamer possibility, chokes some people up with its exposure and demands.

She just looked at him, but paper and pencil were put away and without seeming to move, she was suddenly on her knees on that bed.

"My daddy bought me this blouse." She flicked at a tassel hanging off the sleeve.

"From Mexico?"

"That's right. He took along some woman he shouldn't have."

Blood rushed in his head and arms. What kind of permission did that information give him? Things were going different here from what he had thought and expected, but he came forward, ready. Get to the slap and hiss part and be on your way. Let her hand fly, then get out. He sat on the bed, uninvited, ready.

"Look at the overhead curtain," she said.

It seemed to breathe in and out, something to do with the light behind it, he guessed, even as his heart was now stirring up enough commotion to bend spoons or do anything.

He was looking up when she pounced from behind, with her arms around his neck. "You want to do it to me!"

He was sunk. This close it was true, Lord, true. A man responds, sure. Don't let yourself notice she's a baby playing pattycake. Humbly he said, "With you."

She sprang off the bed, stepped back, and stared at him with the eyes that bloomed like flowers. Now she had a mermaid look, those belled jeans so long her feet were covered. She was just curve and swish from the waist down. What was she murmuring, her face in lantern-low light, hair burnished, eyes fast? Soft, though. Christ, she was a soft-looking one. That white blouse with short puffed sleeves was not tucked in. It hung loose and any movement showed skin. Those tassels dangling off the sleeves. Cheramie came up to her from behind and straddled his legs wide to grip her within. He took a tassel in his mouth and chewed it into a spitball. He breathed on her neck, hair; breathed into her ear, with his hands across her front, feeling breasts push out, stomach and thigh curve to him.

He unzipped her pants. That quick rough sound caused them both to suck in breath. He pressed his hand there: now he was touching the flutter of blood and chanting nonsense to it.

She slithered all around in his arms, and here came the little mewing sounds; hands all up in the loose blouse, holding her arms high, a little girl letting it slip up, off. White, white breast with the blouse off, rubbing him. It was too far gone, whatever the plan. He couldn't have dreamed this. He gripped her, still in her split-open jeans, falling, falling of her own free will onto the bed and rolling, that hair like spun candy wrapping her, fanning her back, covering her breasts, and in the lantern light he could see the nipple gems show through the parted hair. He pulled off the jeans—no resistance there—and knelt before flowered triangle panties. Life was that sweet on the Mississippi River; she rode it up and down, cooked dinner and drove tonnage with these flowered panties riding low against her skin. He ran his hands all over her and hooked his fingers into the panties and pulled them low.

"Here, I brought something to use," he told her. And though he hadn't dared consider this situation and had been sheepish earlier rummaging for it, he said, "I'll be careful." Here he was reaching into his pocket. She covered her mouth like a child and spluttered at him from between her fingers.

"The rubber." Oh, she laughed. She laughed and rolled away. As if she was thinking, Five wives and not one child—who needs it?

Well, he tried to laugh along past the rush of heartbeat in his ears. Then, "Del Mae?" he wondered as her voice went higher. His throat hurt. And he finally just stopped her with a hand over her mouth. Now this was out of control, not the way it should work. This glee that did not fit in with her having the hots or submitting to a worldly man. Just have her this once, though. If she would stop squirming, he just wanted her once.

"Come on, baby."

He had to corral her, not that she was bolting, but this glee put her downright slithery all over that bed. "Little eel, come on."

From the quick hysteria he caught her down and steadied her against him, and she shot directly to the moaning, thrashing shriek thing of a woman's bliss. And long before the magic end-time, when a man gains supernatural strength and the woman is boneless beneath, she crashed and sank, was, he feared there for a moment—forcing himself to think real thoughts—out cold.

He finished quickly. Who had ever seen a girl go on, just go on so fast like that, faster than yourself? He rolled to her side. That radio went on still, with all the news of Chicago, Illinois, something more on Chicago tearing itself up, cops and kids mad on trying to make or kill a President, you couldn't tell which. Del Mae lay spent, and over and over she licked at his bat tattoo and he had to fight down the panic of knowledge: she was a child after all.

"That's enough there," he told her, and even more unnerving, she stopped. He freely wondered what he had never heard a man speak of: about the feel on a woman of different men. A big soft body, Johnny's, must sort of sink into her and wrap around, and then how would it contrast, his own short knotty self jerking up and down her, face in her neck? How a woman adjusted, who knew? He thought of Johnny down tending his engines and the way dumb love had gummed him good.

"I've never seen a girl get going like you, plow right past me like you did. I've never known a woman able to."

She lay in the dark, he hoped not insulted, so he kissed her and she lay on, quiet, sort of humming.

"I think . . . ," she drawled, in a thick after-sex voice, "I see now that I've been waiting for this thrill."

"Well, girl." He slipped his hand to her warm thigh. She might leap to it all over again. He wouldn't do much, just lie there and give her speed.

"I didn't know what I'd been waiting for, what I needed to do exactly."

"I surprised you good."

"I've needed to feel the way my daddy does. Who would have known how sweet betrayal feels?" she said, making all sorts of swanlike arm movements up toward her ceiling scarves.

Cheramie removed his hand.

"It wipes out the pain of love junk. It's rich enough to live on. That's what my daddy likes."

"It's an accident we got together," he reminded her quickly. No impression was made. This girl was chanting.

"He lives with my mother but is lovers with the nurse."

She addressed him, but with eyes he could walk right through, that took you down a hall, slamming doors behind.

"You're still high. I'm afraid you're going to feel bad later."

"No," she said. "I feel great. You don't know me. I'm nasty enough to have wanted my daddy. I wanted him like this, all the way."

And, little chanter, she went, "Delana, Delana, Magdelana."

Cheramie was about out of words. "Don't be creepy with me."

"Johnny knows." But she stopped there, as something rigid happened in the remembering. Her voice got brisk. "It went wrong with Daddy."

He pushed her away and sat up. He grabbed for his clothes. "We went too far, Del Mae, and now you're way off. You are way off in your thinking. Damn, you're creepy. Don't drag me down. I'm not him, and I don't need this confession. The problem is, you ran away, like girls do, and no one ever came after you, isn't that right? That's what eats you. All year you've been riding the river and no one ever came after you. We didn't have a jealous doctor storming the river for his girl. Del Mae, fucking an older guy isn't going to change that."

She was up in a second and biting his wrist, hanging on like a gar, biting deep and hard, and in the pain he saw what the next few days would be: toothprint bracelet turning purple, throbbing, then comes the yellow-green of healing, which looks even worse. Married five times, he knew the course of a woman's bite. He would keep his shirt sleeves buttoned and for once give thanks for his short arms, the way his cuffs rode low for good cover-up.

"You've wanted to do that," he told her. "All your life you have wanted to bite some man. Well, I'm obliged. I gave you reason." He scrambled to dress and gain the door.

"Go to Johnny," he called over his shoulder. "Get tight with him and forget this. When you come up to me to learn your piloting, don't act loony, girl. This thing happened and it's over. I lost my head. Man, I sure did."

"You just acted off your belly," she threw at him. Tease.

"I say we stop the talk now, right now. We're like family here. We forget and move on."

That was wicked relief lighting her face, too, when next she said, "Oh, yes, family." That look the whole earth gets, is going to have, river and all, after a huge rain stops. The silver look. After the New Madrid flood, God surely had that cleansed and done-up look. Del Mae was pure, pungent, wicked relief.

And now she's eating cookies and talking about dying. New mother, she stands with the wet bull's-eyes on her front, saying, What if I die now? That's what's rotten about being a parent. "You've got to really consider it. Suddenly your own death is just there."

"You could've fooled everyone as to exactly whose death was under consideration on this trip."

"If I die, she grows up with my sister Marcia."

"Johnny's nobody?"

"You can't take a baby on the river. If I die," Del Mae stressed, "Robin will grow up Catholic with Marcia. That's exactly how it will go. In our family, death turns a girl Catholic." There was a whip of passion in her voice.

Cheramie paused, then massaged her shoulders. "Del Mae, relax." She groaned. Of course her body still ached all over: stitches were working their way into her most female flesh, to fade there—he knew that much; and some lonesome points like the shoulders found now they had been aching for touch. She rolled them up and down in time to the radarscope's bleeps at her side. That first time up, she had touched the radarscope and then told him it reminded her how once when she was little, her daddy's wet-lipped nurse had shown her an x-rayed heart. For some reason she was waiting in her daddy's office for him, and the nurse took it upon herself to occupy her boss's girl. And she wondered, grown up and eyeing the radarscope: Whose heart? Whose green-dot heart?

Questions Cheramie had had no answers for. Rivermen, they were used to old cooks, tough weary souls, women full-grown. From the start, they none of them knew what to do with her, a girl coming on, all frisking fierceness.

His fingers went to her temples and rubbed; and they rode along, four miles an hour. They rode in silence, and from behind Del Mae he was taking the controls now. His voice barely brushed her ear.

"Mate, we've been places together. We've been about everywhere together." He hugged her. "Do you forgive me for that time coming at you? It was bad of me, and weak."

"Ummm," she said, "that was minor."

Christ, she was steady. He pressed up quickly before pushing himself away, and immediately he ran his palms back from his temples, so fast, feeling like an animal cleaning himself of a trap.

The picture of the sister lay on the panel. He picked it up. That look around the mouth asking a question, asking, "When, please?" Woman long past having her children, who hangs with a priest, it can only mean one thing: she's somehow kinky, this one.

"She's one of those charismatics," Del Mae said, flicking her tongue so fast at his ear his mind raced to catch up with the little breeze, the words going in: "Her goal is to speak in tongues." Then she let out a coyote laugh, which seven years on the river had not tamed one damn bit.

BUTTER CREAM FROSTING," Marcia said. "I ordered extra-thick butter cream, not mint. Yes, with a border of blue flowers. Any kind. Just squiggle on something."

Bluebells, chicory, anything would do. Pink roses on top, the size of real sugar roses. *Roses rugosa.* The bakery had gotten that part right. Just checking, they said, before icing the cake. She whirled from the phone, to find her sons hulked behind her. "What is it?" she cried sharply, seeing for a moment only bulk, foreignness, invasion in the telephone nook. "What do you want?"

"Can we call Aunt Delana a hobo?" the twelve-year-old asked. "Can we tell our friends?"

"She's a pilot on the Mississippi River, coming home."

"Mom, when she came for Grandma's funeral, she told me all she owned was a radio and a scarf. She wore men's clothes."

"She was a mess, slinking back here and hiding from Grandpa. That was six years ago. It's history."

"Come on, say she's a hobo, please?"

"I will not."

"She lives on a boat."

"Mike, she maintains a home in New Orleans, a major city."

"A radio and a scarf, Mom. That's a hobo."

"She's not married," said Jackie Junior, two years older, cooler than Mike. "She's probably a hippie. Isn't she calling the baby Rainbow or something?"

"Robin, Jackie Junior. Robin." And as she said the name, truly it sounded much too light and free, and what saint, honestly, was the name Robin derived from?

"Have some decency," she scolded. "It's too hot. Don't stand so close." She waved her arms high, shooing, shooing the chickens.

The younger boy shrugged and did something unnerving with his lips. Obviously, even this one, her baby, Mike, at twelve, had already kissed a girl. Kissed *girls*, most likely. Marcia flopped into a chair.

"Everything's ready for her. I've done what I can."

At the coolest early Mass, Father Dan had rocked back and forth, speaking right to her. The Saturday gospel was from St. Paul's letter to the Corinthians. "But if they cannot contain, let them marry, for it is better to marry than to burn."

She had rubbed her legs together, loving the slick feel of her nylons. She abhorred women who wore pants in church. Though genuflection would certainly be easier when wearing pants, in fact the ritual had all but disappeared in the wake of change. And now people slouched into pews and talked across the aisle as if waiting for a lecture, as if five years of Vatican-approved meat-eating on Friday nights mandated every laxity imaginable. But as for hats, now there was a decent change: good riddance. No, she did not miss hats and their absurd successor, the doily. A doily perched over a brush bubble haircut! Where had they bought those doilies? She could not remember, only that real hats had gone out years ago, when the Jackie look died. And when the doily gave way to the tissue square pinned at the side of the head, a cunning way to keep the hairdo absolutely unharmed—pink or yellow or blue tissues, but never white, were plucked out of the box and onto the head—it seemed that God Himself was endorsing hair spray. Even now in Italy, they were periodically reminded for the sake of feeling gratitude, it was still unacceptable to enter a cathedral wearing a sleeveless shell top. Bare shoulders are taboo. Shoulders were another part of her body left sexually unattended by Jack. *Married, yet I'm burning, Father Dan*. Father Dan, Marcia had prayed, beamed, hoped to reveal through concentration: I am a sexual tenderfoot. What about that?

She looked at her boys and saw thick-necked wolfish half-growns wearing puberty like a rash; and she was moved to recite from her old Baltimore Catechism, a clear and disciplined approach to life, which they had never known. *Who made me? God made me. Who is God? God is the Supreme Being who made all things.* Before her stood two of God's *things*, who had sprung lively and needy from her womb only to screech and burst their way into foreignness, well, this *athleticism*, and TV mulish contentedness; and it turned out that they got it from Jack, a man who knew electricity inside out and therefore never did take to the argument of God, as he had sworn he would do at the time of their engagement. For a self-employed electrical contractor, mystery was solved by connecting wires, poles, accepting negativity, shorting some things out and plugging in others. Explosions, even a house being struck by lightning, had their origins in the particles, not sin and omen and confessional release. Jack Rose provided food, clothing, shelter, and the teaching of intricate knot-tying to his boys. He gutted fish with them. And he discoursed on his high-school glory via the yearbook that barely featured him.

It was not even noon. Today, finally, Delana was coming home, but it was not even noon.

On her last day home, a teenaged Delana had looked at their father's friends—Sky was playing host to a frolic of men—and asked Marcia simply, "What happened to their passion?" Marcia could have told her: one day skin is just skin. You smell the wrong thing, and the rhythm of his most innocent breathing, the sleeping sounds a man makes, hurts your teeth. A cold ball bearing strikes the heart, thighs, the ankle bone. The knee refuses to bend. It's over. The immediate aftereffect of sex then is embarrassment (what else?), in light of his resumption of dictating plans for a car purchase. "Which model car, I'm wondering. Which one?" He scratches his chest. The velvet and stars are gone. Were they ever there, or did she just see them with a girl's long and longing eyes? Probably that, but Marcia did not say so to Delana, seventeen years old, going to rid herself of virginity. Delusion is one thing she had not spoken of on Delana's last day home.

"You're bored," she told her boys, "moping around the house. Big bored boys. We need to occupy ourselves."

The boys flexed their muscles and shook their heads. They thought themselves too sophisticated for her plans, but especially despised her obsession with broken bones—her warnings and scenarios. They despised the way she had tested the high dive before letting them jump. And she had walked first, embarrassing the family like mad, on the cinder track to tell herself it was safe; safe for her boys to run around in big sneakers, flashing bare knees, white shorts, with the others. (Jack had exploded. "Fucking inundated with safety.") In their childhood, all cabinets were kept locked. The boys had never even glimpsed Ajax or sponges except in their mother's hands, and for them, the result was to take every chance, just break out. Said Jack, "Delinquents or athletes is what you get from that worry. We fell on the lucky side." And with their beef- and milk-fed largeness and uncanny agility, they succeeded, surpassed, won prizes and got headlines in newspapers. They behaved, Marcia Rose swore, like superhuman, disregarding ingrate fools, and the world clapped, egged them on with those newspaper headlines: S.E. COMMUNITY SWIMMER STILL SMELLING LIKE A ROSE; ROSES ARE RED, JEFF HIGH IS BLUE.

Swimming and pole vaulting. The younger one was built of brick, and still (this could not be natural) he would knife his way through water, go silent as a shark in turbo patterns, looking fine even under the horrid lights, with chlorine rising in fumes that gagged the onlookers and frizzed their hair. After twisting in midair, he would knife through the water, maintaining the showiness long after going under. Spectators ogled his finesse: Mike taking his sweet time, lithe and wavy below, breaking surface with his eyes already open. And Jackie Junior, a freshman at fourteen, was the one who went running into the air totally upside down, dependent on a spindling pole—*a reed*—to keep his back from breaking. His legs kick at the sky. He will die surely, but then another twisting kick, and he arcs over. For a split second with his head tossed, coming down he is just a big baby bird who will not learn to fly, and Marcia in the bleachers stuns her face impassive by pressing on her cheeks. Jackie Junior's hair is so short that it remains the same, no matter what, right side up or rushing the ground. He breaks a record with his beautiful skull intact, hair unruffled, and they all go home.

After a good night's sleep this Jack Junior will go detassel corn for the bare minimum wage and prosper; he will walk steadily on the earth doing hard work, and he will not even feel strain. His mind is on pleasure and the body is endlessly springy. The body takes in food, food, food, and does all its tricks. Alone in church Marcia has prayed about this. She knows the detasseler is having a fling, has a girl. And it is sick, sickening, this young girl with blooms on her cheeks, her loud voice snagged on the snapping of sugared gum; the way she serves lunches at the Nauvoo Hotel on Saturdays, with a smirkiness fluttering her lashes, as if adults don't know that signal. Marcia went there to study the girl, and to think, but she held back once the plates were cleared. She did not say, "But he is my baby!" Lightly holding a napkin to her eyes, she refused the girl's suggestion of pound cake.

In the last six years of marriage Jack Rose has caused her feeble pleasure, once from a dangling hand moving so slightly she just clamped herself around it and—prisoner—it gave up pleasure to her. After that, an alarmed Jack Rose kept closer watch on his hands. The other time, having to do with the leg,

Jack never knew about, being asleep. Marcia gained the definite (but low) thrill of a pickpocket; cheap thievery not worth repeating.

She pictured Father Dan over at St. Clement's basement room, where the charismatics gather for Wednesday-night prayer group. *Holy, holy, holy, Lord God Almighty*, as the old song went. With Father Dan finally came some heat. Finally something good post-Vatican, after a period of sickening pale songs and a trial stretch of guitar Masses and the awful look of progress: St. Clement's sleeked down to a kind of Nordic chill. With walls plastered gray, the high crinkled light that comes in through stained-glass windows now seems to dissolve over the congregation in narrower jets of yellow, like a weak winter sun. Gone, gone is the crucifix, big bloody life-size Christ with nails riving hands and feet. Bloody Him, nail Him, but *not a bone of Him shall you break*, was the prophecy for Jesus. Due to the reforms, every parish in America now had stashed somewhere these great bleeding Christs. Marcia had recently seen a "new" crucifix in an Iowa church across the water, which, though not abstract (not some Mexican no-face whittled-wood thing), was hung at a height and angle to suggest a marathon runner coming over the line. Arms were spread in victory, head up, one knee bent; certainly the feet were not nailed one on top of the other. Here was Christ yipping at the altar, a figure for the Wheaties box. Marcia swore for hours after ingestion that the Iowa host had given her jitters.

What a shame to grow up without His blood in your eyes.

Father Dan had brought the charisms to Nauvoo, a wild new action to the Church. He said, "Call me by my first name." The end of Monsignor Deutsch; goodbye, Father Finney. Father Dan led parishioners to believe that anything at all was possible. There would be healing prayers, the laying on of hands. And when he promised that some would speak in tongues, Marcia had prayed to get loud in it, shouting loud. If only . . .

Father Dan, she had prayed this morning, watching him go through the communion ritual, raising the big host (chewing it ostentatiously to let the old folks see reform), I am a tenderfoot lover, age thirty-two; I have had my husband, no others. I believe that a deep sacred connection between a man and a woman *is* possible and, I confess, I am wishing for a spark in the physical realm. I pray to know it. Movies, gossip, the Saturday-night kitchen fights reported in the news—they have not made it up. I do my duties in the Church, serve at the Altar and Rosary Society lunches, all of it. I read biographies of women who have prevailed over suffering. And, yes, again this week I am hosting a lingerie party. Father Dan, I have the lingerie shipped to a post box in Macomb, where no one knows me. Driving back to Nauvoo, I've imagined the trunk springing open; bit by bit the lingerie works loose and sails behind me. I'm a knowing, naughty Gretel. I leave a trail. True love will scent the trail. These butterflies of love will draw the male's nectaring love.

For the occasion of introducing the subject to her priest, she had made use of the new face-to-face confessional approach he had instituted. "Father Dan," she had pressed from her folding chair, not unaware of the lick in her voice, "is it being lustful or dutiful to the marriage or just enterprising to sell provocative lingerie?"

A splendid pinkness spread up to his baldness and down to his neck. She rushed on. "I buy for myself too, at discount."

The priest's hand more or less snapped at the wrist and his fingers twiddled. "Are there any unnatural accoutrements—oh, such as fastenings of a kind and—"

"Fastenings?" she repeated.

"Unusual . . . metallic, like . . ." his voice dropped to a crooner's low. Did she hear him say *keyholes?*

"Nylon underthings, Father Dan. Packaged, if you wish—"

"Go now, dear. Go in peace."

She pictured how she must have looked sitting in the woven chair that time, wearing pressed pants and an overblouse. How could I have told him? Still, a thought swung down as if from a trapeze: He must wonder. At times, since that day, he must wonder what I am wearing underneath. Sweet Mary, help! I crave my priest.

"Oh," she cried.

The boys looked at her. "Now what?"

Her eyes raced over the console TV, the end table and goldfish bowl, the window clogged with hanging plants, and her deep carpet with the plastic runner leading in from the door; she groped to comprehend what she had just admitted. She blurted out wildly, "Working this river runs in the family. And it has nothing to do with hoboes. Why, your grandfather worked on the river over in Muscatine, where they made buttons."

The boys hulked over her and sniffed suspiciously as she found herself retelling with great urgency why Muscatine used to be called Pearl City. For years the tiny town on the Iowa side was button capital of the country. To think that the mother-of-pearl buttons found everywhere in the nation came from Muscatine. Freshwater clamshells were dug out of the river's muck by the thousands and transformed into cheap good buttons. "Boys your age made plenty of money scooping clamshells out of the river." There, that was a point worth getting to: work vs. sloth. But her mind raced. *Unusual fastenings.*

"I already know the button story," Jackie Junior said. "Mom, it sucks."

Jackie Junior had long ago grown the cool eyes that flickered with men's thoughts. He was only eight when they all went to the grape festival and rode the Tilt-A-Whirl. Round and round they sailed in a mesh basket, riding sickening waves and sudden drops. Before it was fully stopped Marcia had jumped off the ride and rushed from its metal smells. She watched as Jack came along, an arm around each boy. Jackie Junior gave her the cool look, and she thought: Dear God, what had an eight-year-old boy learned that she hadn't from riding the Tilt-A-Whirl? Jack sent the boys on to get corn dogs. He was still transfixed too, with some rolled-away stare sweeping the grounds. "What is it?" she demanded to know. Jack rubbed his chin and pushed out his lower lip. "That ride makes your penis feel funny," he told her. "The boys noticed too." Marcia looked away to all the screaming people on rides, then back. Her husband's face was lit by neon, his Kewpie smile turned inward. So there at a carnival was the proof of eternal mysteries. Throughout the rest of the day, and often afterwards, she would look on the three of them as the triumvirate alien.

Buttons, snaps, toggles, loops, cuff links, zippers, Velcro, laces, bows, eyelets—nothing she thought of in the way of fastenings sounded like keyholes. She had heard Father Dan say *keyholes*.

"Mr. Boepple stepped on a clamshell and brought it up to his face," she shrilled. She could hear the same warble in her voice that she used to make fun of in her mother's. "He was furious at that clamshell the way you are when you stub your toe. But he looked closely at it and saw button possibilities. Anger turned to industry. Work was love." She could clearly picture Mr. Boepple, that frowning German immigrant, cussing the shell. *Her* age group had learned all about it in school, even in Catholic school, maybe especially in Catholic school. They reverenced miracle, self-denial, and work. I still do, Father Dan, she thought. You know I believe. I just want the gift of tongues and . . .

"But digging in the river sucks." Jackie Junior yawned.

Marcia ignored this rudeness; she ignored the frowns on the faces of her boys, who stood before her wearing, as always, she suddenly realized, nothing that required buttons. She had to keep the shrieking laughter inside. *No fastenings, Father Dan. None at all.* Their clothes slung over their bodies: hoods and drawstrings; T-shirts stretched across those chests. Zippers, not buttons, gleamed.

She recalled the industrious Mr. Boepple's demise. He stepped on another clamshell and this time got blood poisoning. "It happened before antibiotics," she said. "Nothing could save him."

"Big ones," came from her Jackie Junior. "Sucks big ones."

"Did he hit an artery? Did it gush?" Twelve years old, her young Mike was born to love gore. His neck was thicker than Jackie Junior's: a tree trunk. Another arrow in her heart, this mass. "Hey, Mom," he said, "the art teacher thinks I look like Marlon Brando when he was young."

"Ha, ha," croaked the older boy, slouching. "To Gutsy Fat

Legs anything looks good." Jackie Junior was the snobby one, with aspirations of a kind that she and Jack had never known or wished for or heard of until now: spring break in Florida, air force training the minute he would be out of school. His vaulter's body might have been made of slats. "Marlon Brando," he said, crossing his arms. "That's a good one. A *big* one."

"You love the Avon twins," retorted the young Marlon.

Their croaking voices as good as sucked air right out of Marcia's lungs. The sound they made ached inside her. Yes, Mike had great lips, stars' lips. And girls were calling him. He was only twelve, in seventh grade, and huge girls (the Avon twins?), impatient and much older, fully developed girls, were calling Mike on the phone.

"Find something to do," she insisted. She got up and began shuffling magazines. "Entertain yourselves."

Like old men, the boys limped and complained around the room. Mike turned on the TV, flipped through channels, then snapped it off. Jackie Junior went to the kitchen and returned lofting a melon in his hands. It was a smooth white-green globe, its skin as alarming to touch as a person's. He tossed it to Mike, who feinted to Marcia. She threw her hands up like a shield, crying, "Don't!"

They passed it before her, back and forth, laughing the croaky laughs of boys, caressing the melon with their hands and cheeks. Famous Muscatine melons. Every town around there had some drastic history of enterprise and dreams; then, incidentally, prize fruit that belied the tragic. Nauvoo, where the Mormon leader Joseph Smith was stoned to death in the last century, dripped with religious history and blue-ribbon grapes. This year's grape festival would begin just as Delana arrived home.

Marcia went into her bedroom and the boys dove into the refrigerator. Someone was pouring milk. She lay on her bed in the room decorated with violet print wallpaper and violet print bedspread. The white sheers breathed against the windows. On went the new jawbreaker voices:

"You love the Avon twins," Mike was taunting.

"Fuck off," said Jackie Junior.

Marcia cried out, "Stop it!" The boys began whispering.

"Well, who are they?" she called.

"Ah, Mom, just these ugly sisters with stuff caked on their faces."

"You love them," said the younger brother, known for his clean, quiet knife dives. "You love them in the mud. Oink, oink."

She heard a scrambling. A glass fell and clanged; it was aluminum.

"Fuck off, Mikey."

She ripped open the J. C. Penney catalog and felt disgusted to see women's underwear advertised as foundation garments. Well, truly, this stuff did not qualify as lingerie, these encasements and armored breast cones. All the shining hardware amassed by the sisterhood of fear. Out in the kitchen, on went the thumping and taunting. "You'll lick it off their faces and then suck—"

"Shut up," she yelled. "Have some decency."

But everything had changed since her own teenage days—the words, everything—and she knew for a fact that her older son's girl, the fling (her name was scary, nonchurched: Belle) a full grade ahead of her boy and already sixteen, took the birth control pills, and the idea of swallowing chemicals every day of your life, having them dissolve throughout your system, go into your blood and turn it neon with negative attraction in order to somehow block pregnancy, was too gruesome, unreal, too horribly new. Imagine your blood all lit up and sensitized to stinginess, as if the wrong electrical pole resided within you.

They did it under her roof. She was sure of that. Upstairs, with the door shut, and everyone else right there in the living room . . . upstairs, right above her head, they carried on. And the girl, Belle, would come down looking like picked new corn, the silk fallen all around; shucked corn with the silk left on carelessly, falling softly. She would come down the stairs shimmering like Silver Queen Variety corn—oh, the pearliest—in the noonday sun.

Admit, though, a tiny sigh of contentment. First of all, it wasn't *her* blood taking on the pill's damage. And maybe doctors would know how to reverse whatever bad thing had happened, strip it out the way they strip varicose veins, when these girls got older, if something showed up wrong. And mercifully, you could just forget any trip to Booth Memorial Home for Girls for this one: no Belle girl would be giving away a fresh new Catholic baby to the Christ Child Home. Booth had been a long-standing feeder stall for those nuns. Oh, how it had kept them in orphans, as if there were no other lost babies on the planet. Occupied and pious, long black nun figures handed over the fresh new Catholic babies to screened couples as if the babies were pies from their own tart recipes, thank you. Citrus sharp.

Her good friend Celia had ended up at Booth. And though Celia never returned to St. Agnes Academy, she stole over to tell Marcia about Booth. She came back with one shoulder raised higher than the other, and when she laughed her head fell against the high shoulder, as if to fix the laugh somewhere, to wedge it steady. She brought a can opener and beers, which they took into the woods at the side of the house.

It was sex jail, Celia said. Everyone was sluggish and sweating and peeing and dripping one thing or another all over the place. She said the best you could do was claim love. The girls who claimed steady (really ex-steady) boyfriends rated high in Booth. They would claim, even under severe jeering, "I love him, I love him," and have a tale of how it almost worked except for the despising parents. They rated, high-passion girls who knew what they wanted. They prayed their boys' names aloud. In the night the whisper killed you: Louie. Craig. Thurston. Thurston, what's that? Thurston, with no nickname, bitch.

"It's just like a jailbreak when a girl leaves," Celia said. "She's cut up and hollering."

In the hospital, a girl's baby was born and rolled away pronto, incubated like an ornery tulip bulb; and the girl, if she had even been alert enough, awake (so many were out cold when the big moment came), felt fire in her arms and then lead, then just a freezing paralysis there in space, as though her arm ended at the wrist but the hand was still there, full of raw shock. Some girls screamed bloody murder. "I want my baby!" But it was gone, honey. It resurfaced as a fresh orphan pie in the arms of a nun. The girl's mother rushed in, saying, There, there. She described a fresh start, forced visions of mohair sweaters on the girl, like ether. Wonderful, wonderful outfits for public school. Which is where Celia had ended up. And public school boys, she claimed, walked on springs around her.

"They're deep down horrified and amazed and hoping to lay one of the bad ones without throwing up."

Celia said she saw a black girl just take her baby on home, a parade of women in hats waving dahlias around her. Laughter had trailed down the hall. "You know why farm girls have yellow-faced kids with buckteeth?" Celia gulped that beer. She said she truly loved to drink beer, that she was very good at stealing it. "It's their dad's," she said. "Their dad was the guy."

"No," Marcia had pleaded. "Please, no."

"They said mine was a boy," Celia said, shrugging. She sucked at the beer.

Marcia found she had been squeezing and squeezing her arms across her breasts. She said, "I'll never have one."

God is the supreme being who made all things. How many times had she recited this from the Baltimore Catechism? She lay on her bed remembering being with Jack in the dull-pink Ford called flesh tone back then, that she was spared from being like Celia: her baptized boys swearing in the kitchen came out of marriage.

Delana Mae was coming home with a new baby girl. A new-generation Walsh girl, a wild miracle unimagined. You did not imagine a new Walsh girl; you did not imagine Delana a mother. After Mass, she had lit candles. She had prayed: Delana, marry him and baptize that baby. Father Dan had sent her home, assuring her that God would be with that baby, no matter what. True, Limbo was out now, but . . .

Lying on her violet bedspread, Marcia thought of doll shoes, the blue plastic shoes that her mother had found for her favorite doll one summer day during little sister Sally's last season. They found the shoes in a family variety store up in Oquawka. Then Dovie had turned to little Sally, only four years old, holding her dirty gray stuffed elephant, and told the sales clerk, "We'd like shoes for DoDo too." Marcia remembered her embarrassment. Anyone could see that the elephant did not have feet. But she looked at Sally and saw how her eyes burned. Sally took hold of some largish white shoes, round-toed things, the Mary Jane strap that looped down on a little nub, and with her tongue stuck out for better concentration, she proceeded to stuff DoDo's big blunt stub-legs into those shoes. They all walked out, the proper doll in her blue shoes and DoDo under Sally's arm with each foot at the cavalier angle you see even to this day coming off a prosthetic leg, however nimble. Dovie, Marcia remembered, was singing softly to herself, thrilled absolutely and royal in having accomplished something so fine and concrete for her girl. Two months later Sally would drown. Within the year Delana would be born. What doll did Delana ever have? Marcia could not recall one single doll and felt hot and uncomfortable. What doll? What doll, little sister? Then Delana grew up and ran away to the river, and Dovie screeched at Sky, "Why, why do you drive my girls away?" Nothing he said could dissuade her. She spat, "Your voice is a sausage. It holds in the guts of your lies." She had called Marcia over immediately, a daughter twenty-four years old, with two babies; she had called her—"Come right now"—as if serving supper years before. How Delana would have liked to see Dovie with teeth and claws. A high-heeled shoe lay spike up on the kitchen counter. The pincushion was a clot on the carpet, glowing. It might have been Sky's heart torn right out. *Sacred Heart* —here, take it. She remembered the pictures in her old books: blood, flames, and thorn. Knife, knitting needle, pastry gun, stapler? Who could tell what Dovie had used on him? The house was open menace, room to room, curtains tangled, TV antenna a long horizontal jab. The ugly stuffed chair with little pigs' feet was humiliated, legs stuck in the air. All she could think was: Finally the house is seasoned; finally it looks lived in. Sky attended to his gashes and the next day he worked. Nothing showed. He even delivered a baby. And it was understood that the letter-writing would be left to her, Dovie being out of words, capable only of sending sweets. It was she, Marcia, who wrote to Delana, telling how after dark Dovie would plug in the old clown night-light as if it could call home a girl. (She had seen their mother step away humming, sure of her effort.) How funny it was, she wrote to Delana: love and defeat can look exactly the same on people's faces. Dovie and Sky could be mistaken for two old people in love.

Through a misty view of violet flowers it came to her again: I crave my priest.

She had grown up and not moved but twenty miles from home, and now she heard coming from her kitchen, "Both Avon twins will sit on your face at once, turkey. You'll suck double time." She closed her eyes to dream the dream of parting and pain that was the only true business at hand. Sisters, one on the water, one off, were steaming in the memory of how it once came to be Delana's time to leave home. Just as in the old St. Joseph's Daily Missal, with its left-hand pages in Latin, right side in English, and something exotic and unreadable in the gap between languages, she understood they would each have her own story. Marcia prayed, "Little sister, I'm going back to that time. Let your memory face you too. Bring it up wild, and in your mind lay hands on its darkness. Let's give it sun, finally, Jesus."

SUMMER 1967, you had to be hopeless to watch cities burn on Saturday-morning TV. Cameras stayed trained on cartoon-pink fire, hours and hours of fire. Jack Rose even followed the green flecks of interference, as if reading a code of action into them. "I'm going over to see how Daddy and everyone is doing," Marcia told him.

"Now?" Jack whined without taking his eyes from the TV. Both kids were sprawled on the floor, exhausted TV troupers with pillows, little Mike in undershorts, one hand in his pants. TV light flickered over all. Color TV gave Marcia a headache— the flashes of concentrated light and the accompanying crackling buzz. An announcement blared: "The Mustang is supreme." The singing voice of Diana Ross cut into the car commercial as if the Detroit Chamber of Commerce had gone lunatic on TV, begging viewers nationwide to see that the Motown holies, music and cars, were untouched by ghetto flame. *Come see about me.*

"With all those beekeepers coming, Delana could use some help," Marcia said.

Jack shifted around as if his hemorrhoids were bothering him or he needed a sandwich: she was to understand that a severe attack of helplessness was about to hit. Make a plan to go away, and panic nabbed the zombie triumvirate. The boys looked up and opened their baby-bird mouths.

"Brush your teeth," she told them. "I'll be right back." And to Jack, with a history of regret: "Detroit is burned up. Can't you see it's all burned up? Why keep watching?"

Her little sister did not even hear her come up the stairs. There she lay on a throw rug at the foot of her postered bed, wearing nothing but a half-slip, the small round fan on the window ledge cruising its slow, slow face back and forth over her nakedness. The breeze lifted her long bangs to show Delana's star-bright eyes. Lavender blue, they were, a lovely shock against her gypsy-black hair.

"Delanie, what on earth are you doing? Are you OK?"

Delana's head lolled toward Marcia as the fan swept away, and it was kind of frightening, she looked so lush: berry nipples, and the way her lips were parted. What was coming?

Delana stuck out her tongue and wiggled it. She said, "The beekeepers don't have any real passion. It's been *buzzed* down to bee size. They love bees." She thrashed her head around, and how she laughed, the one tan knee poking up. She choked, laughing, her long hair—those bangs—hiding all expression. Marcia touched her own hair, short and sprayed against disturbance.

"What are you talking about, passion?" she said.

Delana went into hiccuping, her naked torso rising. Ribs, then breasts, rose up white out of a tanned surface, white cresting breast-wave turbulence. Her twitching shoulders seemed to fight the source of this convulsion. Lord, she was ripe.

"They're all still at the hotel giving talks and Dillworth is coming here to help. You don't have to stay around, Marcia. He's turning into my boyfriend."

"Dillworth Lanier. Well, that's . . . nice, Delanie."

"He doesn't know yet." A fit of giggles overtook Delana.

"Oh, little sister." It was not right, the way she talked wearing nothing but a half-slip, and Marcia wanted to cry, "Cover your breasts." But Delana did, shockingly, with her hands, and Marcia felt her face knot up. When had she last talked to Delana about anything important?

Delana lay there, those hands on her breasts, Lord. Pressing, pressing them. Pressing hard when she spoke. "Daddy would have liked a son, don't you think? He's taking Dillworth and his brother to Las Vegas."

"To shoot pool?"

"There's a tournament."

"Well, what's that mean?"

"He could have taught me."

"Have you ever expressed an interest, Delanie? For goodness' sake, let Daddy take some *boys* somewhere, and who cares? *Boys*, who cares?" Marcia repeated. "Baby, you haven't even told Daddy you want to go. I can see that much."

"He should ask. He should say, 'Delana, how would you like a trip to Las Vegas?' "

"Seventeen, you're underage. It doesn't matter. Delanie, put on your blouse or something. Sit on the bed and let me do your hair like old times."

She knew what it was like to be up here when the roar of beekeepers rushed up to and hovered at the floor right under your feet. You walked over the voices, but they could not be crushed by anything a girl did. The fan, so loud now, would be mute against that noise.

Marcia took a brush from her purse. Delana sat on the bed as always, her head lowered now, but you could see right there in her even spine (at least she had put on a bra) some new knuckly growth: aloofness shone; armor was worn on the outside, like a regular sea scavenger. "Oh, Delana Mae," Marcia whispered. Her hand passed down Delana's remote young spine. She took her sister's head in one hand and pulled the brush through gently at the ends; she worked up toward the tangled scalp of girl's hair, all mussed as if by sex. She would seek to be conspiratorial, girlish, to warn Delana, find the right way to protect her from herself.

"You want to be smart with a boyfriend."

"Huh," said her sister.

"You want to be safe, if it comes to that. I know so much more now than when I used to talk to you about boys. When I was a girl talking about boys, I couldn't imagine the truth." She paused, pulling hard, then she brushed and brushed, and in her memory the raucous murmurings from below, on beekeeper day, were childish-sounding, an annoyance.

"I wonder what the bee-lovers will be hot on this year," she said.

"I've seen their schedule of talks," Delana said. "Making honey pop is their weirdo dream. They picture it right up there with root beer and orange."

Marcia laughed softly. The dreams of men! She brushed and brushed and craned her neck to see over the fan to the light outdoors. It was too early for the true urgency of crickets, but the grasses and the trees on such a still day rustled with the small electricity of living things chewing, calling to one another, nestling and living short lives furiously, and the river glinted, taking the flattest kind of sun on its face. Some rays were thrown onto the chrome strips and bumpers of cars in the circle drive: her daddy's whisper-pink Cadillac, Dovie's cream Mustang, her own paneled station wagon.

"If they had passion once," Delana asked from way back in her throat, "what happened to it? How does it die? How can it just go away?"

A vision of her husband in bed, a sleeping mound of Jack Rose, blocked Marcia's mind from conjuring up anything pink, satin, or movable. She spread her fingers as if to reach some point of contact. "Well, it's just movie talk to so many. I guess that's what it turns out to be." She thought of the lingerie ad in the back of a magazine, her desire to order, to hear a glad man's voice call her, just once, a French slut. "Boys have their urges, Delana Mae, but remember, they were not raised on romance. They don't trust it. Did they learn to dance? No. They get life all set up. They marry a woman and before you know it they want to be a kid again. They never outgrow needing mama."

"Ouch," Delana cried.

"Sorry." Marcia moderated her brushing again, but she worked nervously. That glistening water outside, the vision of Jack, the sure onslaught of the beekeepers' roar, it unsettled her, thrilled her oddly. Her clothes felt heavy. Dovie and Sky were down there with the radio tuned in abruptly. Voices on the news rose and subsided, almost causing a seasickness, an imbalance in the mind. Strangely, Delana had plugged in her old clown night-light, Marcia's night-light in the first place. In midday, why? Well, it had been a long time since she had sat here and brushed and brushed her sister's great length of dark hair. Six years, two babies. She had neglected Delana Mae, little sister at the far edge of virginity.

"If you think it's going to happen," she said, feeling her voice go so soft as to dry and tickle her tongue, "think first. Make him use protection. The worst thing in the world is getting sent away pregnant. I'd break down. No, I couldn't let you go to Booth Memorial."

"Rubbers are gross," said Delana, stretching. "I'm not using a rubber my very first time. How would I know if I like a penis if I can't even feel it?"

"Be serious, Delanie. It only takes one slip-up. How do you think you got here?"

Her cheeks stung, the words had rushed out so fast. That glad light outside, the murmur in her head of the remembered bee-keepers' voices . . . She couldn't erase the words, and Delana's back had stiffened, and she turned now so she could burn her deep lovely eyes at Marcia. Oh, Lord, out from beneath the bangs came eyes as bright and whole as Dovie's before the drowning. Yes, the exact same periwinkle eyes.

"For all of us, of course, just the one time—"

"But you were talking about me. What are you saying about me?" she demanded.

And the intensity in those eyes was not unlike Sally's. Maybe little-sister eyes have a certain kind of life. Little sisters have to send a sharper beam or they are sunk imitators, shadows from the start and forever. Marcia looked down at her legs, all goosefleshed—the worried knees, once delectably taut, now lumpy and skimmed by culottes. Candlelike, the flesh had melted downward. Her knees made their own little shadows. A radio below sent voices rushing through the ceiling. Dovie was blasting the radio suddenly, getting ready to leave, getting out before the beekeepers came. A noisy commercial danced at Marcia's feet.

"I heard them the night you were conceived. But a seven-year-old wouldn't know what she was hearing, really. I got it all mixed up. I imagined murder."

"Marcia," Delana said in her lowest voice, "you tell me exactly what you know about my conception."

Oh, the two little fists that ended the smooth line of bare arms, what truth could they fend off? Marcia's heart flopped down. If she could kiss away the owie in those fists as she kissed her boys' elbows . . . She would not lie, but the whole story in detail was not fit for Delana's sweet ears, could not surmount or balance on the narrow slope of her back or snuggle on that nylon froth of slip.

"You've never told me about this. You've never mentioned this." Delana's voice was controlled but alive with hunger.

"Well, here we are, talking about boyfriends and I guess I'm reminded, that's all. You had to grow up first. Now I'm reminded." She spoke to the far side of the room, where she had always dreamed of gay, gay parties. Delana did not so much as sigh.

"It was a few weeks after Sally died, about a month after. I woke up soaked in tears, the way I kept doing. They'd rigged up a little bell at my collar to halt my sleepwalking, another new habit after Sally's death. The bell must have fallen off. I went to their door like I always did to call out to them." She tried to laugh. Because of the hair spray she had to reach way in to scratch the itchy part of her scalp. "They were carrying on. I thought I heard murder, but it turned out to be passion.

"Let me keep brushing, Delana. Come on now, relax." But Marcia's own hand trembled. She remembered hearing those voices and thinking that whatever raged behind the closed door was not her mother and father but something chiggery and mean. And dangerously grown up. She had curled up outside their door, letting go of everything but the instinctive urge to dream adulthood before her time.

Behind that door people were throwing fits at each other. She thought maybe they were throwing pillows too, from the flat muffled sounds of it: "ugh" and "pfft." These old crazy people had invaded and they had no idea in the world that she existed.

"You need an injection," the man voice was saying. "You're hysterical. Here, get the light on. I'm going to inject you."

A shriek went up strong enough to break glass. A witch's shriek. Electrical currents raced along Marcia's scalp. "Don't you dare," said the woman voice. "Killer, don't you dare try to kill me too."

"Shut up, will you. Shut up, dammit."

"How perfect. Shut me up, go ahead and try."

The warbling voice reached higher. It pushed up into the throat, then shot out to run around the ceiling. There was an explanation for this: The woman was jumping on the bed. She was! Her heart and voice and feet raised way up, then came down. The words were squished to jelly, then they rushed out long and sliding. Up and down, up and down. Marcia sat on her knees, then slid lower into the splits, an ability she was to lose a year later, one of maturity's rebukes. Troubling thoughts fled in favor of imagining the great free thrill of jumping on a bed, jumping and jumping, the forbidden jumping on the bed and getting to call out and *keep* jumping up and down in summer shortie pajamas. Someone was getting to jump on a bed and she wanted to do it too. Now she curled into herself, her pajama top stretched like a tent over her poking-up knees. They jutted out from the scalloped neckline, and catching a point of moonlight, in the dark, just shadowed, they could pass for breasts. They really could.

The woman was jumping on the bed. A mean silent man was circling with a terrible needle winking off the moon. He hadn't said it was for polio or anything. He hadn't said it would make that woman get better, just "I'm going to inject you." And no crack of yellow light escaped from under the door. Everything was happening by moonlight; in fact, the lopsided, almost-full moon had probably helped wake Marcia as it spun gold onto her bed, made her insist that her hard knees were breasts she held before her. If she could press breasts right onto her front, she could leave this instant, walk out strong into the night. She could walk away in victory, not having to hear a single other thing, be ready for firsthand action. She whispered, "Sally," but nothing happened.

Behind the door, demons were bargaining, accusing.

"Everyone knows what's going on, but when did it start? You can tell me, come on. Even this twisted river has its dinky beginning, Lake Itasca. Words confected out of Latin: *True head*," chided the woman. "Where is your true head?"

"Nonsense. This is nonsense." The man's voice, so deep, rumbled under the words. It was turned away from the woman. He sat on the edge of the bed, turned away.

"The luxury of nonsense is gone, you fool, dog, fool," cried the woman.

Her high shriek slammed across the room and ended at the other side with a great elephant thud. A moan. Marcia heard crashing and grunting. The woman who was faking her mother must have flown off the bed and leaped onto the man—onto his back?—and sent them staggering, going down: now they scuffled on the floor. Words were gone, used up. No words rose up off that floor, just the scuffling noises and panting, grring, rolling, and slapping closer to the door. She looked at the crack under thc door, where the sound slipped free. From down there the man suddenly protested, "No, hey, now, for God's sake, you grabby witch."

"Losing my baby," panted the woman. "Losing her, huh-uh, it's not the end."

Huffs, more huffs, then mean moans escaped from under the crack in the door. The man, Marcia could tell, lay on his back. He talked deep into his chin the way her daddy would do whenever she and Sally got him on the floor playing mountain and they were down at his toes, climbing up. His chin was tucked. Next should come the fee-fi-fo-fum. She heard: "You shocking vampire."

Then he was dying, of course. Huffing so fast, he was getting out all his very last breaths. No more words. He was out of words, and the woman's last sounds were those of a cat. Brace for the fate of the storybook gingham dog and calico cat, the tearing to bits of the two behind the door; any minute now expect to be alone forever in a big house on the river without even your sister. Remember that she was the first one dead.

It ended. Some last wheezes came from inside that room, the sound that mucus in your throat makes. They were dead, of course. Mother had knocked him out cold, and while strangling him good (those moans), Daddy was injecting her with a killer shot (her final shriek). It was all over, and Marcia sat staring at the door, with her hard knobby knees, her fake breasts, useless before her forever. She bit hard into one. More black time went by. Ten minutes? Hours? Then it issued from her, a very soft lament: "Mommy. Daddy."

A tandem howl went up; live people were in there. And Marcia screamed in response. Now came a scramble and an urgent cry by Daddy. "Honey, are you there?" In the world where people still lived she was out there, one knee white with teeth marks.

And something, that deep knowledge shifting under the skin and nails and pricking at her eyelids and clapping at her ears, the urge that had made her sit down and listen in the first place instead of calling out—the need to know her future—made her shield all of them. She whispered, "I just got here, Daddy. I just woke up."

"Lord God," came a big sighing voice.

Dovie went, "Hmmm, hmmm, hmmm," from that other world.

"You can go ahead and use the bathroom and get back to bed, honey." The Daddy voice was issuing up from the floor—he was talking toward the door. Then, "Ugh," he said, lower. "Hammerlocked me. You got it, now move, you devil." Bottom slap. "Oh," he said, loudly again, his voice turned again toward the door. "Back to bed, Marcia. Good night, honey. Let's all go back to bed."

In the morning there were no bruises, only smiles toothy enough to crack walnuts, smiles to make up for the adult eyes that were turned down like small umbrellas against a windy rain, recalling one of those humid Sundays in March that make you long for pink shoes and short sleeves even though the dirty salty snow remains and chains on the tires kick up hard slush. If you could walk in pink shoes, nothing bad would touch you. It was June. Marcia put on her white patent-leather Mary Janes and trembled, stepping around the beetly mulberries fallen to the sidewalk. And her mother was a little buzzing bee of a lady, with her hair set in pin curls all day long.

That morning they had sent her to church with the Cronin family, the plan to put her in St. Agnes already hatching. The statues, she thought, all those pale-colored statues looking at her, and especially the bloody Jesus nailed to the cross, invited her to release the terror. Maybe bloody Catholic Jesus assured her that love and murder *are* one. The bad thoughts fell away for a very long time. In August she showed up at St. Agnes committed to the miraculous.

She told Delana, "Let me stretch a minute," and walked to the window. The reflection of light on the river had toned to sepia. A daredevil waterskier flew into view, one arm waving.

"I didn't remember a thing about this until a long time later, the night that Jack got all the way to the little string belt against my skin, that silly thing the nuns had always insisted we wear like an alarm against boys' desire. I was saying yes, go farther, and he did. Then I guess I suddenly remembered the commotion. I could see the gingham dog and the calico cat tearing each other apart. I heard the shouts. I saw myself torn apart like stuffing. In the middle of it all with Jack, my eyes locked."

She rushed on. "You haven't heard of the hysterical conversion reaction syndrome, have you? Well, neither had I. Father Dan explained it, bless him. Baby, it's an affliction that came on me the first night of . . . passion, as you say, with Jack. We were in that pinkish Ford. Remember that car? We called it flesh tone back then." Marcia took a deep breath. "My eyes locked wide open. We actually had to come get Daddy— the only doctor for miles—and Jack was crying, begging, and pleading. I could hear everything, but I couldn't see a thing; I couldn't shut my eyes or turn them or anything. Jack swore to Daddy that he had been 'normal' with me. He swore, 'Doctor Sky, I have been safe and gentle.' He cried. Daddy said, 'Shut up, Rose.' Well, it was the worst thing, me hearing all of it but not seeing anything. And my eyes were locked open. An injection brought me out of it, and no one ever spoke of that night. Just recently, after confession, Father Dan explained it to me. He's very modern, with an extensive counseling background. Hysterical conversion reaction syndrome, that's what I had. The syndrome delays the effect of the real shock, the primary shock, which was, he realized, my hearing your conception and thinking murder. The syndrome comes on triggered by a lesser shock, which, in my case, was losing virginity. Oh, Delanie, you seem so normal. You don't have to get shocked eyes or any of that. Let me hug you."

But Delana was holding herself in her own golden arms. Marcia attacked with the brush, stroked and stroked it through Delana's lush hair.

"I just don't understand how they got around to doing it, Marcia. You're sure they were arguing? Then what happened? Did Daddy force her?"

"Delanie"—and the liar's blood sang in her ears—"Daddy had fallen on his back, see." Her throat was closing up as in springtime. "Mother made it happen. Really, I think she just absolutely knew you were waiting to be born. I can't say how many times Jack and I did it before little Mike came along."

Delana considered the news, with her round eyes moving slowly dot to dot. Down below, the radio was playing something brassy and big band, Dovie's selection always before going out alone. Delana's eyes were clear chips of glass. The light, it was slanting in on them. . . . Her little nostrils quivered as in childhood, just like the time they sought out the celestial perfume that dead Sally had left behind on the river. She was learning something, something past Marcia. Marcia prayed to herself, Have mercy, God.

"I was conceived in a fit," Delana said. "All in spite. Dovie raped Sky."

Marcia was on her feet. She grabbed her stiffened little sister. "Baby, they were very confused. You'll see how it gets once you and Dillworth or some other man get together. It all goes together, little sister. Kiss, cuss, it's OK. At times it's OK. I swear she knew you were waiting to come out, and she just *convinced* Daddy however she could."

"One night of deviation," Delana said flatly, "then he went back to Miss Steinbach, didn't he? Now I know where that look on their faces comes from."

"He has always come home at night. Always. We're a family, Delana."

But bring out a Bible, and she would have to swear on it that she had bumbled upon a lone night of marital fidelity, its open rage; recall that silence followed. Whenever she padded to their door (yes, she had gotten the memory clear, speaking with Father Dan; she had to say that now, facing the fan and feeling her resistant sprayed hair lift), she remembered how, always, their door stood open to reveal Dovie and Sky sleeping in figured silk pajamas at the opposite edges of a massive bed.

"His nurse is a killer and a mother," Delana said, rising. "She's a smooth sucked bone."

"She's nobody's mother, baby, nobody's. And Daddy is culpable. Remember, it takes two—"

"If I hate Miss Steinbach totally I have to hate being born. I have to hate the whole fact of my life. *She* caused Sally to die and me to be born. Miss Steinbach is devil and god."

"Delana! This is not how I meant for things to go. You're talking crazy. Quit it now."

"I'm like her daughter. In a way, I'm really her daughter."

"You're Delana Mae Walsh, daughter of Dovie and Sky. I don't care how it happened, baby. We're all accidents, God-given mistakes and freaks."

"Girl Lazarus," Delana cried. Oh, from a deep well of anguish she cried and grabbed off the bra she had been wearing. "I'm not some girl Lazarus." She stood and stomped on the floor. The beekeepers would never hear such a cry over their own ribald voices, Marcia knew, but it was the dream they were all dreaming, having come to Nauvoo, not expecting it but dreaming of racy sport miles from home: a girl on a dais holding her breasts, Lord. Her cold fury would drive them bananas.

From downstairs Dovie warbled, "Sky, here come your shriners. I'm off to the garden club's tour." At the height of summer, she would be positioning a dark saucer-shaped hat to her head, a little veil crumpling over her eyes.

Hot in the noontime sizzle, Delana looked down from her bedroom window to see the first of the beekeeper businessmen turn off Great River Road and up into the circle drive staked by oaks. Zealots who had managed to get a job feeding their obsession, they always drove the same kind of cars, with wide gnashing grilles, to offset any doubt that a love of bees was too delicate a thing, a diminishment of an American man. Bees only buzzed; their cars roared like tanks. Some cars came fitted out with special horns; she heard one play the opening bar of "Pop Goes the Weasel"; then a school fight song started up. You *heard* bee-keepers coming, was the thing. They came together as loudly as they could, their loves being so tiny, just a poem. There were pennants and white wiggling hands thrust out windows to signal the cars behind. They had driven from all over to rural Illinois, where the five-generation Supree family business—the largest beekeeping supply house and information center in the world —was quartered now in an old brick warehouse set away in ash and linden. The beekeepers got out of their cars. One of the pennants declared: *The keeper of man's most useful insect.* Ask any one of these men, and they would vow: The honeybee will save you.

Delana looked out on the river's brown ripples and thought of old ladies' leathered thighs, what these men might sleep with. She lifted her long hair from behind and let it fall. The hairs on her arms seemed to quiver still with Marcia's news.

And now, as if they had followed their queen, a steady stream of cars was backed up out there, forming a shiny bracelet of the asphalt drive. The men got out carting boxes, waving pennants; they hitched their pants and slapped each other's backs. Hands ran over balding heads. They had sex? They wanted it? Delana chewed on her lip. She looked hard at a man wearing flip-up sunglasses, his tie a split tongue, and she touched her breast hard. Huh-uh. Down to her panties. No, felt nothing.

From reading her father's printed schedule, she knew that the men had been down at the Nauvoo Hotel in the multipurpose room, sitting through lectures and demonstrations on topics such as "Let's Make Honey Pop" and "Candles, Yum!"

She had just put on a green linen shift and eggshell-colored shoes, dotted cologne between her breasts as she had learned to do out of the pages of a beauty magazine. And she went down-stairs to greet the prideful beekeepers, thinking that Dillworth had better show. She wanted to watch him eat and breathe, and when they were alone upstairs, with the best of all guises (bee-keepers under them), she would see if it was true, the shiny things

Marcia had told her before, before all this, when she used to share her secrets breathlessly, all the good and wild things Marcia seemed to have forgotten, as if she had become some kind of beekeeper, left with only the tiniest knowledge of passion. Delana wanted the old stories. She remembered the vivid boy talks from long ago, and she wanted to see it all for herself, see Dillworth get a peek of nylon, then lose all sense of gravity and time. *A boy's eyes will roll back like someone in a fit—a sugar diabetic. You won't know what he's saying. You won't believe what blasts out of his head in passion.* It would be, Marcia had said back when she loved offering boy news, her voice hushed, the true beginning of life, the heaven and the hell. "That's where the nuns are wrong," she had said, "making God big and poisonous, like He really wants to sandwich Himself in between all that. Ugh!" She had shaken her shoulders. "He wouldn't want to scare you any more than's necessary by what it already is. But a nun can't *know* these things."

Everyone exclaimed when Delana came downstairs.

"Well!"

"Looky here!"

"Sky, she has grown right up!"

And on and on. She smiled and held out a hand. "Hello, Mr. Ackly. I'm fine, thank you, Mr. Brott. Hello, yes, Mr. Furmeister, it's me." The air was filled with guffaws and the melodious breath of the longtime smokers. Papery palms rubbed together. And underneath her shift, despite the workings of Sky's big fans, the nylon slip clung to Delana's thighs.

As a group, the men were about as shapeless, slick-haired, and chortly as any group of men, but their faces were peculiarly sharpened and they had extra-busy eyes, always flicking something out at the edges. Something trained to bee rhythms, not human, not female, Delana sensed. The missionary zeal—a belief in honey—made them rosy, made them grandiose as sunflowers. I'm old enough to know what they've lost, Delana thought, and truly flirted then, leaving her mouth always slightly open, her eyes dancing toward her daddy.

"It's you, Delana Mae? Well, you've changed form or something. How, uh, tall are you?"

"Yes, it's me." She pressed the hand of a man shaking his duckling head. Yellow fuzz of hair, mostly a perfectly smooth head. "I'm five foot six, Mr. Zunn. I'm seventeen."

"Seventeen!"

How tender and wise and willing, these men all helplessly jovial, their fingers encrusted with class rings, fingers that knew the fur of a bee's back. They loved to touch it, the tiny quivering bee back, with their polar-white thick fingers.

"Delana Mae," they said in toast. "Goodness gracious sakes alive, Sky."

They had come from all over, from every branch office of the Supree Worldwide Beekeep Supplies Company, from Minnesota and Missouri and Ohio. One man had driven straight through from New York State on a thermos of coffee.

"Young lady!" they cried, not having glimpsed her in a year, and their eyes, trained against the lavish, had never experienced feasting on such gorgeous green slenderness, her tan smooth shoulders hard and risen ornamentally, like something familiar: your banister; and their fingers twitched. The squash heels with grosgrain ribbons across the front, her provoked calf muscles. The headiness of new knowledge, of power she had no idea she possessed.

"She's a flower, Sky Walsh. You've raised a flower," someone was exclaiming, and in the background another man made buzzing sounds amidst the chuckles. Just then Dillworth brought himself loping through the door, wearing the whitest shirt, and it seemed to dash toward Delana on its own, to complete a harmony—white and green go together as leaves and clover. He stopped and looked anywhere but at her. Sky, in wing tips, threw his arm around the boy.

"Men, meet Dillworth Lanier, the best pool player in the territory. If you need anything today, ask him. As you know, my Delana is likewise on hand. *Ad arma.*"

The beekeepers strutted and pushed on into Sky's playroom;

then sounds of the slot machine, the pool balls, the pinball bowl-
ing game, every kind of game, started up at once. Every last one
of them was bald enough as if, Delana thought, extra skin that
could be stung was a requirement for brave beekeeping.

"Now we stand around," she told Dillworth. "Pretty soon
they'll straggle out. We hand them plates and cut into the new
cake and stuff. They won't let me open their beer bottles, but I
bet they'll want you to. Every year it's the same. The caterers
have pretty much set things up."

Dillworth popped two olives in his mouth. "So they're going
to stuff their faces and tie one on. No lady jumps out of a cake?"

"I should," she said. She sucked out a pimiento and stuck the
olive on her finger. "I should rush in smeared with honey."

Dillworth rocked on his heels. A good guilty flush spread over
his face. His squint eye went all the way to a slit, and abruptly
Delana knew the brash reserve of femaleness. Her saying ten
wild things would strike Dillworth mute for a week.

"Here, have a beer. Daddy won't mind." She opened two and
drank as if she knew and loved beer. She tilted the long-neck
bottle way back and drank, and Dillworth followed.

"This is better than I thought," he said. "I'd expected lemonade."

"My mother takes the day off to go anywhere else she can
think of. She's touring gardens, wearing—honestly—a hat with
a veil."

"Cool," said Dillworth. "Mosquito snag."

Dillworth walked hips first around the table, eating, settling
in now, that beer bottle at his hip. The caterers had done the
arranging, so mostly the job was to stand by pleasantly. The
occasional beekeeper came in to stick his finger in a pie and wink
at Delana and chew something greasy, with his mouth still
pointed down toward the table of food. Its scalloped cloth rippled
along the edge, a floor fan directed there. The beekeeper would
gulp another drink as if an entire bar were not set up in the
game room.

"They've invented a drink called honey pop," she said.

"Serious business."

"Have another beer." She felt extremely sophisticated and absolutely in control. Her arms were heavy things until she raised them and showed their smooth undersides in a languid stretch. Arm-raising before a boy was something. And she liked the way the points of her bangs stung her eyes. She watched how Dillworth's body bent and tremored in its male ways. He smelled permanently of the outdoors, but she caught an added aroma and smiled to herself. The popular cologne that suggested royalty. All year girls had swooned to it. A whole generation of girls would someday recall the fragrance as the call to first sex.

"How about some music to tune out the buzzers?" Dillworth asked.

She went for Dovie's large pink radio and brought it from the kitchen tuned to rock 'n' roll.

Dillworth laughed and bent his knees, made dive-bombing motions, and then ran around the table and gestured, aimed, like a pool player, at roll-ups and ice cubes and crackers with cheese. It was hilarious, she thought, these finger-food arrangements. Dillworth raised his beer bottle high and sucked loudly. Delana had seen a baby goat fed like that once, but she had never noticed, well, the sexiness of a boy's neck—how everything depended on it—and the alert tension it held. Next to that, all the game room bedlam was thunder so distant as to be benign.

Dillworth played the table like drums, his lips all scrunched to make the accompanying swish sound. The loose neck made all things possible. After drinking more beer she thought: boys and little kids never stand still, and that's a fact. Dillworth joined in on the song's end: "Yeah, yeah, yeah, yeah, yeahhhhhh." Next came the stupid Green Beret song.

"Well, it's just too hot here, and now they're all settled in." She plucked at her neckline.

"What do they do now?"

"They're mental cases. We can listen from upstairs."

She pulled her skirt higher than she had to to climb the narrow stairs, and she felt the lick of hem way up on her thighs and saw in her mind the jiggered carnival lights of being with a boy. Dillworth was behind, and when he came up to the room and saw that it extended as far left as right, he whistled, "Jesus," and his hands dangled at his sides. He jammed them in his back pockets and, with lips and eyes arranged, went nonchalant. But his neck extended like a spring branch.

"It used to be two rooms. They knocked out a wall," she explained. "Come over here to my side."

She sat down on the varnished floorboards near her window. Soon Dillworth would go to Las Vegas. Where had her daddy ever taken her? Into Nauvoo, to Oquawka, out on the section road when the corn was mid-height, to teach her to drive.

She pushed back a throw rug. She disregarded her stockings and felt the raw floor tweak up and down her leg. She lay with her ear to the floor. "Uh-huh, voices are as clear as if you're down there."

Dillworth lay down too. You didn't even have to put your ear that close. Just lie there with your chin on your hands.

One voice was rising. "Daddy," she said.

". . . and there's a reason why beekeeping has been called the poetry of agriculture."

"Hear, hear!" the others cried out. Strangulated buzzing sounds followed. More jolly laughter.

"Poetry in motion," came a thundering voice. The roar was jubilant with swear words swelling up to the cool floorboards like balloons, the men's voices mingling with the strong raw popular cologne enhancing Dillworth. She had no idea where on his body a boy put cologne.

"You've got on English Leather," she said. Found out, Dillworth looked instantly glum. "I like it," she said. "I'm glad."

They listened for a while.

"Will you see any shows in Las Vegas?"

"I hate to say it, but your dad mentioned Wayne Newton."

"That's so queer."

"I'd like to see a dancing show, a line of girls kicking and dancing," Dillworth said. "You can do anything out there. Even prostitution is legal there. They have these ranches."

"I don't believe that."

Dillworth was scratching his fine neck. "Your dad told me all kinds of stuff about Vegas. We're not *going* to one of those places."

They both lowered their heads as if to listen to the beekeepers full-time. Delana guessed that the minute you lie down next to a boy, everything that has come before is nonsense and cover. She was not shy, just unhurried and mulling over Marcia's words: *A boy sexed—it can seem like hours or minutes pass; you won't be able to tell how much time.* Her gums itched and so did her nipples.

Outside, the sky had gained color, heading toward sunset. A smokiness covered the clouds, pink streaking through like scars. Beneath them, voices rushed the ceiling: "I knew this Tina gal once. I knew her inch by mad inch, buddy." "Marge," said another voice, "never did like any part of it, wanted a towel down at all times. I gave up trying. I bought her a vibrator and said, 'I quit.' She hit me with it. A good mother, but hell . . . I might do it, boys. I might get me a van and take to the highways, just go for glory. Leave her and that damn embroidery hoop, the hell." Another voice rose: "What did the elephant say to the naked man? 'OK, but how do you pick up food with it?' "

Dillworth grimaced and snorted down at the invisible men. When he turned to Delana she understood that wisdom lay, after all, in the young. So much had gone wrong with the beekeepers. They had lost an instinct. She reached out and stroked Dillworth's hair.

Below, the laughter might have been the beloved bees themselves, so high and skittery and crazy was the sound. It ran up to the ceiling; it came on up through the floorboards. A constant metal gnawing and clanging sounded with the din—the slot machine was being worked and worked by some fool one-day gambler.

And when Dillworth turned to her, Delana saw what Sky had identified as the dead spot in the eye, what cannot be measured by professional instrument, something in the green-purple iris that gleams and flames. It was, her daddy told her when she was safely ten years old, what you see only in gambling and in love. A younger Marcia had pegged this as *the fit*. OK. She moved close. I say OK to licking cologne, to bleeding, to whatever it will be. I'm ready.

She had never felt a boy's heartbeat, a tough and thunderous rhythm full of ancient hunters' fears and wiles, something beating too hard to know what it protects. Here comes the power, now watch out. Here comes the abject crazed awfulness that can be *induced* in girls, same as if they've fed you Spanish fly, which makes you unable to stop having sex ever. Ever? she had asked Marcia. Well, with Spanish fly it goes on for ages, this fire, until you ruin everything, just kiss your lips to pulp. Delana had listened to Coke bottle stories. (Don't ever! The suction will trap it. Imagine going to the doctor with it *stuck there*.) She had listened and tried to picture fire everlasting, the only example she knew being John Kennedy's grave, the eternal flame. You wouldn't stop at Coke bottles, Marcia had said. They wouldn't be the worst thing.

She lay right on top of Dillworth and was surprised to find the balancing there so easy. His legs, her legs. His face set toward hers, a clock, and she was looking back, then not looking, kissing, the blurry fan sounding, too, like lips. And when he began scrunching at her, fine, and when he began whopping up against her she hung on, rodeo gal. They seemed to be scooching, moving across the floor on his back muscles alone. And suddenly she knew (you just knew) what a silly weight all the clothes between you were, how drastically in the way of hoppiness. Dillworth with his mouth falling open, then his teeth revealed. She listened in raptures for the voodoo talk, the chantings and the undercurrent breath of the ghost Dillworth who in real life squinted at the pool balls and said "Sir" to Daddy. *They change*: Marcia's words.

He was steady into the chugging when she rolled free. "You can take off my clothes," she said.

"Really, DeeDee?" He hadn't called her DeeDee since she was

ten years old, making sure to cover herself with a long T-shirt and wearing dime-store sunglasses.

This was a new kind of nakedness, of which the air took note, stirring itself all over her. On her back the reverberating crazy hoots from below pressed all along her smooth skin. The buzzing, buzzing beekeepers added exquisite touches to Dillworth's coos and slurps from above. And she clutched him hard when her daddy's voice rose, as Rex, singing a stupid song. A dirty song, she realized suddenly. Yes, a dirty, dirty old-country song. He had practiced it all her life with his teeth clenched, too chicken to sing it except in his dummy's voice. Here he was, old hillbilly drenched in the Scots-Irish song. "Oh, your gold ring . . ." The men were laughing, trying to join in. Daddy with his hand up the dummy's back, Dillworth pulling off panties. Delana had Dillworth, and she began to giggle, which turned into a long choking laugh. Dillworth mumbled through some kisses. "Shhh . . ."

"Well, listen to him," she said. "Sexy Rexy!" she called out.

"Huh," said Dillworth. "Huh, huh, huh," in his new sexland rhythm. "DeeDee, shhh. You're supposed to just lie there and feel me, OK? Don't talk." He used his whole body to sort of nutcracker her legs. Her half-slip was a ruffle at her waist.

She had to grunt. His weight was on her funny. This pressure on her chest.

He moaned, then: "Here, you need me to tell you things, let me reassure you that I don't want to hurt you." He blew her hair off her face.

"I know that." Her back arched at the very idea. Dillworth groaned again.

"Just let me say it," he said.

"Well, go ahead," she said, feeling the sweat between her breasts, the crush of nylon at her waist.

"DeeDee, I don't mean to hurt you. This might hurt at first. Think of shots, like immunization. Then, you—oh, God! Jesus! And . . . you're OK. You're . . . shhh, oh, shhh."

"Like polio is licked," she supplied.

"Ummm."

"I'm going to get up stronger once we're done. Walk different."

"Ummm, yeah."

"People will be able to tell?"

"Touch it, touch it."

Rested in his hand, his thing looked all mutated, blind. Bobbed up, pointing. "Like a morel mushroom in the woods," she said.

"Hey, DeeDee, DeeDee."

With that capped look. The surprise of one . . . except of course it was not honeycombed. She touched the part that looked like the wrong end of a stuffed olive. Nothing had ever been so leaping glad to be touched. "If it was honeycombed I'd scream."

"DeeDee . . ."

She held it in her hand while his hand went fishing. His hair was fallen on her breasts.

"You're ready," he announced presently.

She felt a mean stitch followed by a generous pause for adjustment, which lasted until her surprised gasp dimmed to steady little ones. Dillworth kept searching her face, then lowered heavily onto her. And of course next came the plunger effect she had been told about. Now feelings seemed to come up along her backside, be shot up to her from the men's voices, a room full of them. She was settling into a nice lulling rhythm when Dillworth suddenly cried out, then flopped still. In the room below, the mad ringing of pinballs went on; her daddy's voice there swooped and conducted. How he loved to run a show. Dillworth was now smeary-eyed, gazing at her from unfocused eyes.

She emptied words into the little pink ear set to her cheek. Until that moment she didn't know that ears were anything special. Of course they were exquisite, the most important little purse of love. That's where music chimed into the head, where the breath of sky and water collected and sang.

"You'd better go."

Dillworth fumbled himself into his pants. She heard the zipper as a sexy sound. He stood at the window, looking down to the river, the setting sun's pink spread of peace. He kissed her quickly goodbye. "I'll get you a promise ring," he said. "I'll bring some rubbers. Then we can keep on."

When her daddy came up the stairs and looked in at her with his head on a side swivel, his smile liquor-red, Delana knew his secret dimension. Maleness. Maleness shone out through the clothes and in the smile. It sounded in the trudging of his feet. Skylar Walsh was her daddy, but more he was a man. Breast-gobbler has nothing to do with love or hate. An older Dillworth, a man. His sweat would slick down a woman and dry on her cold. Before and after, he would give her the sound of that zipper, the fine metal ratcheting toy sound. His eyes were dizzy with drink, the hair waving back as game as ever.

The bra that Marcia had commanded her to wear for the hair-brushing was tossed on the floor after Dillworth, along with the green linen shift. Delana lay in her half-slip, propped on pillows, the cool sheet bunched under her arms and running off the bed like a sail. Her brown feet lay free.

"Just thought I'd check on you, catkin." Her daddy's little name for her. Huffing, he dropped onto her bed. His solid weight sank it, so that she halfway rolled to him.

"Give me a taste," she said.

"Why, this is peach brandy." But she held his surprised look and reached for the bottle.

"Well, it's been a long day," he said, shrugging. He released the bottle. She drank and drank. "You're not too exhausted, are you, catkin?"

"Huh-uh, the opposite. Dillworth was up here." She handed back the bottle, watching her father. She wiped her mouth with the back of her hand. The room jerked left, then moved back in place.

"The boys liked him. Yessir, he's a find. In Vegas, why—"

"He ended up here with me, Daddy."

"I didn't see him leave. You tell him thanks?"

"I did." And Delana rose halfway, breasts floated free as summer light. Here I am. Here. She waited through his frown, his wincing-away look. What is real? swam in his eyes. She was sure her nipples glowed.

"Christ," Sky whispered, and doubled himself slowly over the edge of her bed. White patches, like perverse hives, covered his face. He looked at the liquor bottle in his hand and squeezed it hard. Her daddy was a man with a sloped stomach who once had simply had a lap for seating a daughter and a strong leg that played horse and rider. Voices drifted up, bloated in the weight and stillness of the night air, lazy voices darkly thrumming from the drive. Car doors slammed. A musical horn trailed its tune down the road. Beekeepers were headed into town, back to the Nauvoo Hotel.

Sky smoothed at his wavy hair before looking back at his daughter, but the stunning irregularity of this sight turned him away again. He looked at all the fingers on his right hand spread out before him, the instruments of his profession. "You're a pretty girl, Delana Mae. You should talk to your mother." Delana snorted; Sky shrugged again. Yes, he knew it was a ludicrous idea. "Well," he said, "in these times . . . everyone needs someone."

She sprang at him, arms open, and locked him in a fierce hug.

His hands had to go somewhere. They held her bare back and pressed slightly; a finger rubbed and she held on, moving against his shirt, feeling it sting her nostrils with cigar smoke and charge her nipples.

She held on tight and whispered, "I want to talk about being born, Daddy."

She hung on, but Sky was prying her fingers from the back of his neck. "Whoa now, honey." He pushed; she fell against the pillows, arms flung wide. Sky reached for the sheet and covered her. For a moment she lay so eerily still, he leaned to her with his doctor's hand automatically lifted.

"If some baby had to be born after Sally, it should have been a boy, don't you think, Daddy? Too bad I wasn't a boy."

"A boy?" he asked softly, smiling. "I can see why that thought might have come to you, but we didn't expect anything. Honey, that was a long time ago. We've always loved you. You're my good daughter."

"I've spent my whole life being your good daughter. I'm an accident that came after the drowning."

"Delana Mae, stop."

"Marcia heard everything the night Mother made you do it with her. That's how I got born."

Her daddy might have forgotten her entirely, the way his eyes rolled up blank, and only the whiskey sweat, pouring and pouring down his face, gave off signs of life. His head hung for the guillotine, hung down. The bottle dropped and rolled. Sky jerked back and bellowed a long hard sound that wrapped and whipped the room, his eyes shutting tight, then popping. Delana covered her ears until, finally, the winding down, his voice creaky as the bottle rolling on floorboards: "She doesn't know anything. She's just like your mother, a true hysteric."

In the silence that followed, he seemed to wash his face with his hand—over and over, the dry papery sound of his hand washing over his face; he jerked at his necktie, then grasped his knees. He let his hands dangle; clasped them; muttered. She chewed on the edge of the sheet. Sky set the bottle upright. Liquor had dribbled a path to the window, where her little fan perched on the ledge and shook its fat round head back and forth, mesmerized in disbelief. Knotty-pine walls gleamed in the dark, and high humidity had brought out their aroma of varnish. She said, "I can handle it now, Daddy. I'm pretty mature. I'm Dillworth's lover. We did it right here, on the rug." She added, "He really wanted me."

Sky sat there slumped and breathing heavily through the obstructions of memory, liquor, and confronting the shock of a sexual daughter.

"Why do you need Miss Steinbach? See, I can say her name just like Sally did. Miss Steinbach. Miss Steinbach." Delana thrust her head up and down like a pony, repeating the name. The room was a mad swirl. This is what you saw, swirling down, down, down in the river.

"We should be enough for you, Daddy. I want us to be enough."

"Baby," Sky said, "it's OK. You're my angel."

"Give her up," she whispered.

Sky's eyes held the world. "You are my angel."

"But give her up," she whispered. "And I'll get rid of Dillworth. We don't need them, Daddy. Not at all."

He tucked her in, his doctor's hands wanting to smooth but instead rippling the sheet. He put it way up high at her neck and inhaled loudly, running his hand up and down his tie, which was hanging loose from his neck. The mutterings began again, a raspy humming he seemed not even to control, as if Rex were upon him. He was licking his lips. And she wiggled ever so slowly and edged down the sheet, and there it was again, the rosier-than-before nipple, a ripe young breast, frank, refusing to be ignored. Sky stared at it.

"Are they really beautiful?" she asked, in an innocence that would drive anyone mad.

He hung there so close she felt his hot breathing, how it began to rile the breast, and he saw that too, the nipple puckered. He was man-close, caught, gone dumb. Lips parted. A silver-haired man, still with dimples, flushed. He hung there, and didn't his mouth just now brush down whole and warm, pressing hand reach below and wonder . . . push up and encircle the breast and therefore own it. Put the salt of his tongue there, and there. Down along her thigh, the same sensation as Dillworth's body. And who was saying, Love, here's love. I can show you love.

She broke him by breathing, "Good, Daddy."

He snapped himself upright and whipped the sheet to her neck again. "You don't know what you're doing." He took her by the shoulders and shook gently, gently, with everything covered up save the face with the staring eyes; he shook his daughter harder, his fingernails just reaching in the flesh of her shoulders.

"God, you're everything I've feared." He leaned away, but liquor smell was everywhere, swooning Delana. She choked and sat up. Sky the doctor paused. She caught him by the tie and pulled.

"Angel, stop," he cried, and hauled himself up fast. He stood over her, working his hands open and closed. "Do whatever you want with Dillworth, but don't tell me anything about what I already know. Don't act like you know. You're not that grown up, not by a long shot."

Sky lurched down the narrow pine stairs, built for girls. An engine started, the car dug into gravel and spun, was gone. And in moments Dovie came driving herself home, her car as light as a cricket out there. She toddled into the house, click-click on the heels, and would not see the mess, or smell the cigars, or wonder about the private confessions made up of home movies and celibate nights and business junkets. With a brand-new baby come right on the heels of the dead girl, she had bought years and years more time to approximate a family. Years and years of it. Seventeen years, Delana was thinking.

Out of season as always, in August Dovie sang at the top of her lungs, "June is bustin' out all over."

Seventeen years of it, my life as ammunition and rebuke.

Outside, the river was as black as the end of time. And from there, that old Sally fragrance, the sophistication of disappearance, came licking up at the window. Sally, Sally, said the river. She's your sister too. Come on. And the idea stung like a fragrance, stung as her eyes and breasts were stinging, and took Delana down in the green linen shift. On her knees, at the riverbank, she cursed, chewed and spit out a clod of dirt for every year of her life, and she lay through the night tracing the course of shooting stars and owls.

O N THE FIFTH DAY, water had been rising fast. They passed through coal country, Carbondale and Murphysboro, Illinois, enduring a sooty sky and the cranky sound of birds caught under it, heralding dusk. Outside the cabin Delana smelled St. Louis coming up on the left: malt pumped out by seventy city blocks of Anheuser-Busch. The earth seemed to heave from that effort, the far horizon pulsing white. And the river had turned pink-faced and teary, as if surrendered in love, as if, she thought, tamed by the power of its own performance.

Johnny and Cheramie were off-shift, sitting inside with the baby, giggling.

"Go relax," they told her. "She's got a double date."

"Wow, Robin," she teased. She was fuzzy with lack of sleep. Memory kept taking her deep, and what others mistook for purposeful mystery was a napping kind of disorientation she carried. She clenched hot hands to her hips.

Downstairs she found Opal plunging her bare hands up and down in the mixing bowl.

"You're cooking this late?" she called, coming in. "You've been cooking nonstop this trip."

"Just getting ahead. Didn't you use to?"

"Sometimes." She remembered the prickly feel of the hair net and realized that Opal wore hers on board whether she was cooking dinner or playing gin. It was likely she wore it in her sleep. But at the end of a run Opal was known to surprise everyone by disembarking in a splashy flowered dress, white saucer earrings, the hair waved over to one side—giving a look back over her shoulder as if to say, "Now the real world." And when she came back on, thirty days later, perfume trailed the decks and sometimes came up off the first day's soup or potatoes. People wondered, but no one ever asked Opal, or anyone, what had happened on shore time.

"It's my jiffy salmon loaf. Empty a can, throw on eggs and crackers, a titch of Worcestershire and minced onion, lump together, and bake." Opal moved over to another bowl and started beating white sauce. "Where's that baby?"

"Johnny has her."

"For a change, good. You feed her too much. Don't let her rule. Feed for a half hour, then wait for two. She'll get what she needs. Otherwise, you'll never have a life. You'll come to hate the baby you love."

"But when she cries—"

"What woman knows it all on her own? I'm telling you to feed for half an hour, then wait for two. Your family women will set you straight on all this stuff. They'll give you the history of where her toes come from and all that. You need womentalk."

Delana imagined Marcia finding religion in ten tiny girl toes. And Joy Steinbach waving an inoculating needle.

"Remember that woman who helped you out in New Orleans?"

"She talked me through it, then left me."

Opal whipped that bowl, triumphant. "Womentalk. You needed the sound of her voice, that's all. You needed womentalk.

That's what got you through. I go on shore and there's bingo
and church and women up and down the street. They sustain
me. Roaming with Johnny has kept you apart. Say goodbye to
that stuff. Roaming's over. You're double-strength female."

She admitted that Johnny seemed to be fading. "It's like I
can't even see him sometimes now, he gets so dim."

"That's the baby's work, her survival instinct. She needs your
attention, so she's scrambled your sensations. Johnny looks sorry
to you, but he hasn't gone down one bit. You're double-strength
female, which subtracts the man. Don't you know simple sums?"

"Is there a way for us to be together?" Delana asked herself
more than the cook.

Opal raised her spoon. "No marine company would stand the
risk of bringing on a newborn. Don't even think of it."

"I'm thinking of shore work," she said reluctantly. "Something
for Johnny."

"Oh, yes, indeed." Opal beat the bowl hard. "Bring him in
like a beached whale? Driftwood?" She paused to bang the spoon
on the bowl's rim. Recalcitrant white sauce flew. "Scorn your
man, call him dim, maybe, but don't exploit him too. When I
see those twin evils coming out of a gal, I could spit bullets at
her. What's wrong with thirty days together and then thirty days
of relief, like all the others do? The more coming and going the
better. It's all the hellos and goodbyes that keep the heat between
a man and a woman." Opal's mixing bowl was rocking. "You're
asking the wrong old river rat for sympathy. I don't want you
to break him."

"You're going to break that bowl."

"It's dilled horseradish to spread on your salmon loaf."

"Horseradish again?"

"Speaking of which"—Opal raised her considerable chin—
"we're directly getting to St. Louis, and across the water, inland
a ways, is the little town of Collinsville. They call it horseradish
capital of the country. I wish I could go pick me some fresh."
The cook's laugh shook the kind of bosom Delana would never

have. After twenty years raising Robin, she would not come back on, a full-bosomed cook. She arched her back, jutted herself at Opal as if to say, I'm a nursing mother. Give me that.

"Yes," Opal went on, "things could be worse than passing all that fresh horseradish, dear. Look, I've got you a special iced orange cake with real fruit wedges all through it. Oranges are very good for you. Now scoot. Go out on the tow head and greet St. Louis. Put your face toward that spectacle for the last time. Then turn away and breathe toward Collinsville. Smell that strong, good air and let it work you. Go on."

In the dark she made her way along the left-hand row of barges. A two-foot walkway was built to the side of each long barge car, a safe walk fenced and with good tread. Moving toward the water's voice, she crossed from the first to the second, hearing the groaning of the chains that attached them: three deep and three wide, barges settling like old men disturbed in their naps, and just as crusted and smelly. She walked way out to the far end of the third barge, where the sound of creaking cables gave way to rushing water. She stood one thousand feet away from the towboat and looked behind her. Against blackness, the yellow-lit wheelhouse offered a mad piano smile high in the sky. A young sub was in there piloting, while somewhere on board Cheramie and Johnny played with the baby. She heard nothing but the leap of river all around her. Buoys and the Army Corps of Engineers' shore lights flashed on the water: some pulsed steady, others sent clusters or fits of light out onto the water, and she could read all of it, the red and green and white lights that marked bends and channel course and depth. She saw the river markings, she read them like a newspaper—the latest— but what she heard were the percussive songs of voyage and history.

In life jacket, she spread her arms and let the spray come on. It rushed hard here in the upper river, close to home. The river voice filled her ears with riddles and jokes. So, she asked it, if the body is ninety-something percent water, then how does it drown? How can it? The water's voice was filled with elation—

no answer, just glee. Not even her doctor daddy could answer you that one, not really. Shiny things filled her baby's room, exactly as Dovie had always done for her. Now she knew that Dovie's gumdrop trees, her thousand scarves and the flageolet playing, had trumpeted against fear. *She knew the minute you were gone what she had known for seventeen years: she did not deserve you.* Marcia's first written words had had the ring of tossed silver coins; she sounded so clear, so exactly like herself. And early on, opening each thick pastel envelope, Delana had expected parental pleas and promise. But Cheramie was right. Within the pink or yellow or faint blue paper, she looked in vain for sweet cajoles. Sky, Marcia reported, had announced from the start that he would let his daughter find her way home or to the moon. He had boomed with pride, "She's gorgeous and smart. I'll let her be." *Though the dummy was put in the trash. Death to a false voice!* Dovie's best effort consisted of little packets of ginger chips and deep, bitter chocolate, and the silence accompanying those mailings was nothing compared to that greater silence to follow. A year on the water, Delana received Marcia's wire: *Dreamer, come home now. Dovie is (surely) two hours in heaven.* A doctor's wife who had existed on tea and snickerdoodles, Dovie went into a long final stare, and then she was gone, her heart done pumping.

Delana felt the dark rushingness all around her. Her ears rang with water high jinks. Standing one thousand feet out from the tow, she could not hear the roar of engine or a deckhand's yell. If birds or animals called from shore, she wouldn't know it. Only the water's leaping phosphorescence allowed the knowledge that she moved through space.

"Jaundice water" was how Marcia remembered the look of the water that day Sally drowned. "It was taut and full of yellow."

After Dovie died, another year passed on the water before the news came that Sky and Miss Steinbach were married. They flew out of the Quad Cities on a Frontier jet to Las Vegas. Sky returned wearing a chunk of ruby. Sisters agreed that the ruby ring could be nothing more than a lavish deflection of shame.

She held her masthead pose out on the tow head. Her hair

vined to the wind, one thousand free thrills. Her hair was damp now, limp, her face soaked with spray, and the water kept up its spoof. How does a body, a little girl's body, ninety-some percent water, *drown* anyway? No answer, it joked back. No answer here at all.

On the far bank, St. Louis, like all cities after dark and seen from a distance, was a vision of diamonds. The malt aroma created an added lure. And built right down by the shore, against black sky, Gateway Arch looked like permanent lightning stunning the earth. It commemorated the first white settlers who had floated themselves across the river.

But the *Pat Furey* had no business with St. Louis and so kept to the far right of the channel, even pulled over and hung there, waiting for downriver traffic to go ahead and pass, and it lolled under the shadow of ancient Indian mounds. At one time, more Indians had lived here than anywhere else north of the Rio Grande. Nearly a hundred mounds preserved the remains of temples and ordinary homes. A vast community had thrived on the river and then vanished. Perhaps, Delana speculated, the dark vanished people had sensed a future of doom. She pictured one moment of mass ecstasy and faith: everyone leaping to the Father of Waters.

The city had fallen behind when the world did stop. The water went flat; engines had cut out. In the stillness an owl floated its velvet question into the night. The river did exactly what it always had done, despite oar, steam, or diesel forcing a path. It rumbled low, spread itself wide, and showed a magnificent disregard for human predicament.

Delana turned back to the tow. Its cable creakings protested loudly in the whole-world stillness. Figures began lining the decks as she picked her way back along the barges. Johnny would not be in that group. Down with the engines, he would be having no thoughts in the world of anything but engines, no sense at all of her moving through darkness toward the yellow light. How

odd it would be to look out on this river permanently from shore,
smell the lilacs and blackberry ooze and the dark-tea aroma of
the water that was gusting up all around her, then turn from it.
She held the history of Dovie and Sky in her heart, her eyes, and
her outstretched palm. If she stepped outdoors to taste autumn
on her tongue, wouldn't it be just a variation on waiting for the
man, some variation on Dovie's fragile plight? A mother herself
now . . . You move closer to your own, even if she is dead.
Yearning, Delana could almost believe she heard Dovie calling.

A deckhand's voice rose above the others. "Engine swallowed
a valve. Melody says the cylinder walls are torn up and the piston
head's a mess too."

Off the galley deck Delana found Cheramie madly swooshing
Robin through the air to stop her crying. "Good, here's Mama,"
he said. "OK, dolly, time's up. Go to Mama." He handed the
baby to Delana. "I've got to get myself back to work now."

"He's chicken," Opal called before Cheramie got out of range.
"Johnny went down to check and Cheramie came running with
that baby like she was TNT. And guess what the big problem
was? A poopy diaper. Don't you deny it!" she called loudly after
the captain's retreating footsteps. Opal was putting the last
touches on a parfait mold.

Delana took Robin upstairs and fed her. In a short while
Johnny came in, grease-covered, and announced, "We can't run
good on just one engine. We'll shut down for the night and then
limp on to Burlington to dock as planned and get repaired. If
we run into trouble tomorrow, at least we'll have daylight. I'm
calling it quits now."

"Clean yourself up, dumpling," Delana said in her private-
song voice. "And hold me tight till morning."

On one engine they crept close to the Illinois bank and an-
chored, lights out. Blazing above them were the steep limestone
cliffs of Alton, three-hundred-foot-high white cliffs topped by
fine, buff-colored loess lining this stretch all the way to Grafton.
In the dark, the high land jutted forward like a giant's chest
feeling the night air: here was the earth at rest, unclothed, ex-

pecting no one. In the morning they would pass along these great cliffs that spouted junipers at the peaks, trees whose trunks and red and blue berries preceded white men by hundreds of years. Johnny was describing them, his lips playing all along the length of her arm, raising hair, making the flesh too lively for its own good. Along here a huge tree had been examined and found to be more than six hundred years old. So Johnny said. He kissed and nuzzled and tasted her skin. Just days before, she had thrown him off. Sinking his teeth into her would be a justifiable act, he had as much as said so, but he was loving. And falling asleep, exhausted, he swore on the divinity of that tree, said that the world had a pact with itself: outlast everything; death should not be the big deal people make it. His whispering voice jerked into sleep: "No person . . . nobody is . . . I am no more important than a tree."

Now everything was still, but in the morning, along the white cliffs, kingfishers would resume building nests of fish bones; killdeer would scoot around; cedar waxwings and bank swallows would come to life high-speed. At dawn turkey vultures would scavenge, and by dusk the *Pat Furey* would lock in at Burlington, where Delana would bring her baby off that water.

PART

TWO

A CAVALCADE OF MEN walked up the steep yard, their courage and mission fronted by females. Delana carried a little tent of gold lamé with bright stars pasted all over it and on the black booties sticking out beneath. Marcia walked hunched, ogling the month-old baby, every step causing a white pocketbook to shave along her hip. Johnny crowded in on Delana, and crickets sang of the coming dark. Opal and Captain Cheramie chinned as much as walked their way up the hill, and they were waving pinwheels against a late-day sun that put the glint in everyone's eye. Cheramie wore his shirt with epaulets, and Opal was splashed with perfume and flowered silk, as was fitting, she believed, when love is the trial.

Marcia's boys pranced around Delana's skirts, touching the folds. *Pirate Lady*, they named her on hearing how she had thrown Johnny in. They took kisses from this aunt with long girl's hair and stayed close with their upturned faces to let her know they could stand some more. They believed in Johnny's supernatural strength and were eager to tell their friends, "He

fell into deep water with fish worse than sharks and he survived."
They tested their elbows and even fists against his large sturdi-
ness, and he walked on, a bear unperturbed by chipmunks. They
sensed the strength of a man in love and hopped along after
him with a million questions in their hearts and the first fear-
someness of maturity ramming their spines. Jackie Junior already
looked ahead to Christmas and vowed: No more pie tins and
coaster sets for Mom. I'll give her some frills.

The sky was paling, and deckhands stomped on firm, brown,
governable land to warn off any sudden femaleness that might
vine right up the legs, wrap and drain their strength. Look away
from hip and white pocketbook. Don't lose your river wits in the
first hours on land, or you're rooted. They had flown over the
old suspension bridge crammed into two taxis, boys hanging like
dogs out their mother's car before them. They had beached their
duffels in the drive and, craving party food, stomped on behind
Delana.

High above the Illinois bank, in the middle of nowhere, woods
surrounded the house. Huge, corky oaks were done up like
women: oaks in high blush, every leaf set against the sky, splayed
or curled, all the same tease. Henna, rouged, wax yellow. Laughing, sighing gossips overreaching a man's house as if the strength
of its brick was nothing next to leaf and twig. Crewmen kept
their eyes moving because everyone knows if you look up at a
woman in a tree you're sure to go blind.

Delana stopped and spoke directly up to the loudness of leaves
at dusk. Hands on hips, she said, "I never knew how female you
were."

"Sister," said Marcia, "what does it mean?" She ran her eyes
back and forth between Delana and the oaks.

Marcia's older boy, Jackie Junior, turned to the deckhands,
all bunched behind now, and coolly announced, "I know the
difference between male and female corn. I'm a detasseler."

Men stopped. Was this boy taunting them? Walking up higher
and higher, putting the river at their backs, already tested them

plenty. They looked around, uneasy. Sexed corn? No one had
reckoned on sexed corn. Apple-perfumed air slugged at their
minds. They suddenly felt old. What the hell kind of Saturday
night . . . ? New street talk and radio trends were one thing.
Who'd think you needed to know about corn? A field of corn
looks male, pure male, all those full-fruited husks sticking out
at groin, breast, and face level, just fine. What's female is all that
leaf up above, that dressiness and flounce. But some corn really
is male and some is female? Like a row goes boy-girl boy-girl?
What does it *do*, sexed corn? What is the taste of female corn?
went through minds. They shook their heads at this new information brought to them, wouldn't you know, by one of Delana's
relations.

Up the steep hill of yard, looking smaller than real people,
three figures stood under the big yellow-and-white awning Marcia had managed to rent even though the Nauvoo Grape Festival was on. Under the tent a woman's figure swayed from the
hips.

"Aunt Delana," Mike explained, "we call her N-Joy."

Jackie Junior cut in, "Turkey, how's she going to know what
that means?" He said, "The N stands for Nurse."

"My boys broke the ice right from the start with this nickname," Marcia explained, now clutching her white bag to her
chest. "She was thrilled."

"Mom, I can remember when they came home married," Mike
said. "I was six."

"You were a twerp," Jackie Junior told him. "You called her
Grandma Nurse."

"N-Joy fixed us weird food at first. Remember the oysters?"

"Well, she was giddy," Marcia said. She looked ahead and
groaned. She let the pocketbook fall to her hip. "Now, what's
Daddy got Jack doing? Honestly, my husband's in some kind of
idiot regression. Lately he's the dupe for Daddy's games. Daddy
calls him the dauphiness," she said, lips tight. "If he calls Jack
the dauphiness in front of everyone, I'll scream."

"They won't get it," Delana assured her. She touched Marcia's necklace. The boys, too, were wearing strings of bulky shells. "What are these?"

"You don't know puka shells? They're everywhere this year. On land, I mean. They're from Hawaii."

"My dad can't ever beat Grandpa at games," the younger boy, Mike, told the crew. "Not even at Chinese checkers."

"Looks like something in him needs to feel suckered," Cheramie said. He had been keeping pace up front, close enough for a whack or two from the white pocketbook.

"Do you think so?" Marcia asked seriously. "For years they didn't speak much and now he's suddenly this fall guy."

"He's finding his penance," Cheramie told her, and when Marcia veered toward him, her white pocketbook jammed itself between their hips.

Delana's heart was kicking. Oak chatter soothed, and spindly walnut trees threw down their meats for the fun of it. Land was alive, open and giving. Apple smell plumped the air, and much of the fruit lay downed under trees as if stupefied by its own power. And it had to be grapevine upwind that put something slangy in the air. Such air, she swore, was too fat for shame. She was the replacement daughter usurping a dream of herself with the real thing: girl baby coming off the water. Her heart kicked, and her cheeks were hard as apples. Any shame around here belonged to a man. Any red shame.

Jack Rose stepped back from a row of big cardboard signs staked before him in the yard. Moving closer, Delana saw Sky's face duplicated on the signs; six or more smiling blue-dot faces, with red stars above and red printing she couldn't make out, all of it bordered with white. Behind the photos stood Sky.

"Oh, no," Marcia said. "He's got campaign signs. So he's really serious about running for county medical examiner. I can't stand it."

Getting closer, Delana read: SKY'S THE LIMIT; GO SKY HIGH.

"When he came up with this a few weeks ago I wouldn't listen. I was sure it was just another scheme, Delanie. Now what am I going to get dragged into?"

"It's a game," Delana said. "He's set up the staring game so he'll beat me. Poster eyes don't blink. He's making me blink first."

"Sister, Lord! You still read everything too deep. So blink first, will you? I know you mean to, Delanie. You're the prodigal girl, remember? Your blinking is under way. We'll have a fine reunion, don't worry." Marcia hedged in so close the puka shells scratched along Delana's collarbone. It struck her that Marcia had a fearlessness in the realm of human possibility: she actually expected miracles of change. Plotting for them would spoil the fun, but Marcia was fiercely expectant and ready. That was her generous side.

"Come on," Marcia urged in that big-sister way, pressing Delana's arm. The back of her head tickled.

Johnny scoffed, "A guy doesn't put signs like that in his own yard. They belong other places."

"I'm for him," Opal announced. "I like him already."

Delana skimmed toward Sky wearing a full white dress so dazzling it was meant to blanch guilty eyes. The star on her forehead was blue. She had imagined her daddy flung down before her, some kind of weak Moses ready for supreme instruction, but how could white-whiteness work against unflinching photographed eyes? Of course Sky would have thought out his own strategy; of course Daddy the game man had brilliantly prepared to play harder than stars, to hex back. Rigor left her limbs. She had that white-whiteness and the roaring welcome of leaves. Sky had his looming self. And the odd brilliance of red suspenders. The color of shame, blood, terror, sex, and Jonathan apples strapped in her daddy's bulk, rode and emphasized his form. The ruby ring happily nicked the air.

"He's bright red, Marcia."

"It's a look, of course. He's been wearing the suspenders since he got the idea to run for office. I guess it's an election strategy. He wants to look folksy and brash all at once."

Reveling was how Delana saw it. Marcia had written: *When you left, she bled him, I'm not sure how. Dovie attacked him. The pincushion, a clot on the carpet, reminded me of the Sacred Heart.* Sky had covered memory with revel.

The baby's weight seemed to increase as she carried her up the hill. It became a staggering weight, and when Robin jerked into a howl she seemed capable of tumbling out of Delana's arms.

It was familiarity, though, that really sapped her. "Daddy." Saying *Daddy* instantly put her halfway out on a swinging bridge, breeze whistling all through her. Close now, his eyes were clear, dizzying. (She had expected little brush fires in them.) Though sweet autumn smells torrented the air, around Sky she caught a faint whiff of olives and Ivory soap.

Her mad fish of a baby leaped into Sky's steady, open palms.

"How's that for a welcome!" she cried, her voice pitched, she thought, exactly like a fire alarm.

Even before his words came, Sky's voice was immense with sound. "Catkin! I'm already full of jactation. Look at this—fresh from the hand of creation."

It was sound, not the words, that settled Delana, swept away some wobbliness. "Isn't she beautiful, Daddy? And you're looking good. You look just the same."

"And likewise, you're stout." The crew behind made startled, shuffling sounds. Sky called to them. "Foo, settle down. She's stout in the true sense of the word. Stouthearted." He gestured with the baby, her head compassing the crew. "She's stout." He swung Robin around with no more regard than he would show a loaf of bread, so practiced were his doctor's hands. "Baby Lamé. No cachexia here."

"I'm hexed," Delana cried, joining in the old banter, batting back tears. "I'm hexed by all these signs."

When he roared with laughter she could see Sky's face was filled not with the deep disturbed blush Johnny often got but with a field of palpating veins. Even the blood was in revel.

"Nixon is gone," he said, now lofting the baby toward an invisible badness that had just scampered into the side woods.

"Duty calls citizens to act and take responsibility. I've been propelled into a candidacy. I have speeches to polish."

As Sky hoisted Robin high, Joy Steinbach leaped forward with a camera, and Opal and Cheramie's pinwheels rose higher, waving at Robin. The deep slanting sun blotted the gold lamé and all the shining stars. Candled so, the baby was nearly vaporized in the brightness. People saw little more than large hands lifted against the blue.

Marcia cried, "It's an omen. She needs the safety of baptism to give her substance."

"Ummm," Cheramie said, pressing in.

But Marcia's shrill cry had hacked up the brilliance. Sky lowered Robin, looked intent still, but blank. His uncertainty allowed for the first small inkling in Delana that she wished to act with, not against, Sky. Harmony, however that worked, might bring with it some peace.

"Daddy," she said, "meet Johnny."

"My uncle Johnny," added Mike.

"John Melody," said Jackie Junior, solemn.

And like a blade, Johnny's hand moved toward Sky's.

"It's a picture," Joy Steinbach announced, clicking at Johnny and Sky. She exulted, a woman whose hair was the no-color brown of quick, futile dye sessions, a woman in her high forties who did not know enough to stand back and keep still, wear the hopeful, pained, and rebuked look on her face that Delana had fashioned for her. A demure humility, some sign of conscience, would have been a forgiving reintroduction to Joy Steinbach. Instead, here she was stealing a family photo for herself.

"How much does Baby weigh?" Joy asked brightly. "How long is she? I'm sorry your delivery was so lonely."

"She wasn't even jaundiced," Delana heard herself bark. "More than fifty percent of babies are jaundiced, and she wasn't."

Sky nodded approvingly.

"Everything on her works. Her fingernails get dirty just like ours."

"I should say, catkin. Of course I'll thoroughly check her out."

Leaves shrieking, that was the only sound. Daddy had gone too far.

Green eyes briefly ruined by their own light, Sky floated the baby in deep rest back to Delana. He seized on all his poster eyes, which might bleed in the rain but would not flinch. He steadied one of the signs. In his late sixties Sky did not need glasses. The family, Delana realized, does not wear glasses; with their eyes burning or frozen, little geysers stirring, the help they need is not ground in glass, nor is vision skewed without it. And Sky's face up close really was the same as she had known it before. And that face was too smooth now. Where experience burned its grooves in the ordinary face, Sky's was smooth. He had the too-rich look of a man untainted by consequence or defeat. Great veininess, swimming blood, and the translucency of skin declared: Nothing to hide, nothing. The mentally ill, she had heard, can retain such an angel face forever.

Jackie Junior broke the silence. He shoved his brother. "Turkey."

"What a day!" cried Joy. "Isn't this great, Sky? It's great!"

The nurse-wife said his name as if she had never gotten over her legal right to do so, as if silver fanned her words. Delana smoothed her white skirt. Right under that crispness she was bleeding. She could wipe her skirt with blood, match and exceed her Daddy's redness. Blood as gamesmanship. It was a crazy notion and gave her crazy courage.

"You still do magic," she said.

"Flummery. My doctor's touch quieted our little Baby Lamé."

"Daddy, I meant this shell game. It's one of your tricks. Come on, show me." She indicated the table under the awning, three centrally placed shellacked walnut shells. *Daddy*. Saying the word was breaking her, breaking up some hardness inside her. She must chant this word, go off into the woods and chant the strangeness clean out of it.

"Yes, indeed. These are genuine Illinois black walnuts I have cleaned, trimmed, and varnished to perfection. I picked them up right here in the yard," Sky said, showing one around. "Does anyone remember that at Mount Vernon George Washington walked around munching pecan meats, calling them Illinois nuts? *Carya illinoensis*."

"We don't know any such thing," Opal cut in on a strut forward. "A broken-down engine has left us here to celebrate your girl's homecoming. I'm pleased to meet you. Just call me Opal. I cook for this bunch."

"Surrounded by roustabouts, am I?"

"Dr. Walsh," Opal said, louder, "I get sentimental on land, though no one of them knows it." She threw a grumpy look back over her shoulder at the crew. "Doctor, I see a family resemblance. I believe the baby has your brows."

"Say!" Sky boomed.

"I penciled those on her," Delana blurted.

"Oh, what fun," added the inappropriate Joy, her fox eyes now tiny lit points.

Opal's chin jutted out. "For emphasis." Her glower told the crew that she had gone right over to land life, never mind where or with whom. The crew was of no real consequence to her on land. A creamy quality had entered her voice and gestures. Land life, it said. Take a look. I'm different. She patted her hair.

"Excuse us. I've got Jack stumped here, and the suspense is killing him." Sky said, "Step right up. Here's one for Baby Lamé." He chuckled over the table, silver hair curling at his neck, and he used those red suspenders for effect, letting his thumbs ride them as part of his country-doctor pose.

"You're telling me to look under that left shell, Jack? You swear that's going to be the one?"

"I do. I swear it."

The ruby ring flashed and flashed as Sky pretended to wonder over the shells. He sang out, "Lucky dog, come to me," and raised the shell next to Jack's pick. There lay a captive pea. The other two shells he turned up empty. Gray streaked through Jack's hair, but his jeans were as blue as a boy's, and that pure intensity is what his stupefaction matched. Sky rolled out the triumph: "Sorry, dauphiness."

Marcia groaned. "Sister Mary Frances. Do you see this complete regression, Delanie? Look what excites my husband—a black-eyed pea. And he has the nerve to scoff at my spiritual life. At home he's an elephant in the living room, an elephant watching TV. Come over and see for yourself. Jack," she said sharply, "will you notice your newborn niece, please?"

"I do. Gee, yes, she's a cutie."

But Jack Rose was more interested in Sky. "The shell game's such an old trick—come on, you can show me how you do it." Sky's open palms indicated perfect control, amusement. He would not relent. "Let's do it again, then, what do you say, Skylar?"

"Hooked, skunked, beaten." Sky relished his victory. "All right, Delana's turn. Step right up, catkin. Show Jack and everyone your sharp eye."

Daddy, Daddy. His voice swam inside her as Marcia eagerly took the baby. His look brought her forward, into the dream of duty. She watched Sky's hands rub and rub, then fly amidst the walnut shells. He worked fast and loud so no one could hear the little pea rattling. Glee puffed and shuddered his sloping front, and his breathing was heavy from weight, age, and excitement. The yeasty aroma of his light sweat came to her over the apple fragrance clogging the air as so much whimsy and wonder. She watched his thick hands, healer hands, dandlers, whisk the shells to a frenzy, and she felt, rather than saw, his pattern of sorcery and surmise. No stranger could match her ability, could possibly tell by Sky's rhythm and his degree of sweating which walnut shell to pick.

When he stopped, she pointed. "The middle one."

"No way," said Jack, his head craned forward.

But Sky swept up the middle shell to reveal the pea. Blood gamesmanship; it worked.

Men's voices rose on a wave of approval.

"You roustabouts see that eye?" called Sky.

"It's a pilot's eye," Cheramie yelled back. "We trained it into her."

"Badinage." Sky swept all the shells into a heap. When he looked up his face matched his suspenders. "She got it from me. I taught her. You all came later. Give me that."

And everyone got hushed in the leaving light, oaks too, and it was just like hearing about the sex of corn again: suddenly no one had any claim at all to anyone else. The crew rippled like a wave around that tent, but no one could step inside under the white-and-yellow awning where Delana stood with her father. It seemed an age that the father and daughter stood there looking hard at each other. They did not touch, had not touched yet, not once. As they seemed to absorb each other's looks, even the boys quit scuffing dirt with their sneakers and watched. Cheramie's hand brushed Marcia's. Opal's perfume vanished with the sun, and apple smell was deepening.

Up near the house, one late cricket held to the tribal pulse, but no brother crickets answered. His lone chirp sounded like hard, feeble work. His voice stuttered and died, leaving everyone still listening, as if hoping for a great crescendo of insect voices, which would thrill them into saying the right things too.

Joy broke the silence. She said, "We've laid in all kinds of things. I've bought disposable diapers." She gave Sky a secret look. "Maybe we've overdone." She slipped a foot out of its sandal; for just a wink of time she showed Delana nails like iced almonds, and she purposely dug those toes into some rasping leaves. The silver nails swished around, and they declared themselves owners of all the delight. These feet own the leaves and everything else. These feet get dirty and cold and kissed right here in your daddy's house. They never ran, these feet, and that's my character and salvation. Mud in my face, and still I did not run. Battling through love had relieved her of faintness. "Lemonade inside"—voice lilting. "Plenty of soap and towels. We'll manage to bunk everyone."

"I'll round up sleeping bags," Marcia offered. She handed the drooped baby back to Delana.

"You, dear," Joy said, pointing at Delana, "need to rest. Your old room is ready. Heavens, Sky, let your girl go rest. And John, you'll carry sandwiches and lemonade upstairs to her." Both feet sandaled again, Joy headed off to her house.

The leaves were roaring and itching to bite. Pure Dovie.

YOU'RE THE PEA under that walnut shell,"
Johnny said. "You're falling. You can't resist him."
His mood was sliding down with the night. He walked around
touching the pine walls of the girls' room upstairs. Oiled, they
gleamed. Their fragrance came out after dark, ancient and cool;
and under the light of one little wall lamp, the thousand eyes of
pine knots bulged, provoked after years of dark sleep, asking:
Who are you? Who are you here?

Delana said, "We'll see what happens."

Johnny walked on in his panthering way. One time when they
landed, she had seen him nearly faint with pleasure from the
morning smell of worms after rain. Change roused his senses.
Now his nose worked and fingers flexed. If possible, he would
catch the very shape of the room, stoke and tend its fire.

Johnny's being here seemed like an immigrant's story, his
presence some desperate act of honor. He did not belong in a
girl's room, and meekness would not do. Forget cobbles and
rainbows; once the immigrant man uses a knife in his own de-

fense, he gains rights. In the shadows Johnny pressed his fist to the wall. Delana ran over and pinned up a scarf.

"Bull's-eye. Hit it. Go ahead," she cried. "It's our room now. Hit the wall."

Let his fist pound, his voice fill the air. The thrill in her loose limbs was music. The house itself might break into a jig. From the vial of river water she wetted Robin's face, Robin who had become a stone on the earth in her seashell cradle, so much so that putting a cautious ear to her tiny T-shirted chest was required again and again; the baby was a stone, and Delana felt weightless, with no connection at all to gravity. Now she was flinging river water into the room, giggling, remembering Marcia's holy-water routine: how she would cross herself with a wet hand, then pour out more and fling drops on her breasts and up into the still winter air, crying, "Humidify, purify, save me tonight!" then plunge under her covers and refuse to speak another word, gasps coming on and, soon, sleep. New noise spanked the walls' rumble. New people. There would be no overwhelming by the past here. There would somehow be peace made, and it had to be made right here.

Without adjustment the dusty old radio tuned in perfectly; it was still set on her favorite station, still giving the world some rock 'n' roll. Out from her boxes came more scarves, and the rock and bone and bottle-glass collection to be gigglingly scattered all around the room, Delana so light and dancing on the trail of music and spells.

Catkin and Baby Lamé. As if calling a girl by her real name was too direct, a sure damnation, Sky said Catkin and Baby Lamé. See the pair of dancing poodles or, better, a cartoon team pranking all over the place—immortal survivors of bricks dropped on the coyote's head. Girls have to sound like foolishness and light because they must be survivors. Nicknames were Sky's admission of hope and fear. Real names threatened real anguish. His lips spilling or lunking back words always had been a clue to emotions not otherwise apparent.

Johnny raised his one hand to make the quacking duck shadow

on the wall. "Do something about that radio." And she turned it up even louder. She flung herself laughing onto the bed. The girls' single beds had been pushed together on her side of the room, the sunburst sheets obviously Joy's doing. The end table held a little glass dish full of perfect, unbroken cashews snugged against each other like creatures. Down in the yard Marcia had arranged men's sleeping bags in a circle; as the sun sank, all the staked photos and the river farther down gave off a luminescent tinge, as if marking the boundaries of the world. History felt alive as the river, moving and frozen all at once: comes on as a backfloat, smiling, then springs up to flood and ravage, if provoked. A desire to purge and mend had led Delana back here.

Outside, someone peeled an orange. Its tang smelled of memory. Marcia and Cheramie were seating themselves together on a stone bench with the slight staggering motions that meant it was important they get the distance right between them. Jackie Junior scuffled with deckhands; from an apple tree Mike whizzed fruit through the air of a soft-spoken countryside.

She pushed herself up, but bounced back on the bed. Some ceiling of energy denied her the power to rise farther. Johnny would have to help. She held her arms out. "Dance with me."

"You know I don't," he said.

"Then here." She grabbed a hairbrush off the nightstand. "Brush my hair."

Johnny stopped his shuffle and slumped. He swiveled on his one heel, that graceful, very masculine gesture that said if ever he danced, he would be darling. "That's another new thing."

"It'll calm us."

He took the brush and walked on, gripping it, knuckles gone pearly in the dusk-dark room; they winked like river and like Sky's photos. They made a point of connection. . . . "You didn't warn me about the way he talks using all those words I don't know."

"It's showtime, dumpling. No one's supposed to know exactly what he's saying."

Johnny snorted and flexed things. "I have to wonder what you want."

What, what, what? shouted in her head past the riling of music. Marcia had greeted her with, "Prodigal sister. Prodigal girl." But reckless extravagance had been the dark charm of only one day in her life, staining her since. She had lived in the shadows of family love and just one day, finally, forced her way into the light (naked, of course, how else?). She had grown up replacing a sister, and the leap to rescue them all, be some kind of step-in partner-warrior-wife, wasn't so great. An outsider crashes the line any old place. She could look back now and see her lavish show of desire as earnest, doomed, and crazy. *In the moment.* But, she reasoned, she was the only one among them with the strength to try for a saving kind of love. That's all she had seen at the time, the gamble and the need to show herself, be somebody who counted in that family. She did not see the doom of a mad act. Naturally at seventeen all action was impulse. Too bad the beating grace of her body, its drastic, desperate nakedness, had had to inflame and repel. Her scrambled idea of hope had flown way out of bounds. She was gone like a moth, a mayfly, before her father's stupor. The enormity of her mistake had hit as soon as he waved her away. She had failed to pirate his love. Shamed, she fled this owl-eyed room. Now the dark knotty pine seemed smooth with truth. She could tell Marcia that the river life was not prodigal. Only that one day was prodigal.

Below, Cheramie was standing now, his hips jutted forward, and from the look on Marcia's face, and her hand rapidly yanking the shell necklace this way and that, she was likely telling her life history, a wild brand of piety. Confession was her love.

It had taken Delana seven years of silence, movement, constant movement away from home, to run off her shame. It took a man loving her naked and clothed; living with a large, suffering doubt; birthing a baby in a shotgun shack the size of Sky's garage. After studying whirligigs and the red morning sun's firing up the live oaks of Louisiana, seeing riverbanks forever gumming water in perfect faith without the slightest chance of securing it, after roaming the South's riverfront towns that spin with the great enduring lies of pawnshops and cue balls and shoeshines, community feeds that are really sly modes of wrath and jealousy, she had piled up tastes and beliefs strong enough to assault the old household's ways of defeat. Finally she felt determinedly bled out of shame. And the more bleeding out, the dizzier, yet lighter, she felt. She harbored a deep unseeable quivering—that's natural, she thought, what any plant in the earth must feel at its startled moment of meeting light; yes, her arms twitched, but without shame, she said. I'm without that weight. And she was knocked down by the loose feel of letting go.

"He's full of pride," Johnny said. "Blazing pride, and that takes some nerve. What's he got to be so proud of? You're not going to fall for that, are you?"

The blossoming air sang, the night was so still out here, country air so thick that noises hung around, gently bumping each other; none could travel, nothing floated away; everything was caught in the clanning air. Delana looked down from the high-heaven room as if peering from a tree house. The bunching oaks posed and yammered; they might have raised this room for their own amusement. Singing oaks say, Take heart. Oaks hold on forever. Of course the mother voice perched there.

Sky's voice rose and fell away as it would with a patient: first comes the joke, then the jab, and at last the serious soothing. She remembered in the candy striper days how she had once heard him boast, "I fathered three children." He was tending a man who had tubes in his nose. The claim was bold and settled on her uneasily. She had supposed it was the allusion to Sally that made her burn, but now in the new-mother swoon she realized how the words had drummed against her instincts even as a child. If uttered by a woman, the man's boast sounds like abandonment. *I mothered* says, *I let go. It happened once.* But children are never gone, and the oaks have grown right up to spy in the window. Mother clings in the trees. Dovie is dead, but there is no past state of being a mother, no matter how inept, Delana knew. A man says, *I fathered three children*. He says, *I sailed*. A mother doesn't feel choice.

And in the girls' room, the sight of stone-Robin drew a flicking anger from her, the panic. The baby sleeps on, at peace, *knowing* in her little spongy self that she will awake to mothering. Little stone-baby on land, this day, seems to have withdrawn into a perfect peacefulness. It drew rage that the baby would show her so bluntly that land is truly their place now.

Johnny slapped his thigh. "I've met him, OK, but sleeping under the same roof with him is nuts. It's creepy. I belong outside with the guys." He came up close and searched her face. "You think you can sleep?"

Pine walls breathed big. Pine walls were winning the arm wrestle with Johnny. To Johnny, pine walls were just so much spring cleaning, containment as strong as the downstairs damask. He couldn't shake that. More proof: nothing would hold him on land. Not a tree house, a baby; nothing. We're splitting, she reminded herself. Mother, mothering, motherfuck. "I'm already asleep," Delana said, each word a bite.

She awoke in the night to the open closet bathing her in a light of memory. She imagined the old night-light shining, Dovie stepping away.

Johnny sat by the window, kneading and crushing in his big hands what she recognized as a once-favorite dress. It was sewn to look like a combined jumper and blouse: wheat-colored skirt and suspenders stitched to a blouse of red calico print; long sleeves gathered at the wrist. Like a museum of girlhood, her closet had yielded this dress.

Hearing her stir, he spoke softly. "You were this girl. It's such a little-girl dress, more like something for Robin."

She had worn the dress new to stand at the edge of Great River Road on a fall day much like this one, so sweet it made you sleepy, one hand being squeezed by her daddy's, the other waving as the LBJ caravan sped by. Classes had been canceled. The black limousine was preceded by sirens: cops and motor-cycles came whizzing around the turns. She saw the long horse face of the man no one had voted to be President. LBJ turned, and a smile caved in his substitute-leader face. He saw her in this dress and his lips moved. He might have seen the flag of surrender, sweet landslide victory coming up like a peek at plain panties. With one hand she held her daddy's, the other was waving free.

Night air was coming in the open window as sweet as it ever could be, the musk of apple and leaf tickled by that late flower alyssum, which fumes a strong honey from its tiny, earth-hugging spores. Johnny kept fretting the dress.

"You were just a girl, and still he came at you."

"Give it to me," she said.

She took the dress and slipped off her nightgown. She caught Johnny's quick glance away.

"Why'd you look at me like that?"

He shook his head.

"If you're worried that my body won't get back to normal, forget it."

He brightened. "Then you expect me to see you. You're talk-ing about a future."

"Figure one out. I know I can still wear this dress." The elas-ticized waistband was merciful, but even so the dress stretched tightly over her front, mashing breasts, and the waistband came crawling up under, a deformed version of an Empire dress.

"Just like a little girl," Johnny marveled. "Like this, Jesus, and he still came at you."

"The truth is right in front of me," she told him, and took his hand. "In this room I have to admit my revulsion and my part. It wasn't all his fault."

"You're lost there. What can a girl know? Any guy knows what happened. Men are born to the guilty side. Any guy you ask would know exactly what happened."

She turned on the radio, veered away.

"You dance," Johnny said. "I'll watch."

She moved around the room to a sugary tune. The day she wore this dress on Great River Road, the sun might have been served up straight from a pan, so flat, round, and smoking yellow it was, begging syrup. To think, again, that all the time she had suffered, Sky was reveling, still waving at parades.

She plopped back on the bed. "Brush my hair, dumpling. Come on."

Johnny tried. He wedged behind her on the bed and stroked the brush through her hair awhile. She hadn't been able to zip the dress to the top, and she felt the hair, the brush, Johnny's breathing, run down her neck and on down her back, where he was tangling the ends. "Sorry." He dropped the brush. His chin dug into her neck so, she realized, he would not shake loose entirely, would not cry, and it hurt, the bone cutting deep there. She wondered if she loved him all the more now that he prepared to leave; if inevitable loss is the real aspect of love that makes it such big business to the heart.

He said, "It's one thing, all the stuff you make up about a guy you never plan to set eyes on. It's easy to make up what you'll do to him if you're sure you'll never see him. I always told myself I wanted to taste his blood. But I shook his hand, and now I'm a joke sitting in his house."

He clutched handfuls of hair off her neck and stroked the beads of sweat on her spine. She felt his red trembling and fantastic heat as a grave encroachment, but she told Johnny, "That's good. There. Hold me tight."

As long as Johnny kept touching her, fine, she could bargain with this room, break up its watchfulness. He found a rhythm and kept on.

"You have to remember what young girls are like," she told him. "They don't know their power. I grew up in a day in this room. I made a play for my father."

"He fell, baby."

"Not entirely."

"Come on, he was right at you. A man and a girl. The seesaw was straight up, dammit. He had the weight."

"If you just keep brushing . . ." She remembered running in the night from this house. She remembered morning, buying a sandwich somewhere but not eating it during that skip of time between home and boarding the river. She remembered flinging water on the green shift, trying to smooth it down, mustard-seed necklace foggy against her skin. The girl at the Hale Barge office was vehement against her plan. "You want the river job? Thirty days and thirty nights on the river? They're used to old cooks. Old women do it. I'd worry about my menstrual cycle. I'd worry about turning hard. They told me I could get someone else for here in the office. You don't even have to type good. You're not a runaway, are you?"

"Suddenly I was in the galley, with you waving celery in my face," she reminded Johnny.

He unzipped her, clutched her hips. "Here, get out of the dress now. I'm going to touch you everywhere and declare my amazement."

But he crossed his arms over her front and kept holding her from behind, dress bunched at her waist, sleeves tugged down but not entirely off—still capturing her wrists, the dirndl skirt hiding her stranger's abdomen. And when he laid his hand on her heart, she knew he thought he was claiming it, nothing more. And feeling its beat was a call to action, demanded a vow: Yes, I'll battle. "You came to me from this house," he said. "You came straight to me." He squeezed her breast as if he could empty it of memory, as if the pain of his want could perform that trick.

I WISH I COULD guarantee you a baptism," Marcia said as soon as the priest was settled in her car. She pulled out from the rectory, a low brick building graced with ornamental ironwork donated by a parishioner from Italy; frilly white benches winged the front door. No sooner had she acknowledged to herself that she had loved Father Dan all these years than she surfaced on the other side of that business, sleek and sparkling as a seal. She, too, might as well have come up from water. Cheramie. The captain had taken her hand and called himself Cheramie. She heard "Share me. Share *me*."

Blame the euphoria on—praise!—Holy Communion. This Sunday of all Sundays, Father Dan had chosen to institute the drinking of wine. Blood of Christ going down. He stood where reformers had removed the pulpit, and told his congregation, "They've been doing it for three years in Europe."

"Delana may strike you as a mess," Marcia warned now. "She has no sense, wrapping that small baby in rigmarole outfits. And she's done herself up like a package, with glitter on her face."

Her unlined face . . . Of course age seventeen to twenty-four is
a grace period. The change was in her eyes, the swirls there, and
her bearing. An enormity of strength was suggested by Delana's
hands alone, though giving that baby over to Sky nearly collapsed
her.

"We'll see," said Father Dan mildly. "I've brought holy water
just in case. When fervor springs free I like to see it. You know
I like to cause it." And he laughed through his nose, a high
whistling sound.

"Oh, when she breaks," Marcia crowed. "When she finally
breaks!"

Yesterday she had taken her sister down in the grass, there
at the landing across the river. Delana's dappled eyes shone with
the freedom of being a little sister; the freedom to blossom into
a wild-thing violet, go anywhere, be anything: a pilot on the river
resting her head in Marcia's lap. And Marcia had cried, "I'm just
so stuck being good while you ride the Mississippi." She had
ripped up a handful of grass. "I've been here all along, stuck
and being good." The older one. Just good. And she ripped up
more grass to avoid a scene, realizing she was a breath away from
clawing Delana's glamorous long hair. Then from a sort of scaly
feeling at her ribs she remembered that she was wearing bikini
panties and red underwire bra. If only her blouse were boat-
necked, something might show. She calmed.

"Do you love Johnny awfully much?" she had whispered to
Delana.

"Yes." The word was breathed into her lap, cupped there
hotly, and like everything else in the moment, it stirred Marcia
madly. Her skin was ripping off her hands. That handshake,
everything, things she didn't even know yet, were ripping fire.
Up in Oquawka they had Thursday-night male strippers now.
Celia of the high-school disgrace was back from a long Chicago
exile and urging her, urging all the women at the lingerie party
(which, really, Celia had set up), women modeling baby doll
pajamas on Tuesday night, to see the show: "Everyone has a

riot." The women, who up until that moment had been content to jiggle around in ruffles and confess their desires, sat down and clasped their shamed and vivified blue knees.

She had pressed her little sister in the sharp, tall grass. Tell me how, how? How do you show your love?

"I licked and pasted stars all over his chest. He let me. He rode up the river made over with stars."

So there it was. Beyond lingerie, which Marcia thought was as far as you could go, waited stars. She could not have imagined stars beyond lingerie. What had she ever known? she thought, stroking Delana's thick hair, wild-thing little sister curled in her den of tall salt grass, next licking her fingers for effect and telling how, how it was she had first recognized love. One day over a satin-pie recipe she quit resisting the redheaded man. She was clarifying butter and saw on her hands what a sweet shine it was. She saw love. A man's love, Delana murmured hot into her lap, is like that: a film so light and sweet, it's barely there. (Oh, delivering angel!) Marcia had breathed, "My Jesus."

And then Delana rolled over and took a clod of dirt in her mouth. She was eating dirt. Maybe she had turned into one of those women who eat dirt for its mineral strength. But wasn't that a special red dirt? This was the regular kind here, and Delana was eating it. But she looked awful, her little sister, a mother beloved of a man (a man, she noted, who was engaging her sons brilliantly, letting them hold the baby, naming their jumpy boy shadows "pelican" and "roadrunner"), Delana with her eyes closed to do her chomping. It didn't go with the white clothes. It didn't go with the stars. Delana spit out the dirt and grinned. Her tears came only from choking, not sorrow. Marcia looked up to see that Cheramie had been watching. He was nodding yes, yes. And he was bending down. He took her hand and kissed it and walked on, and she had no choice but to plunge that burning hand into Delana's hair, crying out, "It's not even winter, and you've got enough electricity here to run a radio." And she twisted and yanked hard for the thrill.

Delana said, "I loved him enough to throw him in the river."

Oh, love, Marcia breathed. *Love games.*

She had received Holy Communion at early Mass and was driving the priest to Sky's house. They turned onto Great River Road, where a stretch of dog-headed willows swayed to the river breeze. Later, the boys would arrive with their father. The triumvirate did not attend church, but they came alive for food, and they all wanted more time around the rivermen. With Communion still fresh, she thought: Well, a woman is more Christ-conscious than a man when you get down to it, to the deep blast of the transubstantiation bit of body and blood. A thought too private for Father Dan. Bleeding Christ and bleeding women converge at the altar, mingling sorrow and renewal heat. Even nuns had that intimacy, and maybe it kept them just back from the lunatic edge. It explains why women take to church in droves, crave that sacramental flesh, more so than men. It doesn't have to do with suffering some drunken lout at home, now bow to your savior. The secret is passed on, tongued to them: how good the sweat, the hot suffering. She could tell Delana, "Women have religion whether they know it or not. You *do*." In this, her fourth decade, Marcia was rocked in her monthly cycle, made demonish in the urges that seemed to turn her skin to tissue paper and her tongue so mad for salt she would awaken four days in a row sucking her finger. Some days she couldn't touch herself; even pulling down panties, her palm smoothing along her hip enlivened her skin as if riled by some other's touch.

Oh, liquid desire, You! You rile me now, Christ.

And how the drinking of wine makes up for, oh, more than makes up for, the lack of a crucified Christ hanging on the wall. When Father Dan brought the chalice to her lips, she sipped the kiss divine. It was He, firing down her throat. Nothing short of Christ Himself had triggered her physical determination for love. He as much as said: Touch Me through man. *That man over there.*

She shivered in the sunlight blazing through puff clouds. An accusational sun, if anything. She had taken Communion that morning and now, after Mass, drove toward Sky's house with perfect zeal for the party and her untamed sister and Cheramie's

hand. "Cheramie," he said. "In Cajun it means 'dear friend.' "
She had looked to the water. Autumn was unfurling itself as a
carpet of willow leaves, minnow-quick gold slivers flashing like
mad. How dizzying to look . . . anywhere. "Just call me Cheramie." Share me, share me, whispered off his tongue.

When he had taken her hand, her eyes turned upward. Overhead a scrap of red sailed by. She had cried out and pointed. "A
kite," said the captain, still holding her hand. But she had known
what he could not: the trunk had sprung open. She was driving
back from Macomb with her party cache, and the trunk was
spilling silk. Then, "Cheramie," she had tried out twice. A name
both hushed and ripe. Silk in high wind.

How annoying the priest could look in the passenger seat with
his perfect egg head, his hands in the lap—albino beetles on
their backs. Priest hands, they are young forever, bearing, oh!
the larval stages of manhood.

Her speculations rolled with the burst cattail clouds above.
She drove, reminding herself that Father Dan always rode thus:
suppliant upturned hands fingering what? Dreams only. Being
a firm environmentalist, he drove no vehicle. He had met Sky
just once for consultation. As a newcomer to vegetarianism, he
was concerned with iron loss. Afterwards he had remarked that
Sky was a sort of grandee of past-century proportions, a doctor
of perfect authority and ease. Father Dan came away with a book
about balancing protein through rice and beans, and the planet's
shrinking nature. His new Earth Shoes, as spanking black as any
oxfords, had looked woefully brave.

Once Marcia dreamed that in her old school cafeteria, in the
aluminum condiment trays where pickles and mustard should
be, swam dozens of Communion hosts in water. She thought:
How fine, and sampled two, then regretted their diluted taste.

She squeezed her hands to the steering wheel. She was un-
accustomed to a handshake. Cheramie's had felt as intimate as
prayer. She got the humbled sensation that comes from giving
away before you exactly know what and to whom. Faith, but the
foolish kind. She remembered sending Jackie Junior off to school

his very first day, seeing a teacher—an actual hen of a woman —open arms wide enough for a whole class to perish in her realm. The handshake took you closer, really, than any kind of eyeballing. What dishonesty could pass between two people who, clothed, in daylight, had exchanged pulses? And in that handshake there was no mistaking the song of honey and lust.

"Father Dan, how can a vegetarian justify taking the body and blood?" she teased her priest. *How can I take this man?*

She detected jolliness in the priest's sweet breath of hesitation. "The host is holy. And of course the wine is too. Ingestion doesn't happen simply on the physical plane, Marcia. You know that."

"But taking Him in isn't symbolic. It's the real body of Christ when we eat it. When *you* eat it."

"Oh, well, transubstantiation is exactly what it is, but now remember . . ." And here Father Dan winked, and his head was so perfectly white and unblemished, so baby fine and virgin, her brand-new love urged she kiss it, though she would not.

He continued: "The offertory saves us. We're not talking about penned veal calves."

"Certainly not." In her back seat sat a tray of ham-and-creamcheese roll-ups, pickle in the center, for the party. She drove on, and the clouds ran off faster, smaller and smaller, looking exactly the way she made Jack's snores look in her mind. If not for the earplugs designed for jet engine workers and explosives experts, she would never get any sleep at all.

"When I first learned that special orders of nuns bake the hosts, I was shocked to hear it," she recalled. "Of course they come from somewhere, but what must it be like to bake sheet after sheet of Communion hosts?" Nuns in Missouri do it. She wondered if they punched them out the way she did sugar cookies, with the baking powder tin lid. She wondered what they thought—"flesh, flesh, flesh!"—doing that all day. They must get reckless in March, with high Easter demand, she mused. "They must chew the scraps."

The white egg head had pleasing points of sweat on it now. "I'm sure they sing," added Father Dan.

How she loved all the delicious what-ifs of catechism, the dev-astating comparisons and moral fixes to speak of with Father Dan. Now, years after the fact, she retained the convert's loud and guileless curiosity. In the end—and this felt like some crash-ing, glorious end—the convert falls back on a pagan freedom to sin. Recanting is the convert's ace in the hole. It shivered her, the power. She was separate after all. For all her fervor, in the end it was this: defection by a convert is practically a natural act. Christ, my mischief Maker! He had shown her: love is flesh too. Love is so tasty. The baking nuns would be plump hermits ribald in their tasks. Elfin. *Flesh, flesh, flesh, alive, alive oh.* Singing virgins, like His own mother, turning Him out to cool.

"In fourth grade," she said, "a nun swore it would be better for the whole town of Nauvoo to go up in flames, everyone dying, than for one of us to tell a white lie. That's how serious venial sin was to her. Just saying 'venial sin' makes me think of penned veal calves."

"And did she speak of love?"

"Father Dan!"

"No, we know she did not, poor woman."

She could spot them anywhere, nuns denuded of wimple. The crime of modernity sewn on their heads: hair chopped to per-version, not piety. Their lame crown of thorns. Sometimes Mar-cia fantasized being hairdresser to the nuns, spooling and coloring it and sending them outside, tossing their heads. Style that hair, or shave it off. Poor nuns do not know that women's hair cannot just *be*. It wants life or a cover.

Best, she thought, that nunhood was largely spared this gen-eration of kids, who would (she knew) laugh out loud at the idea of a town burning up from someone's lie. Better that her boys ran free in public schools, where the gymnasium tempered them. Missing out on men's love puts the nuns on canes and dims their eyes early, and no child of today would believe in them.

But how different was she—a married woman, a grand closet cleaner, who, too, suffers the absence of the kiss? Sleep apnea, they were calling the cause for such deep snoring as Jack's. With the earplugs she could cut it to an underwater sound, and while missing the low buzz of crickets up against the foundation, singing the autumn end of their own lives, she at least could get some sleep. The house was a ranch style, whose bedroom doors opened with such force—the cut of pine being so thin—that before you were quite ready, you were tumbled into a room. The lack of echo and the flatness of light on spackled walls were modernities as mortifying as nuns' whacked hair; she had never grown accustomed. She had shown Jack the news clipping. *Sleep apnea.* It could be corrected. "Break my nose?" he'd whined. He refused to see his own blood or endure any kind of bodily investigation. Jack Rose would not remove his clothes and tie a gown to his behind and bow to a doctor's hands. He had asked for Sky's help just once, as a teenager, for Marcia's sake only, as she stiffened in the emergency of locked vision. He had been humbled, handing her over to her father, still flushed from their sex. At that first sexual moment, any idea of fun was replaced by the permanent notion of duty. There had been no choice between them. No choice! All was decided by one quick, sad occasion. Then: years of blundering on. And with that knowledge rising on the crest of snores, a new white feeling, like the convergence of all color in the universe, had opened within Marcia: last night she had awakened, reached for the earplugs, and sailed lovingly beyond Jack's reach. Beyond now, but lovingly. Father Dan, she might cry out, I am in love. Oh, blood of my Christ, I crave You more.

Subtly, so the priest would not suspect, she raised a hand and kissed it. She raised it higher in country greeting to an oncoming car as they sailed along Great River Road, low willows at a bend thrashing the car's hood. Blood of Christ in my gullet, she thought. Flesh stuck to the roof of my mouth—don't touch it, just suck slow with the tongue and down He goes (shriveling, so very human). His blood awash in my own. Mingling, jingling my own.

The car rocked and sped down along the river, which could have been an alligator, it was so still and solid in the morning light, yet disappeared slyly in sunniness against the far horizon. The word *defection* sounded like an intimate act. She loved the Church all the more. And Mass, the pagan glory, though it was wrong to use that word, of course. But bring on the truth, let people feel it: Mass is the drama waiting; just take a part. Get into it, the great final act. Sweat and wail. And the statues with their pale enfolded robes and eyes and sandaled feet, all the voyeurs, the great love voyeurs, of course they charge the air.

Father Dan's egg head spun enthusiastically. "And consuming Christ keeps us so hungry."

Oh, the gladiatorial aspect, the outrage of it really, she thought. It makes me wild, blood of Christ in my gullet: this new development after the Vatican upheaval. Yes, it's better than the sight of a crucified Jesus Himself tacked on the wall. The drink is so personally thrilling.

Father Dan laughed. "And we charismatics take it farther." The priest's shy hands came suddenly to life as cymbals smacking high. "The truth of experience is the oneness of love. Life is mad mystical joy. I insist we use our lungs. I insist our bodies vibrate to the mystery."

I *will* develop my tongue, Marcia vowed. One of these days I'll be gifted with tongues. She wanted to be a star at Wednesday-night prayer group, go flutter-eyed and loose-lipped in the presence of God.

Drinking from the chalice, indeed. Who would have thought they would cook that up—spring it on folks who had been fed wafers all their lives while the priest and only the priest tilted his head back, way back, to drink the blood-wine in front of all.

Wait around and heaven sends down something new, as promised. The God of old tricked and taunted, raised up prophets, sailed babies down rivers, and rammed whole tribes into deserts. Then came Jesus full of miracle—madmen and scorn following—disrupting the earth as He went, a love monster. And the conscience was born. Roll back the rock. Everything, every war and all the tensions on soap operas and your patience standing in a long, slow line for groceries, even the call for presidential impeachment, Marcia believed, the way things are done today, comes directly off His cross, from His example and His news: Love your enemies. She thought of the great whiteness of feeling she had experienced in bed next to snoring Jack this morning. As if an angel of experience had gripped her and moved her beyond him, beyond any blame or frustration, she had been lifted up.

Father Dan did the cymbals again. "Remember always, always, we're celebrating as Jesus Himself did. The Last Supper wasn't all funeral music and Cecil B. DeMille. What we know is so simple it's just too loaded for so many to accept. People refuse to know that Jesus danced with those men. He danced and He danced."

Body and blood and dancing—how they all go together, so forbidden and fine. The severity of the convert would be matched in the end by sinning in the deepest shades of purple. Lord have mercy, Marcia prayed. Christ have mercy.

T HE MINUTE Delana saw the huge copper pots
Joy had hung overhead, so absurdly shiny they
looked capable of signaling allies, she knew the nurse had struggled. Anyone installing shields in her kitchen has struggled and
has feared. The room would not ever be entirely Joy Steinbach's,
and that is why she sat powdered so perfectly. Spying from the
hall, Delana felt a slight pang of compassion, even admiration,
invade her cultivated sense of accusation. No matter how exact
and trifling the nurse, this kitchen would not surrender Dovie.
No knickknack could blank out the light sparkling like a face
through the screen door, a big smile of light full of memory and
dare.

Dovie's kitchen had gurgled with her attempt to boil mint
candy. Caramel apples and gumdrop trees had prevailed. Now
the more reserved aromas of nutmeg and cinnamon fumed from
there as if seeking to legitimize the changes made, as if—in case
she was a madwoman—Delana would be ethered down by such
smells. Joy Steinbach sat at the table, using long white fingers to
stack muffins in a perfect pyramid; Opal at the stove was cracking

eggs like nerves. The morning kitchen was female, and to prove it, Opal wore a housedress and clips in her hair, a laxity she would never brook in the *Pat Furey*'s galley, not even at five A.M., and she moved her spatula on the grill as if art, not hunger, were at stake. Her slow hip was all rhythm as she wagged out her words.

"A man alone is pitiful. When I see an old one stooped over his grocery bag, I think: pitiful. God meant them to spread their grief and go on out. Men left alone at the end are just pitiful."

"Ummm," said Joy.

"You did the right thing. Marriage at any age is right. It means one less old fool out there dropping his jar of beets on cement. I'll say this: when I die I won't bother a soul. I've figured that one out."

"Oh?" So pleasant, the nurse.

And so seldom had Delana heard Joy's voice, especially in the later years, it had been easy on her mind to reduce it to no more than a breath, to remember the silence imposed by her existence and forget that even breath contains humanity: a cough, a sigh, a song half-sung. She moved to the kitchen door imagining she saw Joy's breath kiss the air.

"Unless a thug gets to me first," Opal kept on, "I've got it down. You see, I'm fatally allergic to shellfish, so when I'm ready—more old and worn down than I am now—I'll tell my son, 'Bring me a lobster.' "

"Dear me," Joy said. She clapped her hands as Delana entered. "Look at Baby. She's so cunning—a butterfly today. Is that silk?"

"She slept through the night," Delana announced.

Robin was wearing a gauzy peach drape fastened in back with Velcro pieces from Woolworth's. And though the fabric fluttered wings, Delana thought her baby looked more like a great downed luminous insect that wished to fly—arms, legs straining—if only it had not landed on its back; a beetle, not a butterfly, this baby who had leaped to Sky's arms and been mute and unimpressed with mother love since. Was she imagining this? she had to wonder. Could the baby be sick? But Robin was the picture of peace, and there certainly was something cunning in her look, her closed-down features. As far as Delana knew, being at peace with yourself was bound to be pretty cunning.

"I was remembering the huge turtles around here," she said. "Thirty- and forty-pound turtles that some people love to eat."

Opal's spatula clanged a warning.

Joy Steinbach rebelted her maroon robe. Her voice was pleasant, directed at Opal. "I wouldn't know about that." She wiped at the tablecloth and studied it serenely down her nose, which was a powdered chute. She exhaled elaborately, so that the work of her shoulders and the whistling sighs seemed as fine and surprising as the work of a one-man band.

"I don't eat turtle, Delana, and I avoid other delicacies, such as tampering with your old room. I dust, period. I told Sky I wouldn't touch a thing upstairs. He wanted me to, but I've never disturbed your possessions. It's between you two. Oh," she cried, bubbling up past her restraint, "your closet shelf is full of games. Can you people use them on your boat?" she asked, looking from Delana to Opal. "Clue? Monopoly?"

"Sounds like the progress of my marriage," Opal cracked. "Then he died."

"We played all those games," Delana remembered. "Candy Land, Life, Twister."

"Who played with you?" asked Joy.

The question felt like a trick, the answer pried, but she admitted, "I guess we all did. Marcia came on holidays. All of us played in winter."

"Your parents got down on the rug and played games with you. That's nice," said Joy, enormously satisfied. "Take the games."

"They belong in this house."

"Then do whatever." The nurse spoke as if dealing with a cranky patient whose bedpan nevertheless *would* fill, whose dependence and awe were assured, were built into the routine, the exchange. She would not waste time cajoling.

"Poker's about all the boys play," Opal said, jerking her head toward the outdoors. And the women eagerly turned to the window.

Outside, the moat of men rose from the ground along with the mist. They stretched, looking down to the green vellum water to get their bearings. One by one they slipped into the side woods, never mind a house with two bathrooms extending shade, wafting aromas, women soft and watching. Men had to circle, get their land legs; like dogs, mark territory with their water.

"Ha," said Opal. "Look there. Ha! Spreading their grief."

"I do *not* understand," said Joy.

"I wouldn't take a one of them to a dogfight."

The women laughed together, and for a moment Delana felt the great relief of conspiracy—the three of them safe in the supreme position of remove from men entirely. But the feeling quickly vanished.

"We're laughing, but I don't think it makes us safe," she said. "I don't feel that removed."

Joy's voice came out smooth and low. "No one's saying we are. No one's saying it's all fixed."

"Land life," Opal said, and winked. "Keep moving around in it."

Johnny and Sky had joined the others without even walking through the kitchen—the logical route—without even saying hello, as if in deference to the territorial divisions and a dream protocol that decreed: In a morning kitchen women are not quite ready for a man's wakeful force. Sky stood in elephant-sized pajamas of a cool light blue, Johnny hovering but turned away as if from a voice too loud.

"They really have the same build," Joy observed.

"Built for comfort, looks like," Opal said.

"Johnny's much taller," Delana swore. "Completely different." Johnny's heft was made buoyant by a light walk full of hope and uncertainty. Extra weight looked fine on both, OK, but only one had given her comfort.

When the nurse turned swiftly, bumping her, she called out, "Toot toot peanut butter." The unrelenting cheer that encompassed Joy, her sense of rightness, bit at Delana's nerves. Love had relieved Joy of faintness. It has clobbered me, Delana admitted.

Opal's grunt brought the interest back into the kitchen, where an extraordinary need for occupation overcame everyone.

"Juice these," Opal said, shoving a little machine at Joy, who did slice one orange open and dome it over the top of the machine, for a moment whirring all words away as if into dark, dripping juice. She juiced another and another. She paused and Delana took over, glad for the work, the concentration on bright oranges, though the tang staggered her. Weakened, with her throat tickling as if a thumb pressed at the back, forcing surrender of the one reluctant word or cry, she saw Dovie's old kitchen, a dazzle of oranges on hand. Dovie's way was to strip off the peel, strum the membranes, and then petal back each perfect section of orange as it whispered, papery, against the act. You should know, most definitely, that you were eating an orange.

When Delana finished juicing oranges, Joy said, "There. I was just telling Opal that with someone else running my kitchen after all this time, and you coming home, it makes me think of the first time I walked in here."

Delana looked around, anywhere but at Joy. The nurse did not have to announce on conquered land, in the appropriated kitchen, that her lifelong designs on Sky had been successful. It was enough that Joy Steinbach had junked the room with too many patterns and knickknacks and mottoes about the days of the week. She had put up reflecting copper tile behind sink and stove, backups to the carousel of shimmery outsize pots overhead. The kitchen smelled faintly of bleach. Marcia's letter had warned: *She's brought the kinds of things a person alone would have, I suppose. Smiley little statues that pretend to sing to each other; happy donkeys sprouting parsley from their backs.* Black iron chairs well suited to an ice cream parlor, shaped like women, had replaced ladderback oak. A mound of eggs in a huge blue bowl on the counter rose like a monstrous, delicate sculpture.

"Why all these eggs?" Delana wondered. "You didn't know the crew was coming."

"We didn't know what was coming, and that's the truth." Joy had turned to Opal to speak, and Opal was nodding like mad.

Overhead in mesh baskets were some forgotten onions, green tentacles poking through the wires, weakling captives that cheered Delana. An imperfection. "Those are old onions," she said.

The nurse nodded without disturbing her cap of hair, which may or may not have been brushed. It would lie there no matter what, perfect nurse hair. "I don't use the pots you see hanging; I just love their shine. I love that they can hold food for an army. I bought them just to look at. You know, I saved your father's life right here in the kitchen."

There was triumph in Joy's pause. Her coffee-sipping silence asked: So shall I continue? Opal cocked her hip. Delana patted Robin's layered bottom.

"Well, then." Joy quickly pressed her temples as if calling up memory. "When Dovie died, Sky abruptly couldn't remember what to eat. He couldn't remember a single dinner, what went with what. Correct me if I'm wrong," Joy said, carefully opening her mouth wide as if food were caught in the teeth, "but your mother's cooking was nominal. She favored sweets, didn't she? Well, even so, you were fine." Joy had the decency now to hurry over the rough terrain she had plowed, and she lifted her long white hands to Opal in an expression of the wonder; see the wonder she felt these six years later. "His grief had rendered him a culinary amnesiac. All Sky could remember was steak."

"Steak," Delana said severely, "was the one dinner food my mother had strong opinions on."

"I certainly believe that."

She could picture Dovie standing over a cold stove, preparing for the infrequent ritual of leathering a steak; Dovie clasping her necklace and, as anyone would from these parts, offering her belief that round steak needed to be floured and pan fried; that green beans are naked inedibles unless dredged in bacon grease; then she would leap to haranguing a world that assumes Chicago *is* Illinois, "as if box turtles and yellow snakes do not still claim the land."

"Broiled T-bone steak," said Joy. "He knew how to buy it and fix it. And I guess Marcia was so busy with her own little family—those boys are dolls!—she failed to see what was what. Sky was a mess, and this kitchen looked like death."

Joy made them lean into her great pause, her steepled fingers that unfolded themselves slowly to indicate the cheerful walls, the sparkling floors and countertops, the very space of trembling, which, despite the renovations and nutty additions and Dovie's obvious absence, held something from before. Orange fragrance cut the smell of frying eggs.

"Come on, finish," Delana urged, citrus watering her throat.

Joy laid her hands on the table. "I found a boneyard. That's what was in here. Plates of bone and steak juice. I'm saying *juice*, not blood, because technically, once cooked, it has other properties. Anyway, it was horrid, just horrid. I'm afraid," Joy lowered her voice to say, "he was insanely reluctant to remove them. I did the work. I brought antiseptic and gloves. I swept the clattering piles of bones off the counters and into a giant pail from the garage. And he cried. Delana, he shed crocodile tears as I worked. It was the best I could do for him, removing those bones, and he knew it.

"Who knows," Joy said, tapping a knife for Delana's benefit, "what end he would have come to if I hadn't stopped by."

"Pitiful," Opal muttered at the stove. "A man alone at the end is pitiful."

Men straggled over to the screen door, and Opal was right there to feed them. They ate outside, standing, keeping equally sharp eyes on river and plate. Their heads swiveled like those of the great meaty reptiles from the riverbank. They could have dispersed, gone to the Hotel Nauvoo, but they had followed Delana here. Stood on the lookout for her. That was their kind of love. The loyalty was real, and to see the men she had navigated up and down the river, and fed, to see them now milling around her father in his flowing pajamas, filled her with an ache of hope. We can all come together. Somehow we can all mingle and manage and drift. The line between land and water is illusory: riverbanks are always wet, and the water is heathered with soil; there is no firm bottom. The rivermen stood there waiting for the next thing. They lived blindly with what she knew she had most lacked: trust. Shattered hard, how do you get it to come creeping back?

And in Opal's quick handing of the plates out the door, screen banging to, in the grunting thanks of humbled men—not at all swaggering as on board—Delana recalled the one thing Dovie had done here with great flourish: feed hoboes up from the water and the tracks. The house was marked, and so they came on, hungry. Men came to Dovie for breakfast, and that, Delana thought now, was her mother's triumph. A lone man with a skinny red neck and voluminous bleached-out pants would hunch on the back porch while Dovie fried up eggs. She would prepare a breakfast of amazing heartiness, nothing anyone around the house ever ate; and though Delana could dollop some stewed tomato or beans onto the plate, she was not allowed to serve; she was especially not allowed to stare through the screen at a stooped hobo eating breakfast, being given to understand that this was his sacred time, his reward. After eating, the man vanished without a sound, leaving behind a licked platter. Once, a vivid face pressed the screen and called cheerfully back inside, past her as she was pretending not to stare, "Thank ye kindly, lady-mum." Dovie had whispered, "Bless his soul."

The honest request for a breakfast plate sent Dovie humming and brisk, and afterwards for days, Delana remembered, she would hover flushed, her mouth open, in the kitchen stocked with gallons of milk and special knock-out coffee, ready (come on!) for battalions of need and gratitude. And what if, she mused, Dovie had *appreciated* her daughter's running off to feed men, to cook for ramblers? The thought was so new and startling, her throat closed right up. She drank a large glass of juice.

Imagine, now, Dovie getting the news: her runaway girl is cooking for men. Secret victory: my girl feeds hoboed men. Her runaway girl had landed on a boat of traveling men. She must have comforted herself, thinking: She is, in the end, Lord, exactly my daughter.

Having returned for Dovie's funeral dressed like a man in hobo clothes took on new meaning. In rough serge, Delana had brushed past Sky. Away only one year, she would not face him looking like a girl. (This time she had brought nothing but the softest cottons, drapey skirts and loose blouses, the white whites and printed, nearly transparent fabrics, some with gilt borders, bought at an India import store.) Let the mourners beware, said the pink feather shocked upright from her fedora brim. The black suit had been swept off its hanger at a Baywater charity shop for five dollars and fifty cents. The sex-offending clothes, not Dovie's death (she felt sure), had made Sky cover his face with a handkerchief.

Before taking her into the funeral home, a delirious Marcia had clung to her as she would have a man, even going so far as to tug at her man's lapels. "The ambulance had come," Marcia whispered, her new polyester crumpled against rough serge. "And alone in that house, I felt sick with guilt to find I hardly missed her. Delanie, it's awful. I'm sure if she hadn't died suddenly she would have called you home one day. If only there had been time she would have. Say she had had an illness . . . Oh, if only Mother had had an illness. If only! What a luxury that would be, to simply suffer illness, to linger and ponder and conduct bedside confessions. To hear true words of love just as you go on to Jesus. To die from illness. No, the Walshes are abrupt as teeth in all blood matters. We vanish. Oh, little sister, with your rich long hair, and here I am still looking like Sandra Dee. Come on."

"Shhh, you're upset." She was preparing herself to see Dovie, dead Dovie lying down. She was remembering taking a nap alongside her mother, touching her mother's white leg, the surprise feel of her thigh, cold skin. So different from arms and calf.

And she was reminding herself that a woman's cooling thigh had to do with age, not sorrow. She had read this somewhere, possibly in one of Marcia's magazines.

Marcia blubbered on about the new charismatic movement: tambourines and faith healing, swoons, trances, and some book about tossing down switchblades. This is the year, the time is right now! Her religious fervor rose and rose, all nonsense to one used to river ways. The great surprise of an oak toppled into the channel, that's where the fundamental idea of God resided. How could childhood belief still hold Marcia? As far as Delana could tell, charismatic just meant more noise.

Inside the funeral home, with aching decorum, Sky moved across the room to hug her. That's where the charity shop suit came in. It would not allow a hug to penetrate, to break her up in any way.

Now, with a virtual run on men waiting for breakfast at the screen door, a colossal mirth shaking right out of the trees, she could think that Dovie sat up there kicking like mad off an oak limb, that she roundly approved the wandering men Delana had thrown in with. And sitting there in the stunned familiarity of the kitchen (was the radio on? were little heels clicking?), Delana reasoned that the snacks Dovie had sent in place of letters were a code to mask the pride she felt for her hoboing daughter. She clutched Robin.

"I'm not sure Robin's really comfortable in this outfit," she ventured. "Maybe she *would* prefer fuzz."

"Ummm," chorused the women. She understood she was to take their voices as consent, either way. They would not interfere with minor matters of taste, though she kind of wished they would. On land, remember, there's plenty of room to mess up and try again.

In a thousand ways she would be required to let Robin go, as Dovie had done with her, and she could imagine no nobility in the act. Of course it could strike a mother dumb, even one who saw victory in her loss. Of course Dovie had mailed only sweets. Her coded love let sugar speak for hope.

But what about Sky's silence? There could be no conjuring of its meaning from some little black bag of tricks. A man's natural silence was a far greater mystery than a woman's contrived speechlessness could ever be. Still, the idea was to settle her mind the best she could. Jostling Robin, she spoke through her to Joy. "I thought Sky would feel shame, but I don't see it."

"Sky does not feel shame," Joy affirmed. Letting it sink in, she added, "And for that matter, neither do I."

"You were the awful silence in this house."

"Enough, please." Joy's chin was raised, her eyes cold. "We're adults here. No one, but no one, knows what a relationship between a man and a woman is. No one should ask. After all, I could ask you how you're willing to boot that man John out of your life now that you have a baby. *Run away from a man who has given you a baby. You are truly remiss.*"

"Opal!"

The spatula clanged. "Yes, I've talked to her. Girl, excuse me, but I've been bursting for some womanly gossip on the unnatural experiences around me lately."

"You're here with your beautiful baby," Joy pressed, "and you want to mope in the past. That's completely remiss. We must always look ahead, always."

"Sky never called me home. That sticks."

"And now he has."

"But I don't even know if he missed me. Has he felt something strong enough that means he missed me?"

Joy's hands came down flat hard on the table, long fingers rigid as ivory. "Opal." She raised her voice, as if calling to someone in another room. "Would you say that question is sweet or stupid?"

Delana tried to explain, but Joy would not hear about what a deflection the shell game was, and she would not listen to what Sky's face looked like to a daughter; she made loud noises against Delana's raised voice when she insisted that experience burns grooves into faces, grooves into voices too, Joy. Which she did not find in her daddy. She described the too-rich looks of a man

untouched by life, untouched by consequences. She did not go
so far as to say, "While I suffered he was reveling." Instead, she
offered a diagnosis: "I know the medical term. It's *flat affect.*"

"Look at me. Look at me straight." Now the nurse contorted
her face, causing cords in her neck to stand out. She showed all
her teeth—silver ridging and red gums—and sent out a faint
coffee smell. Her eyes were shooters. She held the hideous pose,
then quickly dropped it. "Should he look like that while examining a burn victim? Have you thought of the *facial* stamina alone
required of a doctor tending gore? Sky wears his bright face.
He's gone deep enough to find, to make sure, he *has* such a face.
He needs it, and it's there. There! That's what a good doctor
does. It's faith and kindness he presents to them.

"Believe me, little mighty one, to see functioning, beautiful
bodies is his real thrill. To walk into the light after some horror
and see laughter and silk hair is sanity. If he didn't have that,
how could he work? He's developed protection, all right. Look
in the mirror. You're gorgeous to him. Of course he looks on
you untroubled."

And when Joy twisted around, calling, "Opal, isn't that true?"
she looked exactly like someone made happy and foolish in playing the Twister game, when the legs and arms are all down and
your head is rushing with blood—you're waiting for the next
spin, the next decree, knowing it will topple you. There would
be Dovie in her open-toed heels trying it, teetering and wind-
milling her bare, dowel arms, collapsing against Sky, who roared,
"Bombs over Tokyo!" They loved playing the games with much
shrieking and delicious, light accusations: wild alliances and be-
trayals in Monopoly, great gambles, all the while the toy train
running through. A time to be loud, and at a break, Dovie would
rush in with popcorn and ginger ale. In a game someone wins,
oh someone! and anyone and everyone had the chance. It was
wonderful to hear Dovie cry, "Beast! Fool!" and then, cuttingly,
announce to Sky, "Miss Scarlet did it in the library with a rope,"
to win the game of Clue.

The screen door slammed. A deckhand needed juice. The

women sat like statues, and though he hurried, the pouring of orange juice made a long, apologetic, invasive sound. He coughed to cover his noise and excused himself, banging the screen door in his wake, the sight and sound that had shivered Dovie's spine with glory and cut deeper into Delana's memory. Again, that bursting smell of oranges caught her. Oranges were the dowser, the witch of memory in this kitchen.

Each hobo had received an orange. "Something for the road," she could hear her mother calling out the back door as she tossed fruit to the men. "No need to suffer the steerage diseases." She meant scurvy, even mentioned rickets and told Delana that the orange was exactly like eating sunshine. While Sky went off early to officially save lives, Dovie waited for need to present itself, for salvation to be gained. Little kitchen god, she gave away the sun.

She missed Dovie. She missed her mother when she most needed her, bringing home a baby.

Delana was up and roaming the kitchen now, hardly noticing Robin floating to Opal's arms. She reached high and pinged a copper pot. She picked up Dutch boy and girl salt and pepper shakers, put them down hard. Cheated, that's how she felt. She touched the needles of a cactus plant that gave no indication at all whether it was dead or alive. She came to the absurd bowl of eggs, way too white, cool to touch, and cracked two into Opal's skillet. "I'll cook," she said. "I'd like to."

"She's got that big new-mother appetite," Opal told Joy.

"Even as the baby seems to wear you out, of course she gives you extra strength," Joy said. "Delana, give Sky your love. He needs it."

"You're quick with advice. I didn't know you were like this."

"You've never known me at all," the nurse said mildly.

Delana pushed the curdling eggs around in the skillet. She picked a fresh one from the bowl and looked out the window to see Johnny walking with his light step down the yard, nearly tiptoeing, his arms crooked at his sides as a big rounded man's must do, and even from back here the elbows with their redness were clearly signaling bruised love. Now he carried future pain with him, and how could she, like Dovie with the hoboes, usher him on when, really, she did not want to? Unlike her mother with Sky, her man tried to stick by her, and still the dream did not work. She lobbed the egg to a far wall.

"I'll be a monkey's uncle!" cried Opal. "Someone beat that girl. I mean it, beat her."

Joy went superior. She folded her arms across her chest and looked amused. "Oh, it's her petulance. Being nasty is a release. It's helped her before."

Delana stopped. Ears were singing, and the subterranean kick of shame, the part of her shame she had never named, slicked through her mind: Sky's version of that night as told to Joy. Of course Sky would have talked to Joy in their nighttime comfort, when words, whatever their day weight, feather away in the darkness. He had gone over it, talked on and on, absolving himself, shedding shame. Through talk he lost shame, Joy holding him, saying, "That's right, my innocent love," and directing him to her sex. He released shame to the masking dark and into a woman. Delana had never let herself think so far, to wonder what Joy Steinbach knew, what kind of distortion had become the tale.

"Whatever he said about my running away is half-assed wrong. You don't know anything."

The next egg caught Joy on the top of her head, surprising Delana as much as the others.

"Ick!" Joy cried, squinting against the runny mucus fogging her eyes.

"Oops, I'm sorry," Delana said, though seeing the nurse grope wildly caused a moment of childish triumph. Here was the small, exact, and harmless gesture denied Dovie. This one moment of helpless disarray was enough, made it even-steven. Delana wiped her hand. Opal came flapping a towel.

Joy dabbed herself. She ran the towel all over her face and, once the coast was clear, pierced Delana with her look. "I *do* find this little déjà vu extremely interesting. Opal, once this girl poured juice in my lap. Dark red juice, and I was wearing a white uniform."

"She lies. It was an accident."

"Opal," Joy said, turned completely now from Delana, "I had just experienced the *aftermath* of an accident, as I'm doing right *now*. I had had an *abortion* down in Mexico, hardly a *glorious* experience. I had been *away*, of course. Nineteen sixty-three, you *know* I had to go away. I'm just back from Mexico, and guess who throws juice in my lap? Now it's *eggs*, Opal. Eggs. Can you beat it?"

"My sad Christ," came from Opal as Delana felt the cry of disbelief burn down through her body.

She sent eggs flying, anywhere but at Joy. She was grabbing them in twos from the large bowl, and in the skillet fried eggs were sizzling, black and forgotten. The sound of splattering egg thrilled her: get the shiny pots, get the windows and douse the stupid cactus plant. Now bring down the onions. They have a way of shrieking as they sail and tumble down everywhere. She aimed at every sad color and trinket, being stunned out of words for Joy Steinbach.

An onion boomeranged down on Joy after hitting the pot carousel. "Stop it," she commanded. "You're crazy."

Opal was rushing to the skillet, holding the baby like a battering ram—sleeping baby with her peach wings flying. She flipped the skillet into the sink and blasted on water. Smoke rose up. Robin came awake in a fit. Opal threw open the screen door, shouting, "Stop her, stop her. She's crazy again."

And crewmen came running, knowing for certain only that this time there was no water below to snare the wickedness. They scowled all around, noting the eggy wall and the onions on the floor. They knew who had done what. She's home, good, so now let her daddy bring her butt down. Have someone bring her butt down. Fucking A. They glared at the doctor but could not catch the big, screwy-talking man's eyes, which gleamed bright as the river.

"What the hell?" Sky demanded, in the lead. In his pajamas, with men bunched behind him, he looked incapable of saving anyone, let alone restoring the dignity of a wife with yolk in her hair.

Joy stepped forward, gooey and calm. "Shoo. It's OK. We're busy in here."

The onion in her hand dropped, rolled, and everyone looked at its lively green tentacle as if it were roulette. The onion rolled under the Hoover cabinet, which, at least, Joy had neither removed nor shellacked to some hideous color. Delana focused on the Hoover as if on some inner light of reason, as if its pristine flour bin and great roll-up drawer and the glass panes and oakwood grain defied all distortion. When Joy showed good sense, it was astoundingly right, as now, cutting off Sky's bluster.

"Caterwauling," Sky grumbled. "OK, everyone out. Out! Picaroons, all of you." To the dazzling song of oaks, men were shunted back outside.

Blood kept singing in Delana's ears. Robin's spluttering from Opal's arms finally drew her attention.

"Is she hungry?" Joy asked, shyly now.

"She is," Delana decided. She ran water on her arms and rubbed off the egg mess, seated herself with Robin and ducked her head down. She opened her blouse and heard across the table a slight intake of breath, but when she looked Joy was only yawning, mouth covered. Opal came up behind and began rubbing a wet cloth into the nurse's egged hair, apologizing.

"Excuse us all, Joy. On shore we usually cut up pretty bad our first days. We don't know how to be. We bop and holler." Opal shot a look Delana would not catch. The nurse's slit-eyes were watching her intently. That yawn had been fake. Everyone is calm, sitting. Open the blouse, both sides, for her, and feed the baby. Give what is needed. You have nothing to lose, not a thing. You did not lose your baby. Banishing the men had completely relaxed everyone. The nurse looked on, a mistress who had run on faith, not shame. In her hunger she made some low, needful sounds loud enough to make Opal cover them with a huge cough.

"I'm sorry," Delana said. "You know I'm sorry."

Joy, looking beyond her, out to the dining room, recovered her managerial self and even smiled. "Well, keep your man, for heaven's sakes. Men need women. They shouldn't be turned out lightly."

Opal agreed. "There's one I'm working on at bingo."

"Fine, Opal."

"Of course I want Johnny," Delana blurted.

Opal cried, "Listen to her. There."

"I've said it before."

"She's said it, but how's she going to rout him? He works the river. That's what a river rat does. She doesn't want him gone thirty days at a clip."

"Oh, the river," cried Joy. "There's a ferry running from Montrose to the Illinois bank. John can go across the water instead of up and down. The ferry gets over there in no time. He can do it ten times a day and still make the dinner hour." Opal coughed, slapped her bad hip. "It won't do?" Joy asked.

"Joy, he'd perish, honestly," Delana said.

"But have you asked him?"

"No, she hasn't," Opal accused, "because what if he makes the change? You see, what if he says, OK, I'll just sit here and shell your peas or do anything you ask? Then what would she have? A sit-down man. I don't think she can take it. If she gets him this way, then what's the worth? Deep down she fears love, that's the problem."

"You want to get egged too?" Delana shot back. "Keep going, Opal."

"Please do *not* bring out the troops again," Joy said. "We'll conspire and think of something. Now, ladies, I want to go put my face on and wash this hair too. They used to advertise egg shampoo. I never tried it. Baby's done eating? Let me give her a hug." She embraced Robin awkwardly and stepped away. "Opal, thanks for cooking. It's as if I'm on vacation. I'm at camp with the wild girls. I've been initiated. I belong."

S KY ADMIRED his staked photographs in the clear morning light, dew making his cardboard smiles downright fleshy. He wore his red suspenders again today and slowly ran his thumbs under them as he looked out over the grounds, surveying the yardwork from a distance. Crows ran right under the pop-up clouds, and the breeze that sweeps night worries away brushed Delana at knees and fingertips and right above the ears as something curious, she thought, something gentle and wondering. Breezy air would be like the kiss of a ghost baby, an untouchable velvet shearing and flushing your cheek. She stood in the raucous yard—leaves alight in the breeze— watching Sky round up the men: "Corvée! We've got miles to go before we sleep." The sad, settling heap of his figure seemed intent on fixing him to the earth, he, kitemaster to all the girls who had flown from him through the years. Delana had streaked away on water; Sally had gone down; his wife wilted with a smile; his firstborn was subsumed by nuns. And in Mexico, Joy had had herself scraped like a gourd. That last one—undoubtedly a girl like all the rest—did not even get to land. It had to have been a sad accomplishment for a doctor, preserving an air of propriety instead of a life. Doctor Sky could save anyone but his own. Every blood female rushed from him as if from hot hell. Now Delana went toward him.

A barbecue grill being wheeled from the garage suddenly required Sky's vigorous direction. It stood like an exotic bird, tall and black on spindle legs slightly spread, ready to serve. And the men looked as stiff and sure, she noted. Two bushel baskets were placed under an apple tree, where Sky next demonstrated the use of a picker for the men. He thrust the pole with its spiky cup up into the tree. He rammed and twisted, adding some growls. She had to cry out. The caging of fruit seemed a terrible, wounding act. But men cheered like boys as apples came down. One turned beaming to her. "Hey, it's not gar." Lovers of commands, after all, they had fallen in behind Sky and now gave her grievous looks of desertion. Out of routine, thrown off, men didn't have a clue as to how to behave. The zeal on their faces was all out of proportion to the little chore before them. Having no one to love, they would rage at those apples. They would gleefully gouge the tree.

Even Johnny, a brooder on river life, had come to a place where he would pound his fist on another man's wall. Pound on her daddy's wall, being thrown so far out of routine. She watched men chomp apples, throw apples, smash the bad ones. You were going to hurt who you loved, that's what it came down to. Only the deranged, the unstoppably lonely, took hurting to the streets.

Everyone ogled Sky's prowess except for Johnny, who had drifted away earlier, and Cheramie, milling around the drive. Her daddy had got some of the crew raking shiny leaves into stylish piles: waves and mounds of color surrounded the bushel baskets and the wheelbarrow and the deep laughter of the men. You had to shout to be heard over work racket. *How did you do it?* her inside voice screamed. *How could you banish that little one?* But as Sky kicked through the leaves between them, strumming his suspenders, out came, "Daddy, what's up? How can I help?" It was just like passing by Fats Domino's home without knocking:

pure adult, ceding him his sorrow, not mentioning Mexico. It was not her business, and startled by the maturity of that thought, she smiled hugely.

"Atta girl. Call out your John fellow and tart up the baby. I've got photographers coming. Voters will love it. We'll all love it. Come on."

Fighting back words, she followed Sky across the long side yard, where a great intrigue of shrub lay between woods and lawn. Balls from all sports—rubber balls, Wiffle, baseballs, and shuttlecocks too—had been swallowed in this undergrowth edging the green-black woods of walnut and oak. Right under her feet cricket clamor rose with the great passion that invisibility brings. Above were the high bushes with red gel beads they had always called poisonberry. Black-eyed Susans and the gangling blue aster fixed stares up out of thickets, and the ragweed, which had never caused one itch or sneeze in any of them, shagged a high golden ridge that ran back into the woods. You could bottle cheap perfume right out of this air. She thought how thirsty the land near a river seemed, how greedy the plants. In comparison, a desert would be the very mark of courteous restraint.

"Blackberries," said Sky. "Look at them."

She bent over the tangle of new bushes. The berries were huge, like a mad idea of themselves. They were bunched in hives, blue-black in overripeness, cauliflowered out, and steaming so into the air—sun shining on their swollenness—they looked pulsing and ready to gush.

"Ah, they're sweet," he said wistfully. He bent to the bushes, but to Delana these words did not seem the true address for berries.

"The berries are scrumptious," she assured him. Even the strong aroma of the berries made her cheeks sting. And the guiltless, admiring father made her cheeks sting. His look was so frankly full of dreams, she had to look away. The fear of uncovering his side of things was about as strong as her need to do so, up close to Sky. But he had called her home to campaign. That's what she needed to digest.

Before she could speak, Sky had popped a berry into her open mouth. "Surprise!" His waved white hair looked merry against his florid face. He was snorting, delighting again, always in surprise and control. "Caught you off guard."

The delicious berry was a drug she fought. "You expect me to help with the campaign?" she cried, all confused. "What are your chances to win?"

"I'm going for a landslide. We're the ticket, all right."

"And so you called us home to help." Daddy had such a full feasting look about him as he picked and ate berries. He devoured those berries with eyes shut and a soft smile on his face, a slow nod to her words. He was savoring the dream of berries more than the fruit itself. *Sweet.*

"What we really need are pails," he said, snapping his fingers, which had not touched her at all as he placed the berry in her mouth. "Bright metal pails are de rigueur. Voters want the whole picture of happy industry."

"And so you called us home."

"Didn't our littlest constituent connive it? Along she comes like a catapult. Boom, and here you are."

"Because you asked, Daddy. You finally called me here. I thought it was for reckoning, not a political campaign."

He played his suspenders slowly, almost in rhythm to the men's cries of delight as they continued to work in the yard. Two had fallen to tussling in a great mound of leaves. "We could go on and on about everything under the sun, but the only thing we can be certain of is that in memory we fork. Truly, that's all we can be certain of. You're here, and I'm your old and amazed father." And he turned a devastating look on her, of assurance, the assurance of the free, rinsed soul, innocent in regard, roundly curious, the look to fix and swoon, his hands now running up and down those suspenders. Berry juice was trickling down her throat. As surely as she had known which shell had harbored the pea, she understood like a stab that Sky had cherished, not suffered, her absence. He had lived comfortably with a dream of her.

"You want pictures of me all over the place to show that I've come home. You want to show off a family, the bigger the better. And a baby added is just perfect. That's what you want, and it's a surprise, it really is." She imagined herself on billboards, blacked up with wig hair and goatee.

"Could you have come home before, without the baby? No, no, no. We're all together now. We're all winning."

As a deckhand came into range, scraping his rake along behind him, Sky boomed, "Families bend and mend."

His happiness, though nervous, seemed genuine, not exactly that of an old dodderer. But, Daddy, no shame, revulsion, or anger? Her eyes on him beat in a rhythm so hard she thought they must be emitting sound too. He wiped his face and began wringing out his handkerchief.

"I see you still don't know your strength. Catkin, you don't recognize it."

"I know," she said softly, "that I am capable of hurting my baby girl. I'm a parent like you."

Her daddy stopped, and so had the breeze. He began flapping the handkerchief, looking around, squinting at the men gone antic in his yard. "Then you're really grown up, and that's why I can look at you. You have the parent's terrible knowledge. We're on the same side, catkin. Rather, Delana." He wiped at his forehead and all over his face. "See now, you've surprised me too." His eyes were round, like lockets, which, if clicked open, would carry exactly some old dream picture of her that she knew he possessed. But all she saw were twin reflections of herself as Joy would see her: her healthy, healthy self.

"You're a fabulous young Dovie. For God's sake, let me show you off in pictures."

Her daddy went forward, weight heavy on the left knee. His body slumped unevenly as he walked. His grin had the same jubilance as the men gouging fruit out of trees.

She called, "They'll draw mustaches on me. All over the county you'll see me in mustaches."

Sky threw up his hands and laughed.

By the drive, Cheramie stood bouncing an apple in each hand, peering down the road. He was waiting for the party to continue, for Marcia and everyone to come back today and play. He could not know she would surely bring her priest.

And stone-Robin upstairs had been knocked out by land life, was heeding all the gone girls' cries, that's what has happened to her, Delana told Johnny, who lay shirtless on the bed, white, white, white. Robin is admitting herself to earth. Cheramie would agree, say to help her by brushing her lips lightly with moist dirt.

"Where were you?" she asked. Wood shavings and Johnny's Exacto knives were tossed down, evidently in service to a half-stripped branch.

"I hitched over to look at the barge. I don't like time on my hands."

Johnny lay like a huge uncooked slab of fish; he looked like the biggest monster of all from the Mississippi River. No wonder nothing bit when she threw him overboard. Lug fish recognized the white sunless skin of one of their own. A last tiny green scrap of star twinkled on his gold-haired chest. She kissed Robin, leaving a berry smudge on her soft face, and the sign seemed as clearly bad as Dovie's hobo markings must have been good: You'll hurt her. You hurt those you love. A parent is helpless not to do so. She wiped off the smudge, and the penciled-on baby brows too. It was time to let Robin look relaxed in sleep. Maybe, she thought, Sky had refused birth to the one in Mexico, thinking of the inevitability of hurting her. She speculated as much to Johnny.

"And the funny thing is, now that I know what happened, I know we're really more of a family—with Joy—whether I like it or not. Poor thing. I didn't know what she'd been through. I didn't expect to like her, that's for sure, but I don't begrudge her. I have a lot of sympathy for her. And she's gutty too."

Against the dark wall Johnny's shining seemed so bright as to be nothing, so bright he was fading, as Robin had done in sunlight. His eyes were glassy, fixed only to himself. He did not turn toward Robin or seem to wonder about her deep sleep now. "It figures he took her to Mexico for that. His destruction doesn't end. Hey, for all we know, he poisoned Dovie to get rid of her."

She slapped him hard. Long white streaks cooled Johnny's red cheek, and his shoulders raised a boulder-like half inch. Damn, here it was: her capacity to hurt him over and over.

"You think I'm taking this," he said quietly, "but I'm not."

She sucked on her fingers, bit them. Surely pain told the truth as nothing else ever could. And so we hurt, we must hurt. Any memory worth the bother reeks of wonder and pain. She said, "We've landed, Johnny. Until now, we've just been playing."

Below, Cheramie had finally started eating his apples, but in a peculiar way. He was hovering by the drive, biting first from one, then from the other, back and forth nipping. He would crane his neck down the road, then nip at an apple.

The slant of light did not register shock; motor sounds drifted over the fields as tunes; a man was eating apples; bird songs, too, were astoundingly undisturbed by her first unreal, unforgettable slap. Which stung like nothing else, divided up her world not by the experience itself, Delana felt, but by the mortal swoon she was left in, a conflict of knowledge and dread. From now on a certain shaft of light, any two apples, motor tunes, and even birds could roar with memory and bring back the sorrow. Yet her stinging hand still seemed full of fight, alive with the Sunday-morning truth that nothing is as erotic as fidelity, nothing.

THIS IS IT," Marcia announced. "From now on, you'll just have to be celibate without me. Jack, you will have to go on *not doing it* without me."

She was upstairs in the girlhood bedroom. Today she had arrived with a load of men's laundry neatly stacked, exotic in its variety and mass, to find Delana had gone for a walk with Johnny. In the two days since the arrival, since the invasion, as Marcia liked to call the landing, lassitude and grace had raged within her.

She leaned on the windowsill, whispering at leaves which, rightly, gasped at her resolve. Coming up, she had passed Joy and Opal in the kitchen, smothering the baby with attention. Jack and the others were down on the lawn, and the side woods ran away to sweet, beckoning darkness. She still knew its clearings and stumps and thrilling pungency of acorns and moss. Through the years of Delana's absence, she had only darted upstairs briefly, but now with the return, with her little sister's strange things set around the room, it felt right again. She had touched tiny bones and extravagant scarves and the absurd outsize pink cradle. She had found a little box of stars and immediately stuck a gold one to her palm. Now she whispered out the window to the faraway Jack, and she added a high note for Father Dan: "You, too, will certainly remain celibate without me." Two men will remain celibate without me. What a great suggestion of promiscuity!

As long as the deep hunger had gone wanting, Father Dan had been assured of her perfect affection. She wondered if it was an amusement among the more engaged parishioners: watching women devoutly in tow to the priest, knowing they were sufferers of the absent touch. Who else would concoct holiness from emptiness? Who would parade it? But faith as a belief in the utterly unknown had always drawn her. She took a summer blanket off Delana's bed.

She said, I glow. I am glowing and my brow has dropped a sexy half inch and the eyes are shocked open with a pleasure that has no memory, a pleasure that does not serve memory or any snag in the past. She thought of her own father being sexual and her little sister rocking on the water in a man's arms, and she considered her older son's bedroom activity, a grotesquerie considering that the adults downstairs—elephant and wife—sat as if nothing were happening. To acknowledge his play would be to admit to their lack. Asexual, she might tell a therapist. Not frustrated, no; Jack is just a man who the deep store of feeling has bypassed. Asexual. Or it was swiped from him. He does not blame me, though he could: our young misfortune. No, in truth our sorrow relieved him of effort. Even at eighteen, more than anything else, he wanted a La-Z-Boy and cocoa with TV. How these children were conceived is a miracle, a dream of effort I do not recall.

Glowing! I am glowing!

Father Dan had accompanied her again today, and as soon as they arrived, Cheramie took her hand; he kissed her on the side of her head as Father Dan walked placidly, brushing her, carrying yet another tray of her little meat roll-ups with the glistening pickle centers—they had been such a hit on Sunday.

Jesus, she said, thank you for the gift of flesh. I'm ready. Roll back the rock. Cheramie. Share me, share me.

She walked downstairs, carrying the blanket. Spotted him. Looks were exchanged.

The river captain's home sat way uphill across Great River Road. From there, from out the windows or sitting in the yard at night, every now and then you could see some extravagance, maybe the *Delta Queen*—an enormous floating wedding cake served after dark as vision. From it laughter was thrown out like bird song. It seemed to Marcia that no one rich or poor along that Illinois stretch of bottomland and bluff had ever completely been tamed. She had not been tamed and would prove it. Roll on, river, do business. From nowhere else in the country could you travel to nine states by waterway—one of her grade school's first insistent lessons, a good Catholic-school lesson: knowing the waterways of man, the pathways of God. Girls should know that they lived along His most extraordinary highway. In Marcia's first year at St. Agnes, a national defense drill found the whole school of uniformed girls flocked like night birds underneath their tables, but the spring breakup of ice floes on the river found a yet more chastened bunch pressed to the windows, Sister Mary Frances explaining, "The hand of God is in all earthly matters. Look on His magnificent wrath." In the flood He sent a deer on an ice floe right before their eyes, revolving sweet as a music box, a little doe quivering, her legs giving out in the splits, her body scooting down, her head slicing under: little deer, dying. A mass fainting occurred. The priest was called in to bless the sorry heap of girls. Marcia was put to bed for a week with rosary beads, a fuzzy lamb, and sounds in her head she now believed had been a child's version of tongues. If only she could dredge them up now. Ha, hey, lo, lo, maw . . . She lived on God's extraordinary pathway, and up that pathway had come Cheramie.

Teenage restless and bold, she waved to Jack and strolled with Cheramie away from the tent of food. She passed Sky's photo, which seemed to glare. Everyone was milling, gaming, waiting for Delana and Johnny to return. How the chaste history pays off! The great advantage to being such a *good* goody-good for so long was the group's absolute noninterest in her walking straight into the woods with Captain Cheramie, blanket in hand. The perfect criminal is the least likely suspect.

"Where are you taking me?" Cheramie pretended to wonder.

"To a girlhood spot. I call it the fairy glade."

Behind, her boys ran among the men in bandannas. A Frisbee flew overhead like some kind of sci-fi ad promising new planetary life. Father Dan was edging toward Opal, who edged around Joy. Joy was holding the baby in a splendid Victorian lace gown Delana might approve. Among strangers, Marcia thought, a priest will always approach the women first, to read the situation. Because how hard, how very hard it is to command roistering men to kneel. Asking a man to kneel is just about the most outrageous request a person, male or female, frocked or nude, can make. She could not imagine her father, a slump of weight, ever kneeling. When little Sally died, when Delana left home, when Dovie passed on, Marcia was certain that at no time and for no reason did Sky ever kneel.

Back in the chuckling oak woods, in her favorite small clearing, where the first spring violets always look terribly polite amid the layers of old leaf, the ground was now bubbled with acorns. Weedy new bur oak offered big splay-handed welcomes. The air was shushing along. And peeping through wherever it could, breaking its fat neck to watch, the river faced up. Today it was static, holding its breath. Lord, let it steam.

She flourished the blanket and sat on an inquisitive, shifting earth. Acorns, of course. She pulled the blanket back and swept away the acorns. Cheramie promptly lay on top of her. The still river-eye seized her own gaze, and her body began to flame. Fire and water were the elements of love divine. She shifted and squirmed. Squirming was a ribald pleasure.

Spy on me, river. Fine, that's fine, she said. Dull lug monster of envy, it could take some away, but it could not leap its banks screaming and point a finger. She was sure it wanted to. She and the captain lay with the river below not giving out a ripple of muscle; it could do no more than bulge with disbelief. It would never scare her again. From now on she would flash it triumphant looks.

Cheramie exclaimed over her lingerie. "Ummm. I like silk things. This is sexy." He hugged her beneath him, and through the blanket she felt earth's little bones and bunions, its sheddings, and a lovely reek of autumn breath. Between earth and man, she thought, I lie in heaven. She felt the presence of the grace of a living God. Her eyes fluttered, closed. When everything had calmed and her eyes opened, she saw waving leaves, the river, motes in her eyelids.

"I can see everything," she said. "Everything!" No guilt, no memory. No locked eyes.

"Ummm," said the syrup voice in her ear. "You are the woman to save me."

Saint Jude.

A plane high up passed through the still air, sounding like a lullaby. She heard as murmurous her boys, the priest, the other women from far off, and it all charged her, the picture of herself unruly against that calm. Her ecstasy was not so different from what she imagined the gift of tongues would offer. It came from the same center of passion and blasted all over her.

She discovered Cheramie's second grace when afterwards he combed leaves from her hair with such tenderness. She might have been a little doll.

They sat up and hugged, then dressed hastily, Marcia following Cheramie's lead, though she would have liked at least to leave off her blouse in order that the scalloped bra might see more sun and take extra compliments. Her limbs were all loose. She was bobble-headed. His voice was more drawn out once he was upright, and she immediately regretted the way a heart protects itself in a clothed chest.

He kidded, "What did you use to do down here as a girl? Practice magic? Make wild potions for growing breasts?"

"I brought my dolls," she answered. "And sometimes I undressed them."

"Nekkid dolls, huh?"

"I was odd," she confessed eagerly. "I remember a Roy Rogers episode where Dale Evans got tied up and gagged in a hay wagon. I was glad."

Her lover laughed. This was as it should be: the little hallmarks and idiosyncrasies of life tumbling out. The man listens. The man delights. He is yours.

She told him, "This is Ember Week, a Catholic harvesttime celebration."

Cheramie twisted all around, examining the sky and ground. He moved his lips beautifully to say, "Uh-huh, it's harvesttime."

"Wine, oil, and grain get celebrated. The corn is bursting ripe for harvest. And the grape festival is on, so people are making wine like crazy. But"—Marcia frowned—"we're missing oil."

"We're carrying petroleum oil on the barge. We brought the oil here and parked it. I brought you the oil. You got Ember Week down pat. Yeah, I can see the bruise of desire is on this land."

The captain took her hand and noticed for the first time her starred palm. "Hey, what a sign."

"That's Delana's nonsense."

"Better hide me away. A star in the girl's palm is serious stuff for a werewolf. He's going to gobble her up."

Marcia laughed at his look, his snuffling kisses to her hand. Even in her passion she knew that no man had that power. She smiled. Love. Love games.

"I don't believe in the palpability of Satan," she said.

"Well," Cheramie said, drawing back, "it's nothing I feature. I don't even think about it. But I know the way evil presents itself, and that's any old way it can."

"I," Marcia said resolutely, speaking from out of the magazines and news spots, "am doing my own thing."

"Dig it."

"I don't feel an ounce of guilt. I really don't."

"A regular Del Mae. A land version."

"There's nothing to compare. Don't say that. Don't talk about my sister now." But Cheramie was all over her with kisses, silencing, poking kisses, and ready, after all, to see the party bra again.

MARCIA CAME FROM the woods twirling like a child, twirling, twirling as in the game of statue, which might end in nosedive or somersault. Her short, rowdy hair told the story she had dreamed since girlhood, since twirling with a gown to her front. Even from a distance Delana smelled the heat of love. Its success fanned the air. Marcia came to her sizzling and floppy and giggly, arms raising up to touch the breeze. Her open mouth invited, even expected, a blackberry. She needed to be taken away before the buzz at men's spines revved to high recognition. Already the priest, keeping his eyes meditatively closed, was kicking up a tantrum of leaves.

Her sister's arms felt tender as a child's and a little damp as Delana smoothed them to her sides and took a last bit of leaf from her hair. She fell into Marcia's dancing step. "Calm down," she urged in a whisper. "You'll blow it."

"You guessed!" Marcia gave the ground a searing look. Such familiarity was too exotic to contain her now. Her plaid culottes looked riotous, being so plain. "I'm wild now. I'm the wild one."

"Take me to Nauvoo," Delana decided quickly. "Let's go to the fair."

"How perfect," Marcia said. "How gritty."

From across the yard Johnny watched. He stood in a slump and looked exactly like a circus bear in training, staggered on his haunches as you wished, but mournful. Now what? he asked. I have come this low, been this tricked for you, and now what? Even at a distance his eyes showed red-rimmed with anger and despair. Trained, now tricked. He was the one who belonged with her, going to a fair.

"We've got girl business," Delana yelled to the yard, to the crowd in general, pushing Marcia toward the car. Joy raised her chin, Opal took a quick uneven step forward. The men kept raking leaves.

And flicking by—a lizard in sun—Cheramie was inside the house before she could evil-eye him. How strangely the sisters were linked now. Cheramie was right: seven was a gambler's number, the age difference between the sisters and nearly the number of years between his abrupt seductions of them.

She wrapped the baby across her front and ordered Marcia into the car, into the driver's seat. Emergency made her feel broadly parental. She supposed a woman is probably never quite so old, so seriously old, as when tending her newborn, the reach of responsibility and dependence never so crucial and consuming.

"But Cheramie should come too. He'd love the fair, Delanie."

You had to be firm with true helplessness, a mother's first lesson. "No, just the two of us are going. We're finally old enough to be two girls together. Tell me everything, or you'll burst. *I'll* burst."

Marcia twirled and twirled, laughing, but got into the car. The bossiness of her religion had prepared her, even in love emergency, to follow instruction, and to confess.

They left behind Sky, coming from the garage with more rakes, shouting, "Corvée." The nephews were dragging buckets and burlap bags. "Feudals, ahoy. One day of free labor, the lord demands his corvée. To the rakes, men. To the apples."

"Boys! You're such boys!" Marcia screamed out the window, then rushed the car onto Great River Road.

The Nauvoo Grape Festival was spread out over a few blocks of dusty highland. They drove in below, along the road where great flat expanses of green Mormon-owned land ran right down to the river that had carried people off after their leader's bloody death; here and there stood small red-brick buildings or log cabins over one hundred years old. Their tight square structures positioned across mower-perfect lawns were dutifully pristine; inside, Delana remembered from the tour, teenage guides encouraged examination of bellows and butter churns and blue-speckled pitchers on nightstands. No bullet holes remained; no trace of tears salted the air; no tooth marks, no rapture. The antiseptic proof of innocence was insufferable. She had wanted hard evidence of life really lived.

"I hit Johnny," she told Marcia. "I slapped him."

"Testing him! Discovering that nothing is bad enough to stop his love!"

Marcia's exultation was that of a person to whom every leaf that dropped in China was somehow related intimately. For her, there was no news that did not pertain to Marcia and to God. Delana's slap confirmed for her the glory of her own fling.

The black asphalt road wound up; down on the flats they could see the last Mormon summer pageant in progress, an affair with women in long gingham dresses and bearded men playing pioneer, their brand-new vans, strange parallelograms, cramming a nearby lot. People stood in a circle. From somewhere they had hauled forth a grazing ox and an equally unlikely covered wagon, which looked on with its bonneted face. Boots stamped and hands clapped. Delana remembered the pageant's inevitable closing chant: "City of Joseph—Nauvoo!" Pseudo pioneers called out, heads raised, as if to dispel the carnival revelry up on the hill, which clashed with their piety.

"I wonder if the Osmonds ever come here," Marcia said.

"Not in those vans, I bet."

"A religious pilgrimage by Winnebago can't possibly be right. Oh, imagine Jesus living and dying in Nauvoo, Illinois. It's too dull to mean anything. These people drive here from Utah—cross a few states—and just like that it's a pilgrimage. At least going to Jerusalem you pay real money and risk your life. Joseph Smith," Marcia scoffed. "There must be a thousand in every phone book. Smith! Joseph Smith. A real prophet is recognized by one name; no wonder the religion is minor. Think of Jesus and Mohammed and Confucius. Anyone really important only needs one name."

"Like Fats."

Marcia touched her puka shells as she laughed her flinty love laugh. "That's right. Saints and stars and notorious people go by one name. There's St. Joan, and then there's Jackie!"

"Elvis and Liberace."

"Cleopatra, Delanie. A queen."

"Yoko. Zorro."

"You're so quick. Let me think." Marcia's eyes were big, her mouth working as she thought out loud: "Last names: Aquinas. Onassis."

"We already said Jackie."

"Got you! I mean Ari," she sang, waving an arm. "Ari *or* Onassis works. Either name stands alone."

"Because he's such a villain to us, marrying Jackie," Delana said, enjoying the sisterly banter.

"You notice how all these one-name people have wild, wonderful names? Of course I'm thinking of Cheramie. Cheramie! It has that whoosh to it. His name is Cheramie, not Bob. Let's do teams," Marcia cried, all the leaves in China dropping before her. "I'll get Joseph and Mary out of the way. Your turn."

"Rhett and Scarlett. Liz and Dick."

"Donny and Marie."

"Come *on*, Marcia. They're brother and sister. That's not romance."

"True." Marcia waited for a family carrying lawn chairs to pass before the car. "And it's a little bit creepy, don't you think? The way they sort of flirt? I mean, adolescent brother and sister. It was different when they were ten-year-old tap dancers. What kind of romance is this? Cuckoo. Jinxed. Good grief, does either of them date?"

Delana admitted, "I've lost track."

Marcia squinted out at the Mormon field. "Jack wants a Winnebago even with this oil crisis. Can you imagine? He's been collecting salt packets and matches from restaurants, and he squirreled away some sample detergents that came in the mail to stock the imaginary van's kitchen, of all things. He drove over to Forest City, Iowa, like *he* was on some kind of pilgrimage and checked them out. He says half the town of Forest City is millionaires now, thanks to the invention of Winnebagos." Marcia paused and looked around, as if remembering where she was.

"Every small town wants a fair," she declared. "Those Mormon pilgrims shouldn't get so put out. But since they *are* here to suffer, this gives them some new reason, some fresh misery besides the same old reenactment of the Joseph death."

Delana calculated. "The oldest Mormons would remember growing up with pretty fresh stories of Joseph Smith. I bet having those stories handed down makes the religion seem more real than some. People like firsthand reports."

"Ugh, Delana. Who wants to hear something like 'My mother once loaned Jesus some gloves'? Who wants to make Him that earthly and talk about His skin tone or allergies or the shape of His feet? I'm glad the Middle East is ancient. I'm glad it's been burning and burning with passion forever. Jerusalem has been sacked a hundred times. Great religion causes great drama. Poor Joseph Smith got killed here and then what? He gets a little pageant in his name, with pagans on a hill drinking wine."

"It makes for good suffering," Delana said.

"They've got a recognized religion," her sister conceded, "and people want something to pit their experience against, something big, or you're lost. What would it mean to me to be with Cheramie if I didn't have the great title of sinner now to go with it? Sinner. It sounds like cinders, like fire. Delana, how do you think of yourself? Who would you say you are?"

"Your sister. I have a few other suitable titles too."

Marcia clumped at her fuzzy hair. "I mean, at least I know I'm a sinner. Sister," she said, with a tinge of spite, "it makes me more than you."

"Really, Marcia." Her mouth felt dry. The sun was beating straight in on the front seat. Patience came slowly but necessarily to the new mother. She was anxious to get out and stretch, even though the relentless exhaustion since Robin's birth urged her to sit, to sleep. Marcia's energy had a mad, after-midnight edge to it.

"You've been larger than life, doing larger-than-life things, but how far can it take you?" she persisted.

"There's nothing larger than life, Marcia. It's huge."

"Even as a kid you imagined yourself as a little Mary Mag outsider. She traveled with men, all right—supposedly the best. And they turned on her like whips. Why? Because dead Jesus appeared to her first. They couldn't believe it. When the Lord showed Himself to Peter days later, the sniveler *complained!* 'Why didn't you come to your friends, Jesus? Why'd you go to a woman?' There were twelve of them counting on fame. They closed right in and took away Mary Magdalene's words."

For a mile stretch into town, cars were parked on the shoulder, but Marcia drove like a queen in her own parade—humming engine extending her energy to all—on into the thick of foot traffic, and found a space. They emerged into air saturated with grape aroma and the sweetness of caramel apples, spun candy, and funnel cakes, and the sour undertones of diesel fuel from the unspectacular rides with their black, whirring motors—a low grinding hunger of sound urging people to take a cheap jolt, get dizzy any way you can. And a pacifist oily heat hung over all, thanks to the contribution of cooking lard and sun. People were on the stroll, so many women in pastel shorts, and their veined legs seemed like a reply to the men's tattooed arms. But how to stroll without Johnny? He, not Cheramie, or Marcia, belonged here. Delana took Marcia's arm snugly. She was used to the sentimental excitement of the stroll. If only it were nighttime. At night the strips of yellow bulbs rope everything off to definite sections of longing and amusement. The border's glare shelters trailers set back in the dark, where she imagined people sitting (as Johnny does now at home) in a daze of weariness. They eat bad, easy food, nothing fried (they are too exhausted for that) but grim stuff like seal-pack ring bologna. Whatever, a private and reassured world is defined and guarded, those light bulbs sectioning carnies off as the river does its crew, yielding a quiet remove. Carny trailers were the life behind the life, which most people shunned at a fair. Fairgoers wanted zinging darts and stuffed pandas, not the cheated feeling of forced contemplation, what they got after going deeper and deeper into the hall of mirrors, full of sport, only to be stopped finally by one clean image of the self.

Of course she and Johnny had loved a fair. Land life, a strange caution to them both, was made real by the artifice of the fair, its little prizes and easy food, its definite hours and yellow lights. Johnny was a pro at winning fuzzy animals, plaster statues, feathered hats, whatever dangled on strings above the skeetball cabaña or propped up the plates on which to toss nickels. If anything, fairs miniaturized and stylized life. Sticking to fairs, they had behaved as if land life could never hurt them, could not crack and toss them down, knowing, surely, that it would. They strolled fairs in order not to test luck. "We were babies," she told him after the slap. "Until now, really, we've been the babies."

Marcia disappeared around the side of a truck selling corn dogs and rushed back sipping and sloshing from a cup. She dangled a bunch of grapes from her free hand.

"I started the day with consecrated wine," she said. "Now I'm downing the unblessed. I'm on the plane of the unblessed, which, everyone knows, is where the true miracles happen. Off limits to a nursing mother. You get grapes. Oh, but I wish I'd seen you throw the eggs, Delanie. You christened that kitchen, I understand," she said, gulping wine. "Even with a baby you know how to be wild, but watch out now, I'm catching up. I'll hop on your boat and leave you here."

Delana took the blue-black grapes. The taste was as smoothly dark as Marcia's idea of sin, the pulpy meat so ripe, so strong, it dizzied her as if she were actually drinking wine.

"Joy's made her place. She never gave up on Daddy. You'd think she would have dumped him at some point." Yes, it was a downer change of mood, but she wanted Marcia off her case and she wondered what she knew.

Marcia blinked at her wine and drank stiffly until the cup was empty. "She didn't expect marriage, so why stop? What would have made them stop? Sally's death didn't change anything. Why would she have walked away? She didn't expect marriage, so what would have made her leave?"

"Nothing," Delana agreed to Marcia's softened features. "Of course, nothing at all."

Over their shoulders the Himalayan Express ride came to a lurching halt, only to start up again in reverse, ramming the passengers back into a dark tunnel painted all around with white-capped mountains. Their screams were tinny against the engine roar and rock music. Delana felt her mind running like that ride, speeding, then lurching back. So Marcia didn't know about the abortion. It hung all the heavier as a secret revealed yet protected. Word games were all that came to mind now to share. Synonyms. She might ask, "What else is a corn dog called?" Answer: "Pronto pup, if rarely, and dog-on-a-stick."

"This is my day," Marcia gloried. "I'm so happy feeling risqué." Her lips were made indistinct from the wine, so what she said seemed all the more oblivious. Her eyes looked familiar but new. No, she did not know of Joy's abortion. She threw down her cup with a flourish.

"Watch out for your boys' sake. Don't be careless."

Marcia's face tensed. "I, technically, am wounding them to

the core. This very instant. But who would suspect me? That kind of hurts, believe it or not. It hurts knowing how little I'm suspected. Yes, if they knew what I've done they'd be hurt, and still I'm going to do . . . my thing. That's why it's good and right that I've consecrated my boys to God. Who can bear the responsibility? Who can? Sometimes I think we screw up just to make sure God is watching. Put Him to work. Let Him do His duty. Let Him give my boys solace if they decide I'm awful. I can't do everything for them. I can't guarantee them much. I love them and feed them, but I can't really guarantee a single other thing."

Marcia tripped away. Delana with her sacked-out baby followed, ears ringing with what seemed a rabid new idea tossed to her as freely as an empty paper cup.

As a girl, sometimes she had come to Nauvoo with Sky to meet Marcia in town for lunch, the nuns conceding a special dispensation for this curious local child who was particularly remembered for her youthful crown of brambles. Marcia described school lunch hour: girls picking at diet platters, then came a mass languishing in a garden of pygmy beech and sugar roses until a bell rang. Like prisoners, the other girls passed Marcia money to smuggle back cigarettes and candy. Once, in spring, after a light rinsing rain that had sprouted pale, marble-sized buds on all the trees, she met Delana and Sky in the Hotel Nauvoo dining room waving a St. Christopher medal on her wrist, a gift for Delana's new bike. She made a ceremony of banding it onto Delana's small arm, speaking in Greek: "Kyrie eleison. Kyrie eleison." Sky wore the stiff smile he always had when her religion came too close and he was forced to look at what he had done, sending her away to become this; he saw what pressure and guilt had imposed. Marcia had kissed Delana and then pleaded with Sky to let her smoke a cigarette, just one. They were sold at the counter for a nickel apiece. "It's posh, Daddy." He refused. She wore lipstick for the duration of lunch and reapplied it twice. Before returning to the nuns she had had to bite and rub her lips like one possessed. They had waved goodbye to Marcia from the lawn and watched her transformation: freckly arms disappeared as sleeves were properly parachuted to the wrist and buttoned. Next, the waistband unfurled itself, and so they lost Marcia's knees. Delana's knees quivered in sympathy. Marcia's walk slowed. "She's meditating now, I expect," Sky told himself, but they were both stricken by the burlesque of demureness, seeing Marcia as not-Marcia; that's who Sky had made her be, putting her there. She minced back to the nuns inside, where the hidden, glamorous, big-girl knees would suffer kneeling and more kneeling. And *their* old knees! Marcia had assured Delana that nuns' knees grow to look exactly like elephant feet: big, wide sort of suction pads that latch onto the kneeler and suck there for one hour at least. *It's a well-known disgusting fact. They measure their knees to see how their holiness is coming along. The uglier the better.*

That day, after lunch with Marcia, Sky walked moodily around the town, reluctant to leave Nauvoo. They sat for hours on a stone bench in the Mormon rectified fields. St. Agnes was on the hill, surrounding Mormon lands stretched out unsacrificed to the inclinations of time. Sky told a new story. Right in these parts, he said, he had once helped a mild gangster elude the law, just the silly liquor law. Back in the glamour days of gangsters, this one had spilled out of Chicago, awarding gold toothpicks to his fans. He wore spats to the country club and carried his tommy gun in a golf bag. Sky had loved recalling the details as St. Christopher stared up from Delana's naked wrist. He needed her to know that though Marcia had been given away, he was capable of magnificent rescue. It was a locust year, and early evening brought them out, massing above. Locusts fell and raged on their useless hard-shell backs, and Sky talked on, getting all the more excited as Delana struggled with the story and her own fears. She had looked up and would not risk another peek at the sky. She kept her shivery, goosebumped knees locked against wobbling. He thrilled at her willingness to sit through fear as the locusts speckled and jittered above, and he watched, she thought, hungry to hold her attention completely, to make her his entirely, no matter what. She understood she was supposed to feel safe with him despite, not because of, the medal on her wrist. She was supposed to be his good-girl sidekick, as always. This was a test: she was actually being rescued. The bugs fell to earth slowly, acrobatically, on a cloud-filled spring day. When a big one landed by her toe, she picked the bug up by its wiggling legs, its creamed white fattiness the ugliest thing she had ever seen, and she dropped it whole into her mouth. She made frog sounds as she swallowed. "My land!" Sky cried. "You kill me, angel." And she was satisfied to see the helpless look in his eyes, something opposite consternation and beyond simple awe. His definite, helpless regard of her exactly evened the score.

Now she walked in Nauvoo, with Robin riding high, wetting her shoulder. The baby was covered in brilliant orange sacking with huge black dots. Her head was a tiny thing, and with all that cloth and the diaper padding, she poufed out like a fair prize. People commented, "Oh, that's cute." Delana remembered how she had picked up that bug and eaten it, showing Daddy she was somebody, and she realized right now, in this moment of seeing family resemblance flood Marcia's eyes, seeing some vast unreachable dream there, that what she saw in Sky's eyes was exactly this look before her. It was the unconditional. Love, nothing less.

"Look at me. Let me see your eyes, Marcia."

"Can you tell? Do I look fallen?"

"They're pure Walsh."

"What do you mean? Daddy's eyes are green, yours are lavender, I've got dog brown, and Mother lost her color before you were born."

"It's a look I've seen on Daddy."

"It shows!"

That look from her father on the locust-eating day had come over Sky once more on the beekeepers' night, her night to flee home. How fearful she had been not to see it. Now, thanks to a flash in Marcia's bleared eyes, she connected the two incidents and dared to believe that his last full appraisal of her held helpless love. What a horror the true heart is when presenting itself, what a dumb, slogging-on warrior. Sky had looked at her nakedness as he did her bug-eating, astonished by love. Twice she had absolutely needed his attention, and each time she had made herself appalling enough to be adored. But all she knew at the time of those wild-girl gut actions was her fierce need to be. She could not read the effects.

"I'm glad it shows," Marcia proclaimed. "I feel like everything has brightened, Delanie. I'm an adulteress and the world looks bright."

"Uh-huh." She indicated the wine. "That helps."

"But really."

"Really, Marcia, I love your eyes. Don't mind if I stare."

"I didn't have time for makeup."

"I've never been as innocent as you."

Marcia stopped primping her hair. "That's true. Like the Mormons, you were born and the suffering was *there*, so *fresh* and *there*. But you suffer too easily. I only gave you the facts. You did the rest to yourself."

Delana thought of the little Mormon buildings preserved for so long. She, like the buildings, was a little bricked-up remnant set toward the past. She lowered Robin and kissed her, dear future in the flesh.

"Delana Mae, it pains you still, I know, all the growing-up stuff. It's like you've been your own religion, like you've manufactured God and punishment inside you. It's not healthy. Here I am, the sinner. Finally, finally, finally. Can't you see it's so much finer to be . . . something?"

Right or wrong, she stayed in God's palm.

"Marcia, for all I know, people are God with skin. I don't know one way or another. Robin is God."

"Give her to Him."

Marcia gulped from little plastic cups of wine sold everywhere, and she rolled her eyes at all she saw, meaning, of course, that nothing could match her passion, nothing. "Look, the merry-go-round. We have to give Robin her first ride."

They rustled past children to grab two big blond horses side by side, with rhinestone collars, stars and moons etched into their gear. The organ music began, and as one sister rose, the other's horse lowered her. They were old enough to be girls together. Delana tried to relax. She leaned in and mustered a light but false taunting voice. "You two sure didn't waste any time. I hope you considered consequences." She thought of Cheramie long ago sheepishly patting his shirt pocket, but had the feeling that this time he had been wholly unprepared. Marcia's eyes were slits, but Delana pressed on, jocular, though her voice felt like a plank.

"I don't know what Booth Memorial would make of you, Marcia."

"It's closed down. The pill closed it down. Girls are all on the pill now."

"Are you?"

"Ha, sister. Serious, serious Delanie."

They rode around and up and down, that wonderful sense of flying which going two directions at once imparts, which always did make the merry-go-round seem more dangerous and adult to Delana once she had boarded.

"My body and soul were in perfect harmony," Marcia called into the music. "Nothing nags. Believe me, there will be no fallout."

"He's not some redeemer," Delana cautioned.

"He's pure flesh."

Marcia's horse rose up and away.

In God's palm, Marcia floated to a tent where a country-western band played desultory music. A lone couple was two-stepping near the bandstand. The jut of her ruffled midriff top advised that the woman was taking credit for this idea. Her man held on low, at the juncture of hip-hugger pants and skin, and he studied his boots. A crowd watched as rudely as if the couple were splayed out cold, accident victims on the highway;

faces showed no sympathy or censure, only a bored rudeness. At the back of the tent two little girls were galloping, hand in hand. Marcia's eyes were round and soft as those of a person who has lost her glasses. She sagged against Delana. "I think the temperature's rising."

Delana shook her. "Come on, let's show them." She could not carry two bodies. With Robin sacked out high on one shoulder, she used her free arm to wheel Marcia forward, and she lightened, swinging onto the dirt dance floor, smiling to herself as her hips began to swivel. She barely touched Marcia, and guided. The band cheered and started up a faster, twangier song, drawing some whistles from the sidelines. Clenching Robin to her front, Delana took Marcia's hand in a jitterbug. Once, a teenaged Marcia, desperate to perfect a new step, would lug a little sister around the bedroom, saddle oxfords clattering. Now Delana guided. In sync, they fairly floated, taking turns twirling arms over their heads. And in Marcia's face Delana saw a maddening, misguided peace. Past her love eyes lay perfect trust in a future that is God's. Marcia glowed: saint or sinner, still answerable to God. God would have something to say about all of it. She would listen to her God. Delana did not know what she thought about God, and now, holding Robin, she thought the doom of parents was that they must take a stance on God. What they say must feel urgently right. With God talk you should be steady. It would not do to tell a child whom you had made pray at his bed, now, on reaching six years, "Oh, well. I don't really believe anyway." That only worked with Santa Claus. Now there were so many decisions to make, pieces of the puzzle to strain to put together. And here was Marcia floating in God's palm. She twirled her a little roughly; Marcia stumbled, but she kept that peaceful look through to the music's end. They moved to the sidelines, her sister leaning heavier now but looking around sharp-eyed again, full of the fair as a child is, straining to get on to the next new thing.

"It burns me that Cheramie moved on you so fast," she admitted.

Marcia's winy lips smacked as she spoke. "I led, sister, I led. What's with you two? First he has to talk about you, now you have to talk about him. Stop, will you stop? The introduction has been made." She ran off, followed by the keyboard player's hoots: "Come back, sunshine. We'll sing your favorites. Everyone come back tonight for our deluxe show."

She caught up to Marcia, standing before a sideshow set up in a tiny tent about fortune-teller size. The barker used an old bullhorn to gather a crowd.

"Ladies and gents, look, looky here. We've got the sensational Frog Baby inside. Don't miss this once-in-a-lifetime opportunity to see nature like you're never going to get on the TV shows. Here's a species even our top scientists can't begin to explain. We've got limited space and cannot admit minors due to the adult aspects of this phenomenon. Scoffers welcome, cuz you're going to come out dazed and humble. Put down a few bucks, ladies and gentlemen. Come on in and say hello to the amazing Frog Baby. Two dollar, two dollar."

He was a man in a loose brown vest, with silver tips on the ends of his string tie filed to the point of danger. "Come on in and see Frog Baby." The canopy showed a smiling frog on a lily pad, a heart above his head. Next to him, on the riverbank, a girl sat reading, with her legs drawn to the side and hidden beneath a parachute skirt.

"Oh, what's he like?" Marcia cried. "Let's go in."

Delana pulled her back. "It's a come-on." She and Johnny had never wasted their time on sideshows, knowing without saying that it *was* risking luck: twice removed from regular river life, in the sideshow, you could expect some convolution; something unimaginatively preposterous and far too shameless to count might shake you from the only dream you had. You might come out stripped of gloss, your very skin left behind. No, they would not risk a sideshow.

The barker said straight to Marcia, "I see a loving lady. And that's what Frog Baby needs. He wants some company, ladies and gents. Frog Baby asts for a little of your time. A hello, a howdy, some companionship."

"I'm going in, Delanie. It's meant to be. I'll go alone; I don't mind." Marcia's hug was so tight it disturbed Robin into a snuffle, and her kiss on the cheek was strong and sour and sloppy with wine. She could not be left untended.

They paid and stood in line, entered the tent, where, once inside, a sneering blond in fishnet stockings used her glitter cane to hold them back. When it was their turn, she tapped it at their feet, raising dust, and mumbled, "Next ones."

The sisters went forward into the darkened tent, found to be much larger than it had seemed from the outside, thanks to an open trailer attachment. A flap to their side billowed in the slight breeze, then collapsed like a great breathing presence. They pushed forward in the small circle of silent people. On the table, lit green from behind, sat a large lidded jar, the commercial size that held mayonnaise and relish for the *Pat Furey* crew. And in it, in water that sent off terrible hospital fumes, at a tilt was wedged Frog Baby. He was a tiny formation, smooth and pink; he sprouted the bulb head of a human, and arm stumps, and the idea of a body swiveled down to a nub, a kind of fin. A giant, giant minnow altogether. With raw eyes open, milk-glazed. As in a fishbowl, the floor of bright rock chips grew one thick strand of seaweed. The lack of a little arch was all that separated the look of Frog Baby's domain from that of a dime-store goldfish.

A girl worked the jar. As people stared at Frog Baby, she tapped it for effect. Now Frog Baby bobbed gently and swam his tiny distance against the glass, then he bounced away from it, the extent of his exquisite commotion.

Marcia cried, "My God, could this come out of a woman? What is it? It's an LSD baby, right? A creature of drugs. Something expelled, aborted."

"It's nothing, and it's our heart," Delana told her, deciding absolutely not to mention Joy's abortion, ever.

"I was expecting something cute." Marcia's voice was slurry, as if the confusion of drink had become more acute up against the limits of reason.

The barker, just come in, began speaking low now, without his megaphone. "You might have looked right out on the Mississippi itself here one day and seen him. Frog Baby, Frog Baby, where's he really from? We got him from down South, and they say he was found expiring on a mudbank. Medical technology tried everything. . . . Imagine looking out on the Mississippi River there where Huck Finn rode his raft and thinking you see a swimming child, then no, he flips and you see the fin tail. You lose sight entirely. If you don't go out of here making pacts with the guy upstairs, you're numskulls. I don't know about you, gents, but I say Frog Baby keeps a man humble. Think before you act, eh?" The barker removed his cap and wiped his forehead. "I tell you, the South is wildlife. I wished I could of brought you up the other one we got, the wife-with-no-head phenomenon. But regulations are that she can't be displayed north of Arkansas. You drive down to the Arkansas State Fair next week, fellows— it ain't so far—and I guarantee you'll see your perfect wife." People snickered, couples poked each other.

"Now here's Frog Baby," the man said louder. "Looky here. He wants you to look. Ast him something. Go on and ast Frog Baby to predict your life. I guarantee you some results."

The girl tappeo the jar and Frog Baby bobbed.

Baby Robin let out a scorching howl.

Murmurs rose. "Hey, the baby talked back to Froggy."

The need to believe, Delana thought. The mind would make up the miracles it expected. And had paid for.

The crowd gained in alertness, moved in closer. Was Frog Baby mourning his own kind, singing his hideousness and capture to the baby? People allowed he was so ugly he deserved to be supernaturally wise.

When the crowd pushed the sisters close to the jar, Robin howled again. More exclamations: "My Jesus. I tell you there's something to this. Something's going on."

"Oh, baby." Marcia's voice was faint, mushy. "I thought we'd see a trained frog in a vest or something. Something fun, Delanie. You know the frog song, remember the song 'Frog Went a-Courtin'? I don't know . . . I thought of him. They had that happy picture out on the canvas. . . ." She turned to the man and yelled, "You painted a happy picture on the canvas! Froggy had a girlfriend!"

The girl of least employment plinked Frog Baby's jar, and Frog Baby bobbed and stared at the sisters.

Marcia reached out her hand. "Don't disturb him." She touched the jar as if to steady Frog Baby, as if to soothe him. Her hand cupped the glass and hid Frog Baby's face from the gawkers. She wobbled against the card table on which Frog Baby was displayed. Following a great burp, she sank to her knees. Her eyes rolled, and she drooled.

Thrilled sounds rose from the other viewers, and general pandemonious calls came: "Cripes, don't mess with Froggy. He zapped her, man." Now a big woman in blue knit shorts crowded up to see. She touched the jar. Then she went down too, splat in the dust. The crowd went to riot.

Delana crouched over Marcia. "Come on, come on," she urged. Conked out, her sister in plaid culottes was smiling. Dust was scuffing up all around.

"Don't break their fall," said the barker smoothly. "The ladies are safe in the state of grace." Frog Baby stared on. When the big woman stirred, two men hauled her up.

"I'm not letting anyone else touch," said the barker. "Little guy's too powerful today, all wrought up. Enough."

Delana put her hand on Marcia's forehead and called, "Someone get help. We need water."

It was Robin's cry that brought Marcia back to her senses. The same men who had hoisted the fat one came to Marcia's aid. Roughly they hurried her out the exit flap. Delana followed, carrying a baby gone rigid in squalls.

"Here's her ten bucks," the one with a kerchief at his neck told Delana. He pressed money folded to the size of a stamp in her palm. "Quick. Move on before they all come out."

"What do you mean, ten dollars?"

"That's what he agreed on for fainting ladies." The men yanked their heads toward the tent. "Thanks. Go on now. Others are coming out. Keep quiet, gals."

Marcia threw up.

Regurgitated wine splashed dust, and all the sounds of the fair seemed to Delana ground down to one: the engine sound of the Cuddle Up ride right there in front of them, big red shellback seats spinning and dipping, full of the cries of brained and breathless riders. She whipped out a diaper to dab Marcia's mouth.

"We've got to get you home."

Marcia responded only with a long look out of her eternally innocent eyes. "Why do I see this hideousness and sorrow after I try to love? Am I jinxed *again*? I'm trying to be light and free with Cheramie, and what do I get this time? Not locked eyes, no. Something weirder! This . . . Frog Baby staring demon thing. If I did it five hundred times with Cheramie, could I break the jinx?"

Delana smoothed her brow, said nothing, just sat there with her.

Marcia caught sight of the girl in fishnet hosiery, now out posing on the soapbox. She charged over to her. "I was expecting a cute thing, a little frog acrobat. Something like that. Not a monster."

The girl shrugged. "You could've read a comic book for that."

Marcia clutched Delana's hand. "I have to wonder, sister. Do you think Frog Baby has a soul? Does something like this have a soul?"

"Limbo takes care of all the fringe ones. They all have souls." Delana was surprised at how quickly she recovered Marcia's religious teaching for her. "Some are just unclaimed," she decided, "like hats."

Marcia sniffled and scowled around at the fair. Bagged cotton candy hung like colored stuffing from one little booth, and there was no evidence at all that it had been made on the premises.

There was no great whirring of machinery, no man in peaked white hat scooping a cone to spin pink fluff seemingly from air.

"We don't talk about Limbo anymore," she said, "and hardly even purgatory. It's not right to think there's a place in the afterlife for everyone except *these* misfortunes. It's too cruel to believe that being part frog or something, what*ever*, is wrong, keeps them out of heaven. That's a man-made cruelty, not God's."

"If there's a heaven, this one belongs in it," Delana agreed. *They all have souls.* It seemed a necessary truth in the face of the frog baby. It was too hideous, without explanation. It was so unfair and ugly and wrong, there had to be some kind of balm. And, true, there was no such balm on earth. Give it a heaven.

"Now I'm the woozy one," she told Marcia. "Let's sit down. Everything is too much."

"I'm jinxed. I'm simply jinxed in love. Me and Donny and Marie."

"Honestly, Marcia. Come on."

Delana hauled herself up. They would all be better off getting away from there, Robin too, who had gone into her terribly sad cry that meant hunger. "Frog Baby's nothing," she said crossly. "It's not real. Come on, let's go now. We're all tired, come on." She wanted to fling herself across the bed in the cool upstairs and promise Johnny that the next fair would be theirs and theirs alone. She wanted to lick the place she'd slapped and fall asleep with his fingers in her mouth.

With Robin drooling on her shoulder, she remembered how Dovie maintained that the departed, too, came hungry to your table. She always left food on her plate and requested that Delana do so: a spoonful of mashed potatoes and that last bite of meat; save your pie crust if you've left any berry goo rimming it, and a wee bit of whipped cream on top if you can stand to let that go. (Leave pie, but don't pass off what you dislike: no canned corn, nothing with mayonnaise.) Dovie left on her plate a tiny proper amount of food for those gone away. She believed there was a need to nourish them. Love the souls. Beautiful whitey-blond Sally; Joy's shadow of a baby; Frog Baby too—all were gleaming souls to acknowledge. When Delana closed her eyes, the sun seemed to press souls against her lids, souls flitting by. The first color a baby knew, once her vision revved up from black and white to color, would be this, the color of the souls whooshing and sporting before her, the phantom Crayola color, sky-blue pink.

I F THEY HAD PULLED up a minute earlier, they would have seen Johnny hot in the agitation of an afternoon roiling with useless activity; Johnny unmoored without Delana, finally facing her father (jibes, ribbing, foreign words), finally, finally succumbing to the shell game. *To show him up*, he imagined. They would have seen Johnny hunched with concentration under the tent. Coming home a split second earlier, they would have seen him duped and heard Jack Rose's idiot laugh, then all the crew's harumphing.

Men had moved in close to watch. This stopover had confirmed it: land life made you the fool. They had suspected they might walk into a trap, and it was being borne out. The heckling trees rode hard on the nerves. Chores got old fast. A woman had dragged them to this when they thought they were protecting her. So let Johnny beat out the old guy at his little game. Give us that, some dignity here. The men moved in close. They would no longer be mocked.

If they had pulled up a moment earlier, the sisters would have seen Sky's eyes go to a glory green, his palm outstretched, forcing that little pea right under Johnny's nose. See that little pea? Take a look, fellow. Sky chose words carefully: *fellow* resides at the far edge of buddy.

The fellow had been beaten at the shell game.

Duped Johnny nods, and the points of his elbows inflame. Only Delana could have read the fire there. In his mind, Delana's lost girlhood hurts. She is that pea. Johnny feels duty. He extends his arm and seems to lay Sky's hand right down on the table, gently, as some kind of handshake. Congratulations. After all, Sky has just conjured that pea from the least likely walnut shell. Fall air is still, porous; the sound of a leaf settling, even a normal, not laugh-filled leaf, could echo in the head.

Arriving moments earlier, Delana and Marcia would have seen Johnny take that hand with surprise, even reverence, seen the look waver as does a shoplifter's, and then Delana would have recognized in his softening features that he was seeing her, feeling her life in that hand. Johnny held on as long as he decently could, and just as his hand began to shake, and one smithereen of a second before he would have kissed the hand he held, Johnny broke the fingers one, two, three. Flipped them, cracking bone. In still autumn air, the sound was a scream before the scream.

To men who would not be mocked it was exquisite, it was sex, hearing Sky's fingers break. They staggered punch-drunk. The bones snapped so wonderfully loud; maybe doctors' bones break especially hard. The healer's hands had not given up easily to humility. Johnny had shown balls, fucking A!

Joy and Opal, rustling tissue as they lifted a bit of crochet from the old cedar chest in the hall, came running outside at the sharp reports.

Marcia had just turned off the engine when they heard Sky's fingers break. She and Delana flew from the car.

There was Sky, bending down only to jerk back up, again and again. He grinned terribly, good hand clasped to his shaky wrist, out of which fingers rose hideously limp.

And the mild day showed itself as a blackheart, with its quiet mediating light, its indifferent eavesdropping quality washing down from an endless expanse of blue, like an audience of infinite desire and greed hushed for drama, like the frank stares of people at the fair who had watched the two-steppers, like people looking on accident victims.

To Delana, love for Sky and Johnny felt as infinite and as coarse. She shook her head when Opal yelled, "Has he been drinking?"

Jack Rose was suddenly on Johnny, slugging air, chin, anything, just slugging wild. Johnny was ducking, shielding himself. Cheramie roughly elbowed him aside and got in return a surprised look, a growl, and a very definite bop on the shoulder. Johnny's large hands hovered over the small, wiry man, then dropped to his sides. His face was a fury, though, and since no one among them was much of a fighter, the poses were mechanical remembered stances off boxing posters and from TV. Johnny's pants had slipped and the crease of his behind was showing. It was all a mistake. While Sky lurched and shuddered beneath the tent, Johnny, Jack, and Cheramie pushed out of it, deckhands surging after. Delana stood rooted, with her arms around the baby.

Deckhands ran forward in a rush, bumping rudely into each other: finally, something to do after all the politeness and waiting. They were remembering that they did not ordinarily tolerate each other on land. The point of land life (all messed up here) was that you moved on away from the bro's, came back with tales that you jismed as manliness for the next thirty days on board. But here, with guys all thrown together, it was like everyone was messing around in your own tale. They felt pissed and duped. And Marcia's boys, in the trees, had begun pelting them with apples, an extreme irritation that seemed fixable only by each man's turning to the next guy and pounding him good. They could not go after a writhing old guy, or a female pilot with a baby, or boys in the trees, so they thrashed each other.

By now Delana and Marcia were running around, calling, "Stop, stop it."

Cheramie took one last swipe at Jack. He looked across the

yard and caught Marcia's eye. It was a horror to her, the man she had just loved now beating on her husband. The picture was wrong, completely lacking in nobility and romance: two men were not fighting over her, and the one's grin was horrid. Jack was flailing away without a clue as to why. And as if to hide his contempt for Jack's ignorance on all fronts, Cheramie turned away and gave Johnny an equal whack, the surprise of which caused Johnny to simply quit. Marcia began beating her plaid shorts, a sound like sails in the wind. Her face darkened and whimpery sounds came out.

"You're not fainting again," Delana warned. This time Marcia would have to hit hard dirt if she went down. Her own arms were frozen around the baby.

"I can't watch," Marcia cried.

When she screeched out of the drive, no one but Delana took notice.

Jackie Junior and Mike in the tree were mean shots with apples, adding confusion below by making rapid aims of great accuracy. Joy rushed to Sky's side, waving a flyswatter at nothing. Opal, with turquoise combs in her hair, was tugging forward a great coil of hose from the side of the house. She took one final sweeping look around and opened the nozzle. It was no riot hose. It hit men not with a stinging, crippling force but with grace; even on land, water brought them to their senses. They separated, yet still Opal kept on shooting water up one man and down another, letting the foolishness hit; and they stood there stupid and new, being frisked by a woman with a hose. There was possibly no greater humiliation.

And from the tree, demon boys howled and threw down apples.

Delana ran to Johnny, whose bruises were cartoonish: a great mark under the eye, hair clumped up, smudges on arms and shirt. His white palms were raised in defense or in amazement of the inexplicable.

"It wasn't an accident," he insisted softly, "but I didn't plan it either. One finger would have been enough." His voice trailed, full of unconcealed pride and relief. He shrugged. He would now take whatever punishment. In fact, he would devise it. He looked at Robin and kissed her sleep-still bald head. "I'll go stay on the barge until it's fixed. Shouldn't be too long now. Goodbye."

"Dumpling."

But he turned away. And in his light walk and his wide strong back she saw his victory over all grievances past and future. Johnny was gone, the bear light and lumbering, going down the hill. Sister and husband were both gone.

Joy was rocking Sky, and Opal had brought a clean towel to wrap the broken fingers. Sky's voice was all husked up. "The nugatory fuck. Get him out of my sight."

"He's gone, Daddy."

His face was wet and purple as grapes. "Bring me ice and aspirin. I'm on fire."

"We'll starve that fever, don't worry," said Joy.

"The pain is killing me."

"Shhh, no one dies of a broken finger."

"Fingers, woman. Three."

"It's your left hand, thank goodness," she murmured. "Skylar, I'm here. I'm right here with you. I'm going to give you kisses and make you better."

"Is nugatory a swear word?" Mike asked his brother as they slid down from the trees. "It's cool."

Not knowing, Jackie Junior rolled his eyes and spat. Right in front of everyone he realized he could get away with saying, "Fuck it, dumb fuck."

EXACTLY WHAT IS the weight of the world? Would someone please broadcast that news? Home alone, Marcia thought: There is no word strong enough for the wrong that sunders me now. She had taken a lover and, for that, seen her husband punched. Any newspaper article would report her as being embroiled in a sex scandal.

The house was quiet, smelling faintly of a gym, as it always did, as if athleticism simmered on the back burner. Everything hurt: her mouth, her body, mostly her mind. If Jack Rose suddenly arrived and turned his amiability on her, she would fall apart.

She moved through her house, and as door after door sprang open, she felt the lightness of its construction as something good. In its flimsiness, she felt essential, snug innocence. A house without secrets, springing you lightly into room after room, that's what you got in a house built up off a shaved hill after World War II. Men, having hidden in foxholes and crawled dark jungles, did not want mystery in the home. No one wanted old dark staircases and squeaky floors and extra, unused rooms filling with cobwebs. Grown, she had not wanted an old river captain's home. She stood at the picture window. Anyone could look in, and the view was of perfect safety, revealing: I have no secrets. The most important thing was to live without secrets. Confession was the Catholic way. You could not live a healthy life with your insides knotted, holding in secrets. Confess, repent, trust. Then comes a flushing out. She could stand naked in her own home, and she did, shedding the clothes, the party-red bra last. She stood for a long time like that. Then she walked room to room again, letting the doors, those light, ridiculously light pine doors, spring from her hand and topple her into each room. This was the most Catholic of homes, unable to abide secrets.

When Jack Rose came home he found her naked in the kitchen. He blushed and frowned. He hooked his thumbs in his jeans pockets and slouched on one foot, knee pointing, Marcia thought, like the high-school girls who grew too fast and woke every day desperate in maturity.

"I'm not hurt or anything," he said. "Your dad's gone off to be fixed. The boys stayed. I wouldn't blame them for being embarrassed, seeing their dad fight like a kid." She nodded. He went into the living room and turned on the TV. He waited a few long minutes before coming back. She was at the counter now, naked at the counter, feeling the chrome strip crease her belly. She pushed hard against it.

"What's going on?" he said. "I mean, what are you doing, Marcia?"

"I'm getting ready to take a bath."

"Of course, go ahead." He was relieved. "I need a shower too. Heck, I'll wait."

"Jack," she said, and planted herself—oh, she was aware of how she planted herself before him and that her skin was nearly translucent in this kitchen light (new fluorescent fixture overhead), her belly like some big slice of pear, her breasts unintentionally alive, taut in memory. "Jack, look at me."

"I know, I know," he said. "Now go on. The paper boy or someone might come by. Go on, take your bath."

She shook her head. "Never mind. Go shower."

She listened until she heard the water running good. She would wait until Jack was soapy. Then she would go naked to the bathroom. Slip into the shower. He could close his eyes, and even so he would not be able to look away. He would experience the alarm of proximity, with no sandwich to peer over or TV to talk to. She would simply stand there with him, and if he turned away from her she would soap his back. He need not touch her. He certainly need not touch her. She did not believe the heaven of sex was their province, but she knew what she and Jack had done all these years. They had raised boys. Reason enough to team on. *Look at me. Some are born to have the prize kept out of hand. And they survive.* She would let gallons of water wash over her. This twosome shower would be just the beginning of a real purification. She would go into that shower and turn the water to hot, hot, hotter. She would steam out the weariness and shock and have a witness, a naked man witness, even if he stood with his eyes closed. She would go to pink and scalding standing next to a naked man witness who acted elephantine but at least was sturdy. He had shared her table, chairs, and bed all these years. At the very least, she would stand there with him and let the hot water run. She was just too Catholic to do it alone. And if her boys came home and found the red bra in a heap on the floor and heard the shower and their parents' voices, let them think what they might. No secrets. No, she was just too Catholic for phony, phony secrets. Life *is* confession. She wanted to purge. And she was just too Catholic to do it alone.

DELANA CUPPED Jackie Junior's head in her hands. "Take me to Burlington, sweetpea."

"I've only got a permit, Aunt Delana. I can only drive with my parents."

"If we come to a roadblock," she said, "just run it."

She followed her nephew's eager look around the dark yard. Men had clustered at their sleeping bags, and Opal, stationed inside alone while Joy took Sky to the hospital, had the house entirely ablaze, as if brightness alone would heal hearts and fingers.

"Grandpa always leaves the keys in the Caddy," her nephew said in a low voice meant to disguise his exultation.

Jackie Junior peeled out of the drive as soberly as possible, Delana holding Robin on her lap. He headed for the bridge, and then they were crossing the water; the boy wanted to follow Iowa's rougher river road up to Burlington. Delana squelched her impatience at the longer ride for the sake of letting Jackie Junior preen at the wheel.

"This is the first time I've crossed the state line driving," he said, and the car veered a bit as if acknowledging the glamour of frontiers. Then they rode up the river to the sound of clicking, mechanical things, Jackie Junior fiddling with the automatic windows, the wonderbar radio tuner, mirrors. Briefly, windshield wipers ran wild. And getting away from town, Jackie Junior remembered headlights. In the nighttime darkness the river was still, and if not for the few amber lights reflecting thin wavy points downward, no depth at all would be registered by the eye. The river could be a great plain of mud, life's secret black origin.

They rode up the river in silence, Delana thinking that this family who dared not put toes in the water nevertheless kept themselves in a frenzy by insisting on living right at its edge. In order to leave home, go anywhere, they were required to move back and forth, back and forth along its rim, behaving like people witnessing a drowning far beyond their reach, testifying again and again: It was far, far beyond my reach! *Penance*, Marcia had explained long ago. *They have to stay right there and do penance.*

"Uncle Johnny's cool. I guess he's pretty tough, huh."

"Yes," Delana answered, thinking now that Johnny's fortitude was beauty, not the hapless, guileless endurance she had seen for so long. His reserve and, now, its explosion—three small cracking sounds—seemed noble.

A great honking of horns caused Jackie Junior to yell, "Hey, cram it. What's the deal? Oh." He switched off the brights and the road seemed to lengthen.

"Uncle Johnny reminds me of *On the Waterfront*. Can you see what I mean?"

Delana was firm. "He's better than the movie."

"You don't think my brother looks like a young Marlon Brando, do you? That's what a teacher told him."

She laughed, looking up to the dark sky, where a sliver of moon showed through like a rip. Jackie Junior's brother at twelve looked like neither parent. His thick neck alone seemed a visitation on their frailties. Only his obvious sense of faith, even if it was entirely in himself, came from Marcia. Delana could not see anything of Jack Rose in him, save an appetite for meat. (In the yard she had heard them raving about bratwurst.) "Yes, now that you mention it, I do see the resemblance. Especially in the lips."

"Oh, man, don't tell him. Don't tell Mike I *asked* your opinion and got this, Aunt Delana."

"I promise." She pretended to think a long moment. The only car on the road now, they tunneled the wilderness, lights sweeping low along shelves of rock, as they twisted up the river. "You, of course, are more the Robert Redford type," she explained.

"Really?"

"It's obvious," she swore.

And Jackie Junior drove on smoothly, gallantly, maybe being a bit too confident trying out the one-handed steering, and she held back from saying, "This is not a cantering horse."

All of Burlington was asleep and bright; round streetlights shining on anyway seemed the glad chaperons of some invisible party. The very busy smell in the air made the town seem like a snapping lively place. She and Johnny were used to entering such tiny ports and immediately catching clues to the character. She had forgotten about Burlington's potato chip factory.

"Yeah, Sterzing's," Jackie Junior said, sniffing, window rolled down. "It's cool for a town to be known for potato chips. You really smell it at night. Next summer I'm going to work there."

While people slept, on went the busy production of potato chips. The small town's industry was based on the notion that you should picnic and dream. With the great aroma of boiling and frying potatoes lacing the air, surely life's rhymes and puzzles complete themselves as you sleep. Here was exactly the place to meet the banished Johnny. This was not St. Louis, with its great but dark-hearted beer brewing; this was not Cancer Alley—death to greenery and fragrance for miles around. Here was a land of munchables. She could almost see Johnny, large before a TV, hand deep in a rattling bag of chips. She could see him content like that. Her home stretch of river was a place of willow rushes and melon patches, corn carpeting and, here, potato frying. Johnny broke her father's fingers and then stepped away to a town that smelled exactly and permanently like a fair. She tried out the wonderbar and hummed along to an old pop instrumental. Surely life was perfect.

"The other neat thing they've got here is a munitions site. Kids in West Burlington say their school shakes when there's underground testing."

"That's an entirely different town," she told Jackie Junior.

On rough gravel they maneuvered down to the riverbank past the lock, which, darkened, looked like a deep cement swimming pool built into the river's side. The *Pat Furey*, disengaged from its load, was a pinpoint of light in line with all the dark shapes that, like strange animals, nodded and gurgled in their water berths, blithering their own river tales.

In true movie star form, Jackie Junior elaborately cleared his throat. "Well, I guess this is as far as I go. I can't help you past this point. You're on your own."

Delana got out and came around to his side of the car. "You won't have trouble getting back?"

"I'll speed. Maybe I'll get my first traffic ticket."

She set Robin down and took his head in her hands. She loudly kissed his cheek. "Be cool."

And they both knew he would post himself nearby. If she was to come flying off that barge in tears, Jackie Junior would thrill to gunning the pink Cadillac off and away, rescue mission complete. And if not, he would wait a considerate amount of time, drive home more splendored and sobered by the car than by sex, which, unlike the car, he already knew past its first handling and could more easily get again.

"Aunt Delana," he called out softly into the air, "what's nugatory?"

"It's a name for a nothing nobody."

"Then Grandpa's wrong. That's not Uncle Johnny. He's like a Paul Bunyan. You watch. Grandpa won't even hate him for what he did. My dad should have pulled something like that a long time ago."

Snake-charming her. The notes Johnny was blowing out of his harmonica were charms. This sound had a purpose. She stood a moment, letting all the fancied potato chip work add itself into the picture of Johnny sitting out in the black air, sitting beneath the shy moon. She thought of the morning after the first time they made love, Johnny stepping lightly down to tend his engines, she being contracted to crack three dozen eggs for omelets, perfuming her hair and her arms to disguise kitchen grease smell, but also the electricity of lovemaking. After one night together he said, "I love you." He did not say, "Give me your big toe; I'll die if I don't suck it." He did not say a thing she could trust, just pillow words that matched his marshmallow-sweet whiteness.

How could calm words mean anything? she had wondered. Now, as she listened to Johnny play the harmonica in the dark, her heart lowered in a dread thrill: she heard a certain jauntiness in the tone of the music and recognized it as a hobo call, the kind of self-reckoning riff that would come before journeying. Through music he told the world and himself who he was. Somewhere under a bridge, men might be nodding and smiling. *Come on.* And in the vagabond tune she heard something utterly free of women. Johnny was ready for hoboing. Because he was up here, the South beckoned. Give him thirty days down in Baywater, and he'll be itching to split. Urges led; logic did not even figure. But she recognized that Johnny knew himself. The river fed his heart. He had no steaming quarrel with it, or his soul, that newly acknowledged entity that put such burning questions in her mind. Their real difference had been there from the start: she was running, and John Melody was already free. His song tonight said he was going to move on along now, keep being free.

She came on board quietly, but he heard her and quit playing.

He sat unsurprised on the stern, turned from shore, that moon above like a crackpot smile. The strong metal smell of hull in still water smelled awful, like birth. She was exhausted, nauseated. Robin slept on. She felt her weariness, and Johnny's peace told everything, the Grand Canyon truth between them. She really wasn't going anywhere, and his contentment lay in motion.

"Tell them the engine's fixed," he said.

Johnny hardly looked like the person of the last few days. He sat in a big satisfied peace, water against the hull sounding like puppies lapping. It was as if breaking Sky's bones had melted down his own. He was soft now, damn boneless. Bring on the jailers: he was now one of those men who would hymn their way to the end. But until he spoke, she could not think exactly what to name the missing poison. "You're calm in a new way," she said. "You're serene."

"It's fear that's gone," he said. "I've wondered what I'd do with all this, and now I've done it. I'm not even the least bit afraid."

"Then neither am I. I'm too racked around. You fought my fight."

"I fought my own."

She sat by him and looked out on the water. Up the shore, the great shadow of a grain elevator made a crazy geometry of the sky, like long-legged cranes gawking and wading. The work, the hope, the cartoon of life was everywhere.

"Dovie would have loved you."

"For doing him in?"

"She loved hoboes. I've been remembering how she fed them off the back porch."

"Did they behave themselves? She found hoboes who behaved themselves?" Johnny looked out on the water as he spoke.

"They didn't bug her. They ate and ran. They hit the road, Jack," she said, and whacked her fist to palm.

"So they were good guests. Not like us. We're some kind of guests, Delana. They better keep us on the water or else clear out of sight." His strange, high giggle set her off.

"Keep us on ice!"

"Telephone us," Johnny said, nearly gagging on his joke, "but it's safer if you write."

"Oh, and if you've got eggs?" she added, with lust. "Quick go ahead and fry them all before we arrive. Otherwise, wham! we poach your face."

"And watch your hands," Johnny said, standing and offering his white palms, which she loved to taste. "My advice is to keep them in your pockets."

"Put on a baseball glove," she offered, hitting again, one hand against the other. The sting was good and lively.

"Baby, only a catcher's mitt is really safe. It doesn't even pretend to have fingers."

"Maybe they could just turn us on each other." Her voice was in a high crazy place.

"Maybe they have," said Johnny softly.

Their stinging eyes gave way to snorts, then honking laughs, then great sobbing heartiness. Delana was reduced to crumpling on the deck, which smelled all the more of dank river and work and the men she would miss. She was sure she would suffocate, Johnny too, like some great half-breaching whale racking his head up, down, up, down, as if feeding madly, gasping air. Such full-strength gut-rolling laughter was unknown to him; his big body tried to keep its rumbling, wild laughter somewhere inside. Finally a huge bellow expelled all of it. Lights flashed on shore. Jackie Junior was gone. Delana charged into a fresh round of laughing, which screeched out over the water like a loon's. Then they both sat panting, facing land.

When the sleepiness that comes after shock suddenly hit, Johnny did not ask for a thing, but she took him to her, saying, "We can be babies or wild things together. Anything." And even as she felt his mouth moving down, Sky's face loomed like a moon in her mind. She pressed Johnny harder. Marcia had said, *You suffer too easily. I only told you facts. The rest you did to yourself.*

The tiny real moon above had enough to do, reflecting what was what. She prayed against a full, fat moon of surprise, the face intruding. How distant, cold, rough, and forgettable, really, that moon. There is no man in it, no, no face, none to touch there, no one like your own, and again she thought of salt, salt-craving with its powerful source, the very taste of our skin. We need the taste, the taste of another's skin. To lose that is the sorrow. Here was offered the gentle substitute: in little parks at the boat landings along the river, in green shacks with mesh windows, you get deep-fried anything and the modest loser's pleasure of local-brand potato chips. Not everyone has love, but pretenders and losers share the need, to lick salt, to heighten and dream on the tasty miracle of skin. Johnny's palm was a meal in itself.

W HAT ARE YOU looking at?" Opal said.
           "Nothing. I'm not looking at a damn thing."
  "Or anyone, I hope. Slugger," she tried out on Cheramie,
turning fully from the sink. "You captained that brawl, all right."
  "Men are fools. You've said so yourself. Lay off now. We all
feel low."
  "Low as snakes."
  "Opal, lay off me. Think of Johnny and Del Mae. How's this
going to play out for them?" Both sisters were gone. *Two* women
at once fleeing his space; that was a record. He was a sleep-over
fool left at the father's house, and so afraid to ask for breakfast
it was nearly time for lunch.
  Joy came into the kitchen, clipping on an earring. "Sky is
mending very well. At this point his fingers don't hurt half as
much as his feelings."
  "Yes, bones knit," Opal said, throwing a huff toward Cheramie.
"It's the hearts that lose out to grief. Break a heart and you don't
know the length and size of its pain, the future spent on reper-
cussions. Go on, Cheramie, go do something with the boys.

They're positively witless now. I tell you, bingo never sounded so good. Joy's taking me to bingo here soon. I'm a teach her to win."

Bingo was strictly for women, and snakes did not always crawl on their bellies, but this was no time to bicker with Opal. Cheramie thought of a simpler time of life: as a kid paddling in the pirogue with his sister, down Bayou LaFourche. She took the job of keeping snakes out of the boat, snakes that wanted to drop down out of swamp trees, and boy, could she swat them straight out of the air. She was the first but certainly not the last female bundle of guts and strength to clobber him with wonder. Seems like in time they all did it to you. Time to move on now, get moving on.

"I've never played bingo," Joy said.

"That so?" he said. Move on, move on. They might be able to start upriver by nightfall and shed this bad skin. He had called the lock office. It turned out that Johnny'd made a mess of the engines, being all mixed up. But no one was going anywhere until Delana returned from that barge. Tuesday. They were full into a day of waiting, and except for women trotting off to noontime bingo, no one dared make a move.

B Y LATE AFTERNOON Wednesday, Delana had not returned from the barge. Marcia had called Sky's house five times, then she went over with fruit and cold cuts. There was a wilting and a shuffling around her father's home such as she had never known. Opal and Joy played gin without comment. Cheramie kept out of sight. The tent looked lost. Sky was shameless, posting a large photo of himself with his bandaged hand high. Beneath, a new motto: BROKEN FINGERS, NOT BROKEN PROMISES! She left quickly.

Back at home, the triumvirate stayed out of her way; they came home smelling of drive-in hamburgers and dove for the TV. The feeling of mute suspension was killing her. She thought again: I am just too Catholic to do this alone. The more witnesses, the better. I have a fund of religion, and now I'll draw on it.

At seven o'clock Marcia waved goodbye toward the TV and stepped out for Wednesday-night prayer group, wearing a dark shift and a scarf tied the way she had seen Audrey Hepburn do in her best movies. It did not matter that the Church had uncovered women's heads, nor that prayer group was not even

Mass. She was off to court, the perfect love widow. She did not wear her puka shells.

The church basement was a low-ceilinged room designated for anything save Mass. Pancake breakfasts were served here; the annual Catholic Girl Scout day of retreat and reckoning commenced with the high little windows cracked for air; altar boys who messed up the Mass were brought down here for scolding.

A bright, basement-blue paint had been applied to waist level. Overhead, pipes ran the length of the room. In winter they made sounds, ominous or encouraging, as prayer group progressed. Sometimes it would seem that pipe noise set the tone entirely, even going so far as to protest a speaker's argument. Speakers had been known to pause at the loudest hissing, break down and reverse themselves entirely. It was as if the pipes insisted truth upon them. In summer, the blurry-lipped sound of the box fans took up the mission. But this was mid-September. This was Ember Week, harvesttime, and the crisp autumn air outside allowed that any voice would be strong of its own accord. Marcia imagined her news spilling into the air as bright and pungent as the fresh blue paint.

Father Dan was dressed in open sport shirt, in deference to the fact that prayer group is mostly a lay person's province. Women far outnumbered the men, and no one remarked on Marcia's dress or the white cotton gloves she would remove for the linking of hands in prayer circle.

They got right to work. They went through the physical ailments first, praying for various family members not in attendance, though, annoyingly, Marcia could not shake from her mind the cheerleader-type hit by Tony Orlando and Dawn, "Tie a Yellow Ribbon Round the Old Oak Tree," which had been playing on the car radio. "Dawn," her sons had told her, was really two women, an incidental mystery that had kept her straining, despite herself, to hear twin female voices. And she somewhat regretted that she could not distinguish the two women's voices, could not hear clearly enough over the bomping music.

Next came the healing. The women who laid themselves out

on red floor mats had worn pantsuits in consideration of their
plans. People knelt by and prayed over the prostrated bodies.
The concentration of energy and belief zoomed the temperature
upward. Someone opened the window. Ankles, forehead, hands,
feet, and heart were touched. Unlike at Mass, here no crying
babies or sneezers diluted the experience.

Presently, those touched were helped up. Soft singing commenced.

Next came the period of silence.

The group pressed in close, and a man known for his ability
to detect worries and troubles people did not yet realize they
possessed now prodded, "Someone in the room feels sorrow."
Sighs. "Someone in the room aches." "Ummm," came replies.
"Someone in the room feels like cheated and cheater both. Someone in the room wants to say it, say it, witness now."

Of course he meant Marcia, with her ears tingling, and had
she lost her voice? The silence was unbearable. Her throat began
to burn as if the words themselves chose incineration over truth.
From out the window, the crickets began. A few, then more. She
concentrated on closing her eyes. First the idiot radio song had
invaded, and now came the crickets cheeping in the same rhythm.

The prayer group sat with eyes closed, holding hands, breathing in deeply. She tried to maintain a rhythm but felt short gasps
coming from her. Crickets had come right up to the windows,
the way they do in late autumn, as if demanding they be let in.
Coming in, we're coming in. They were tooting out this ridiculous song but mainly screaming of their own upcoming deaths.
The cricket voices wanted in. They were asking Marcia to let
them in. The sound of shower water, the scalding water she had
cleansed herself with at home, came to her. She remembered
exactly why she was here and what she must do. She must ignore
crickets and all of the world. She must purge.

A person here and there muttered a junior sin: pocketing
incorrect change, etc. Crickets were screaming. In the shower,
Jack had sudsed her breasts.

With her eyes tight, Marcia said, "I have committed adultery."

The words floated out to the cricket roar. She felt no weight in her mouth. She remembered, idiotically, reading that the tongue of a whale weighs one ton. The confessional words weighed nothing. A rush of light seemed to seal her eyes. She had never seen such a show behind her eyes. She remembered suddenly the rank of angels in descending order in heaven: seraphim, cherubim, thrones, dominations, virtues, powers, principalities, archangels, and the lowly sweet one, angel. She spoke joyously to them. Words tumbled, thrashed, raced from her head as if from her pores, from her scalp, and surely from her ears (that's why she couldn't hear herself). The roaring truth rushed from her in the singsong beat of Tony Orlando and Dawn.

She began wheezing. It felt as if cotton were stuffing up her throat now. Water was put to her lips. People bunched around, touching her face and hair. The leader's eyes roved on her, flecking. Father Dan gave her a look of devouring love. He said, "Finally, Marcia. You finally have the gift of tongues."

She had no voice at all. No tongue, or possibly the tongue of a whale. Nothing worked. She shook her head.

"You had something important to say to God. I witnessed. Bless you, Marcia Rose. Bless you, dear."

She grew even more dazed now. She drank a second glass of water. The crickets were barely peeping.

"You don't know what I said?" she ventured.

He smiled. Tongues, only the jubilant garble of speaking in tongues.

Adultery had brought her the gift of tongues? She accepted a cloth to wipe her forehead, hot and sweaty, she realized. She hid her face, her wonder. Cheramie had caused this, Cheramie. Sister, sister, sister! She wiped her mouth, secretly sucking the cloth, fearful of stray English whoops or embellishments. Torment fled before God's humor. Oh, it was wicked, God's sense of humor. Evidently the more drastic the wrong, the more dramatic God wished its deliverance: tongues testified to the enormity of her misdeed. What a glad conniver, God. She groped at and hugged her fellows, whose admiration was all over her, but their gentleness annoyed her now. She could howl at the moon. Father Dan should be starting up a bash. He's the one who revealed the truth that mattered now: Yes, Jesus danced at the Last Supper. Jesus was full of kick, full of it. And that's the picture she saw of Him now and wanted hanging in her house. Banish forever that other stuff, poor old son of God mooning up toward heaven. Every last picture had Jesus looking like a dog. But He was a man. He laughed and danced. She wanted a picture of Jesus cutting up with those apostles to lead her on from this day. Shed, once and for all, the drudge concocted by men. She smiled at her friends but did not trust herself to speak. Oh, how God loved a sinner, and she loved Him back, believing in the presence of greatness and how human, Lord, it is.

S UNFLOWERS WOULD NOT lift their heads, no matter what kind of spectacle went by. A sign to Delana of her true lack of influence. Here was a dopy, bobbing reminder of the powerlessness she could not shake on land or water. Let a full cornfield whip your legs on a windy fall day and you can feel the truth; put your feet right in river muck and there it is. She thanked the sunflowers.

Here by the roadside were elder flowers that people claim are magic; blue vervain that calm nerves; fat cattails and the gleam of poisonberries pointing home; great listening willows above and a whole field of tall, praying sunflowers, so heavily seeded now, so drugged with their own lifegiving, that they no longer stretched to the sun at all but stooped over pumpkins that preened at their base. Everything she approached winding down Great River Road on foot carrying a baby remained polite and unsurprised, a simple reminder that nature's is a hostess heart: the minute you are out of sight, its mild sympathy deserts you. (A person walking, what's the big deal next to all the other lushness? Divinity is evenly dispersed.) She scooped into her pockets some buckeyes freshly hatched out of their casings, shining like teak.

She had ridden over the bridge in an open truck crating to-matoes. At the juncture, her strong-armed driver insisted he would take her upriver or down, wherever she wanted, ". . . carrying that baby." She told him no, thanks. On the *Pat Furey*, Johnny languished, believing she had called home for a ride from the lock office, that his lying low was a courtesy to all. Today was her body's first day of real strength.

She trooped into a field of corn nearly sucked dry of color and juice, readying for harvest. And she went into the stand of sunflowers, with the no-faced pumpkins snugged beneath. Field mice scattered and crows ignored her entirely, black slick hunger riding their wings, eyes turned back and the yellow beaks stab-bing at crickets or anything, at moving things as big as them-selves. They rooted and rustled over the stalky ground. Squirrels were nut-crazy. Mad in it, they hopped around with their mouths open to scream size in order to carry the nuts. As likely as not they would run straight at a car. The day wore on and Delana walked through it. When she got thirsty she considered some dangling pears, womanly and sympathetic but still green. She bit into the firm, sour crab apples hanging low overhead and avoided stepping on the white mush of those downed on the road.

There was a world of time to fill, Johnny really leaving.

Though she had not made any plan at all, she had expected a different outcome, one in which people huddled before hur-ricane lamps and dealt from new decks of cards. Aces would fly in a world where she absolutely knew how to be. Though John-ny's wrist was wide and definite when he swung his arm, saying, "Thirty days, I'll only be thirty days there, then thirty days back here," its white relief against the dark night spelled the truth: We are spectacularly separate beings.

The mustiness in the air seemed to slow time. Twice, she waved down a car, rode for a few miles, then walked on toward home. When clouds covered the sun, the sweeping air chilled her. She hugged Robin tight, wrapped only in diaper and blanket, she concealed and stroked the baby's baldy head, Robin cooing and clutching, seeming to like the trek home. When the sun came out too hard, she dozed in shadow against a bale of hay.

By the time she made her way to the drive curving up onto lawn, the breezy sky looked like a burst feather pillow: mackerel clouds, as sailors would call it. She turned away from the house. Instead, she picked through the ancient path down to the river, panting hot, hearing a rush of sound in the weeds. The old dock was gone now, but a small clearing of gravelly sand had survived between riprap—the huge upturned slabs of rock that had always looked to her, from the river view, like shouts and warnings. A cattail bed thoroughly striped orange added a strange tropical flair.

Lack of attention had allowed the dock to give way piece by piece; it had floated down the river, soaking and splintering on a free ride to the ocean; and she thought how family history had done as much, that it is not so much the tide, rather the onlookers who determine the nature of what flows. She no longer believed that Sally went down to a trap of vine, was wreathed by weeds or a tire; rather she sped laughing, tumbling wild, whooping the bubbly whoop that fish would know as a joiner's call. Sally sped off in the current, a streak of silver that washed and washed and washed itself against the tide until it simply became the rushing water. Whatever flashed on the surface—you see that knife-silver flash now and then—understand that this is the soul: light from light sheening river water, the soul. And that's what held Dovie and Sky in the house overlooking the river; they exercised a kind of second sight sprung from faith. And chances are they did not even know it.

"I'm so hot I can't stand it," she told Robin.

She took off her sandals and bent down to wet her hands. "This is the real thing," she told her baby, dotting her forehead with water. She waded in, holding Robin. It wasn't too cold on her tired feet. She swished around, aware of the drag of her hem. Her dress was spotty, worn for the third day now. Thanks to a stash of diapers on the tow, she had kept Robin clean. She and Johnny had lived on potato chips from the lock office and tuna from the can. She went back to the bank and dropped her skirt, unbuttoned her blouse tossing Robin from arm to arm, and threw it down too. Now panties and bra. She laid Robin in this nest of mother-perfumed clothes. The bright sun on bare skin seemed like a pact in favor of intensity. Dull feeling would be a sin, always, the true sin. Let eyes and skin burn. Let the mind flame on. She waded in and felt her nerves jangle up to the temples; the water was not so warm after all. Sweat was drying already. She waded deeper, carefully now, through small rocks slippery with moss, which had some kind of erotic thrill to pass on up through the toes, some live wish of their own to impart, given this rare chance contact. She waded up to her breasts, which stiffened against the water, her nipples wary: now what? what is required? Up to her shoulders, then she dunked under completely. She squatted, braced with her hands, and held to the mossy rocks. She felt her bladder open and that warmth funnel down, raising a cloud. She blinked on a thick swirl of brown and held herself there. A glass of water taken from the river settles out one half mud every time. Her toes curled under, gripping rock and mud. Pressure gathered behind her eyes. The hurting lack of air was a poor imitation, a poor attempt at sympathy for the dead. The living cannot be or have the dead. Her choking lungs were furious, filled with the news. *Go away*, the river mocked. It sucked and swirled. *Crazy.* She came up senseless to all but her sobbing breaths.

Robin lay in a saucer of light, that perfect look of serenity such an appalling rebuke to any thought or action that did not feed its trust. The requirement was enormous, impossible, and would not go away. That look of bliss and need. That strange protected baby look which demands the right action, that says a baby's simple business is to haunt its mother.

"Don't count on it," she called. "Spook God, if anything. You're God's business too." Saying *God*, she half expected the

baby or someone or something to choke and writhe and call her
liar, ask, Where do you get off saying this? But only nature
politeness surrounded her, and the river heaved along. She
splashed water on herself and palmed the surface into waves.
She talked on, explaining to the baby on the bank how she could
not do it alone, how she had no plans or means, no way at all
to save a baby from whatever she needed saving from, "which
is plenty throughout your life." Whipping water, she talked on:
about a cut knee in childhood, the mouth burn from her first
pizza, on through to her abandonment to silence. Marcia had
said, *Let God pick up the slack.* The choice that defined the idea
of choice, acknowledged, brought a piercing kind of relief. Fear
had beaten her down to this choice. The fear of not being
enough, not being able to cover for the whole treacherous business of raising a girl. It had beaten her in like tin. Now, she said,
it won't. God help would not look like anything: no gift to un-
wrap, no telephone call or money sent, no magazine list of rights
and wrongs offered. Trust did not look fancy, but it would give
the whole show a little bit of a vacation quality, putting her an
inch away from tight, total, impossible responsibility, feet up.
Bandage the bloody knee, then let skin, air, and time do right
by it. Your part is done; keep out of the way. "No one does it
alone. I can't do it alone. The problem was, I was going to try."
Robin's little mouth was sucking air, just slightly sifting around
in its dream of perfect service, requesting milk, please.

Delana dried her hands on her clothes. She lifted her baby
and took her in the water.

"Just your piggies," she said, wading in, barely dabbing the
baby. Robin stuffed a marbly fist in her mouth. The crease of
her wrist looked like fortune, a sign of her adulthood assured:
baby skin already preparing to weather on, private in its knowledge. "Look at the water-skiing baby."

She bobbed Robin along over the surface. With her look of
complete weakling acceptance, the baby made only small twitching signs of surprise. Water streamed down Delana's breasts and
belly, colder now, the second time in. She held her baby out and

away from her, saw the bulging belly button, evidence forever of their link. She touched little toes to the water and then watched them curl under. Baby toenails were a brilliant shellacked pink. In Burlington, before heading back over the bridge to Illinois, she had polished these nails too tiny to hold more than a speck of pink. She had simply streaked paint over the entire ends of baby feet, the very teeny tips of baby-girl toes. Some little toes were actually stuck together, but this had seemed like a kind of protection, if a silly kind, and now she remembered an ancient photo of Sky that Dovie had flashed once as a taunt, threatening that she would place it on the mantel. Sky had roared good-naturedly, and yet, Delana remembered—she doing homework down on the rug, which smelled salty and rare, like winter soup, researching Abe Lincoln (whom Dovie Lincoln Walsh, lifelong Illinois resident, insisted on claiming for an ancestor)—her father had swiped that gilt frame from Dovie. It was little-boy Sky dressed uncomfortably—as a girl, thanks to the fears of an Irish grandmother, who in this manner had claimed salvation for him. Believing that the "little people" took boys and left weak change-lings behind, she posed Sky in long curls and a dress. To think that Sky had begun life as a little girl.

She hurried Robin out of the weeds, across Great River Road, and up the long driveway. Sky sat in a white wicker chair, fanning himself with his own cardboard likeness, which, judging from its jagged edges, must have been ripped from its stake. Words just tumbled out of her.

"She needs a checkup, Daddy. Don't pay any attention to the nail polish. Just make sure she's OK." She kissed the top of her daddy's head.

Sky scrambled to his feet and took Robin but seemed not to recognize her at all. He turned slowly, a man with a compass, looking out at the men in the yard, then back to her. "Do you mean it?"

Absolutely.

His glance at Joy sent her away and back in no time with instruments and a crisp white sheet. Robin was laid out on the table under that striped canvas intended to proclaim the light-hearted circus possibilities of a family reunion. The baby was laid out as if it was taken for granted that an outdoor exam was in order, a sort of picnic exam would commence. And apples were so ripe they seemed to hum on the branches.

Sky was breathless, fanning fast, the white victory of his band-aged hand raised up. "I've wanted to offer, but I didn't dare. I've hoped I could change a diaper or wipe her mouth, but this is just wonderful."

"By the time you get done checking her, she'll need a new diaper. You can take care of that too."

He used instruments and thumbs, and when he opened the baby's little mouth and used a tongue depressor tiny as a Popsicle stick, he spoke for her. "Ahhhhh." Out came the stethoscope. Catching her heartbeat brought a smile. Measuring foot size made him draw in breath; he kissed each sole, grinned at the shiny toes. Robin was all candy pink, perfectly still now. She had dozed off during the exam. Sky fawned over every inch of baby flesh, and he raised to Delana eyes that were familiar in their penetrating, stupefied dazzle. They thanked a miracle of compassion.

"Such a farrago," he cried.

Men nodded earnestly but looked at apples or anything rather than at bare baby bottom.

"She's perfect," Sky pronounced, his stethoscope bouncing off his chest as his voice rolled out.

"Of course she's perfect," Delana said. "I wanted you to know for sure."

"Dear, you look exhausted. Go rest now," Joy urged her. "Go on upstairs."

T HEY'VE BEEN NOTHING but mopes," Joy said. She paused with Delana's plate of muffins and jam at the kitchen window before setting it on the table.

Delana saw it too, a grim politeness on men's faces, bent necks scandalized: When will this land misery end?

"I'll be out of their hair by tomorrow."

"What are you going to do?" Joy had seated herself across the table and laid her hands out, fingers spread to show that no little pea or other surprise was hidden.

"Eat these muffins. Thanks."

"You're home, that's what's important. Silly that those broken fingers are what it took to really get you and your father together. He didn't know how to do it." Joy was shaking her head and smiling. "There's an election coming up, it's true, dear, but there's no contest. County medical examiner and the water commissioner have no opponents in this election. I don't suppose they ever do. Sky needed some hoopla to hide behind. He needed

a scheme, *signs*, something more than his poor old naked hope
to coax you home."

Delana's heart beat in her eyes as she digested this news: Sky
had elaborately orchestrated her homecoming. He had devised
a game in order that she win. "You mean people might black
out my teeth on some poster for nothing?"

"Pride and fear," Joy said. "It's amazing where they lead us."

To mad surrender, the lucky ones. Surely to the lowest place
of delusional dread, where there is nothing left to do but get
love right.

Outside, those men turned moon faces down toward the river
as Sky swashbuckled about. Delana saw schooling fish: the men
had lost track of what comes next and could not find direction.
As their pilot, she saw duty. It was up to her to break spells and
knit up the bones of uncertainty. It was time to act for them.
She yelled out the window, "Let's get out of here. Let's go test
that engine. I'll run us up to Rock Island and back quick, like
trip fishing. Come on, let's go now." The strength in her voice
felt like a gift, and every little thing, even the taste of the muffin,
seemed like more revelation.

She called Marcia from the kitchen phone and explained that
everyone would ride on the tug. "It'll be better than any sideshow.
I need you there."

She called Father Dan and asked, "Will you come? Will you
preside at a miracle?"

Men stepped lively, but Sky had folded himself into the lawn
chair again, hands turned up to the sun as if he had heard
nothing. Eyes, brows, mouth had all gone straight with relaxa-
tion. She went to him and took his good hand. It was warm and
soft, and his heart beat right there.

"Will you come, Daddy?"

"Now if," he replied, thrusting the rigged hand in the air and
considering it, "if your John fellow had gotten so upset due to
the shell game and nothing else, I'd say put the dog down. With
the rabid there's no choice but buckshot. But this was a case of

locking horns, yearling to ram. That I respect, though his method was crude, rude, and ostentatious. I'll come." His head gave a final snap as if to stop the word flow. Of course he wished his voice had not been wobbly.

She called to the crew, "Get dressed up, guys. It's an occasion." She remembered her first Thanksgiving with them, how they had come bowed and itchy to the table, wearing little plaid sweater vests and string ties, as if at Grandma's house, to eat the holiday meal she had served them after being on board only a few months. She fixed such an extravaganza the men had balked at actual feasting.

Now: action, finally. Relief. From upstairs she could hear their scramble. Closet doors were banged open and shut, and soon scents began to drift up the stairs. Men were getting slicked, tucked, and pressed. She flounced Robin into the eyelet gown Joy had shyly presented and dressed herself in an embroidered velvet blouse that tented down to her thighs; underneath, Johnny's pants, her essential uniform for the last piloting stint.

Finally people stood around, demented from effort and relief, on the great lawn overhanging the Mississippi River. Milling, soughing men. Joy's nurse hair was tricked into the same wave as Opal's, a sign of friendship for women of a certain type. They would be spotted as friends, that was the important thing, friends in a resort town: we're dressed up and we're friends. Just like teenagers, they had duplicated themselves for strength.

Marcia came wearing an elaborate getup, a matching skirt and jersey blouse in a black-and-white paisley design. Dangling from the knit top were black sequins the size of dimes. Scales, they moved and glinted in the light, looking like mourning and allure. Her face was as pink and sleepy as the baby's, coming in close, breathing mint on Delana.

"I've spoken in tongues," she said. "The events of my life shocked me into the gift. Delanie, I love you." She shot a haughty look at Cheramie, who grinned back. He was wearing his shirt with epaulets. "Starched, I suppose," Marcia scoffed, "by Joy."

She needed to make a statement, she said. Wouldn't it make

sense to look different, to look changed? "I'm considering a shag haircut."

Jackie Junior convinced his father and grandfather to let him drive the pink Caddy. Mike swore under his breath and chose to ride with his mother rather than sit with his older brother's smugness. Sky's red suspenders were set against a powder-blue shirt, his hair brushed into thick, wavy fluff. He carried that ripped sign, which Delana noted now bore a black, greasy mustache. Joy caught her eye and winked. Sky checked the carloads: Marcia's, his pink Caddy, Joy's nurse-beige station wagon. "A caravan to the caravansary!" he cried. Against the endless blue outdoors, Delana saw tinted clouds as sleek palominos racing north.

"Shall I walk the plank?" Johnny greeted them from a distance, on the second deck, but his voice calling down was so mild it leaked pleasure. His deer-colored hair shone like a surprise, like a rare sighting Delana would not forget.

Mike shoved past his brother to get up to Johnny. He imitated the stance, looked out on the water, down to the others coming on board.

"We're going upriver a ways, dumpling," Delana called up.

"I'll start the engines."

"OK, but let the sub take over. This is our ride."

Opal shook her finger at Johnny, and Joy smiled immensely. Johnny called, "Doctor, make yourself at home."

"Like you did? Ha!" Sky looked around, marshaling his support. People nodded. "Ha. Go on, go on, fellow. It's enough that I'm here."

Delana climbed to the wheelhouse with Cheramie. She took the controls, started a roar of engine, and maneuvered the *Pat Furey* in line to lock through. There was a slight scraping against one dank cement wall, a deep swallowing sound of water contained by concrete.

"Wait," Cheramie said. "The water's still filling. Don't blow it now, girl. Don't go losing your pilot's wits all in one day." But neither epaulets nor gruffness could cover his high discomfort, his running-off look.

"You've been using your wits lately, Captain?" she asked.

"I didn't mean her any harm." Cheramie spoke low and fast, waving his arm, making brushing motions to acknowledge the entire family of Walsh kin crowded close on the tiny hurricane deck around them, so could they keep this private? "She's a special lady. But I can't offer her anything."

"I don't know what you did to my sister—the works. She's suddenly speaking in tongues and credits you."

Cheramie blushed like mad.

And locking through, Delana swore she could feel the artificial water level rise right up to her heart. The tow lifted, the gates opened, and she was piloting through. She turned into the open channel and sought that three-hundred-sixty-degree bird's-eye view of river. Faces pressed to the glass, watching her steer. All her people ringed around, floating high as clouds, mouths set like choirboys'.

Deckhands stayed below. They were wary but slowly regaining themselves, breaking out in a croaky whoop here and there. They had taken up exaggerated positions of work and loitering, just as if they were in a movie, exactly recalling to Delana the first time she stepped on board. Seventeen, she had breezed along carrying a suitcase jumbled with hair bands, scarves, incense cones, Yardley cosmetics for the eyes, and white cotton panties. Under her left arm she had carried a large plastic radio. When she smiled at the men lined up on deck, it was funny the way their heads hung down. They seemed to be memorizing the slope of a T-strap against the bare browned foot coming closer and closer. No one looked as high as her shoulders, which even she at seventeen had understood to be smooth and obscure as ripening fruit.

Then she had looked behind her to see that Burlington was suddenly exotic and dim, with its swell of land up, up to that growth of houses on the bluffs. Across the river, where the state of Illinois wanted to glare at her sins, past and future, a wondrous mist had descended. And the old metal expansion bridge was opened –it seemed generously so—to let river traffic through, to herald escape. What felt like a vicious nuisance from high on the bridge when you were stalled in traffic was revealed as great generosity from down on the water. The river claimed the main part of earth; land made some kind of pie crust.

They were out in the channel, her family claiming the hurricane deck, this highest of river perches. The boys stayed close to Johnny, exclaiming, pointing to and identifying oddly angled houses. See all the broccoli-bunched trees, the little islands, dark mud river flowing high to the bank and textured like elephant skin, sluggish gray, striated with the creases, sags, and muscle of great age.

The priest looked on from the perspective of one who traffics in uncontested bliss. He turned his face to the sun, and Delana swore she could see the sun glance back, then move on up to settle smartly on his bald head. Robin in a bonnet was as droopy as a sunflower and deep in the dreams of flowers.

Jack Rose strained to look in the wheelhouse at the radar screen, sensing a game, a puzzle. Marcia and Sky had moved together to a corner rail and now stood close, looking down on the water. Delana cut the engines and, giving Cheramie the controls, came out on deck feeling like a concessionaire to freedom. She let stillness announce their deliverance.

"We're not where I think we are," Marcia cried. "We're not *there*, are we?"

Sky was bunched against the rail. "Oh," he said. "Oh, say. Well, for crying out loud . . . I recognize this place." Silence grew as the water stopped its lapping in favor of perfect patience. People moved past each other, clothes whispering, as they checked out the view.

"How can I look?" Marcia cried. "Sally awoke to eternal life down there and that's all I want to remember about that." But she was all eyes, scanning the water.

Sky's head had sunk into his neck like a turtle's. "From up

here the water is very different. That must be the case. It's so clear." He was dreamy yet agitated like a boy. "No, I believe it's changed entirely. They fiddle with this river. That Army Corps of Engineers is crazy about changing rivers. That's all they do. Here's a different river, all right. The Mississippi," he called out loudly, to anyone, "now, it really used to be something, the mighty Mississipp."

"Daddy, it's the same," Delana said. "Exactly the same water."

"Clear," he insisted, holding on to that rail. In fact, the surface looked absolutely the opposite, all crisscrossed and sluggish and opaque, so durably old. And the dark-tea aroma of willows floated to Delana, even though lemon leaves were petaling the banks and branches were drained of sap. And no girls were calling out. Everything was calm.

Sky licked a finger and appeared to calculate wind direction. His good hand fidgeted over the rail, and several times he seemed on the verge of speaking, when only a low rumble came out, very much like the river's deep-trebling fish, the drum. He was speaking down to the water, but the words had trouble forming from sound. They ran together.

"I can't suppose that you realize this, Delana, but when Sally drowned, Joy and I weren't exactly together yet. Nothing was set."

"It's OK, Daddy. Whatever."

"Your mother turned away and I don't blame her. Dovie sort of needed a villain. I understood. I think there was some dignity, oh, some sense to it, if someone could take blame. Joy's name hung in the air. I don't know, but things progressed. Still, I never stopped loving your mother."

"Daddy, I don't need to hear this. I'm just fine." She did not fear his confession and so did not need it. He had concocted an elaborate shield, a way in which to call her home. The tiny thrill of seeing the armor crack was enough. Now facts would add nothing.

"I love Joy very much." Squeezing his good fingers on the rail was a perfect act of earnestness. "I need you to know that."

"That's what counts now," she assured him.

From farther down the bow, Opal's voice rang out as a general warning or call to arms. "A man alone at the end is pitiful." As if in response, Johnny's animal hair flashed, was gone from sight.

Sky kept hanging on the rail, bug-eyeing the water. "I can't get over it. You really know how to run this . . . machine. You *drove* us here. You know, from the time you were a little girl, you've been more fearless than you let yourself know. It's your fearlessness that has always thrown me. You've been fearless, not reckless, as it would look to others. What can a father do in the face of that kind of strength but just love it, love it madly and, well, creep away? Men frighten damn easily. I didn't know what else to do when—"

"Thank you," she cut in, sensing he was ready to spill a hundred words she did not want to hear or even wish to understand. She believed now that there were versions, details, perspectives, remoldings of the story, whatever the story, different from her own idea of how they had lived together and apart as father and daughter, how the world spins: five ways at once; and that belief was enough now, a victory over memory's dark heart. Shine the light, shine on.

"Daddy, there's more room down below," she said, and touched him. "Let's go down with the deckhands."

Cheramie nodded as the family left, Marcia last, who had been standing purposely in profile, chin up and one arm dramatic on the rail. The sequins dangled and shone like fish lures. And she looked more bound to the river than she could know, Delana thought. Marcia was religiously bound to that river.

With everyone gathered below, the priest stepped out of the galley, carrying the silver instruments of baptism. "For administering the sacrament," he announced, "I'll refer to the baby by using a saint's name, of course. I'll call her Rufina."

"Honey . . . ?" Johnny hurried down from hiding above.

"What's going on?" A touch of his old worried self was thrilling to Delana. "What's the deal?" he demanded.

"Baptism, dumpling."

"You're making her Catholic?"

"It's a whiff of safety, kind of like insurance."

Marcia said, "First you brought tongues, now baptism. Little sister, your faith kills me. It always has. Rufina!"

Father Dan murmured, "The true home of beauty is the soul."

"I'm not even gone and she's Catholic?" Johnny wondered, hands raised. "What else will you do with her? How else will she change?"

"We're just going to acknowledge her soul here for a minute. It's like shaking dice before the roll. She'll have more luck on her side," she reasoned. "Just think of it like that. Anyway, it can't hurt her. How can baptism hurt?"

The priest cleared his throat. Marcia restrained him with a hand on his arm, agreeing: "So beautifully said."

"But Catholic," Johnny said. "That's a big deal."

"We want it to count," she explained. "A big-deal baptism is what we want, one with before and after stories, or why do it? Before, there's Limbo; afterwards, there's luck. Maybe it's a courtesy to God. We're saying thank you, that we know He brought her and she's holy and all that." She tried to speak nonchalantly, but it was hard to explain even to herself, and she wished Marcia would quit praying "Holy Mother" and "Amen" behind her.

"Johnny, I'm twenty-four years old, and I don't know everything. I'm tired of figuring things out. Let her grow up and turn Hindu."

"Grow up . . ." Johnny's voice trailed, eyes gone starry before the fathomless years ahead. A deer with no trail, that's what Delana saw. A glimmer of hope.

"Everybody's doing fine here, just fine," Cheramie exclaimed, placing a hand on Johnny's shoulder. Reaching high caused an epaulet to scrunch against his ear. Marcia snorted at the sight.

Johnny opened his big palms and slumped toward the rail, his sign of consent.

It took about a minute's worth of priest-chanted Latin words and a dab of holy water to register the soul. People glanced at Robin-Rufina now as if she might fly. She did not howl. Marcia took her in her arms and hugged and kissed. Cheramie spoke singsong to the baby: "I'm baptized too. We've got this in common," and grabbed an opportunity right under Father Dan's nose to duck and kiss the baby by way of pressing his head to Marcia's breast. She gasped.

Mike cuffed the air in front of Johnny. "Let's go up on the top deck again, Uncle Johnny." The father of a baptized baby girl, he seemed glad of the escape, Delana noted with a heart full of regret.

"She threw you in from this top deck?" Mike whispered to Johnny. "You were up this high when she pushed you?"

Johnny admitted, "That's right." He spat over the rail. "She pushed me in the river."

"From right up here?"

"I was sitting on the rail."

"You should've been standing. You could've really flown. Watch me."

"Hey, Mikey!" Johnny yelled.

People below heard the cry and looked up to see Mike, stripped down to Jockey shorts, poised on the rail, his arms in a great wingspan, the delicate lifting of his heels like the talisman of rapture. Little Mike the diver lofted from the top railing out, out slowly to hover like a bird of prey over the water, his apple calves and the deep well of his back full of shadow and light. Marcia screamed, "Jesus!"

Her boy jackknifed. His back was a table; arms and legs snapped under to meet each other. Then he was a turbo machine, twisting, twisting down, and without a splash he was under the water.

Marcia crumpled against Father Dan.

But Mike surfaced, a pup seal, smooth face streaming water,

pug nose sniffing the air. He opened his eyes and grinned. Delana was the first to clap. "Cool!" yelled Jackie Junior, in a flash stripped down and tumbling over the rail. And forgetting Father Dan, women, and pride, deckhands were suddenly stripped down to their undershorts too. One by one they jumped, frog-dived, bombed, and flew into the water as if fleeing Pompeii. They screamed against its chill, thrashed water and each other. Their white limbs in the gray river waved like flags of mercy. Mike was backfloating off the bow, grinning up at the sky. Cher-amie and Johnny watched, then went down to the low deck and threw out preservers and ropes; and men came on board stream-ing water, bullish as gar, slapping their chests and each other, proud of their shuddering hard-ons, the sight of which, Delana noted, Marcia was devouring: happiness galore peeked straight out of plaid boxers. Manhood regained by the river. And they were moving toward Delana now with that look of the first hol-iday dinner.

Men had closed their eyes and spat and got wishful against their better judgment when she appeared on deck and all over, in the mess, in the engine room, tapping on bunk doors, a steno-grapher's notebook in hand, asking, "What can't you live with-out?" She had accused, more than asked. "Tell me what you're dying to eat on Thanksgiving Day, and I'll fix it." She had stunned them, set a table with fan-tailed turkey decorations riding a length of white linen cloth. Out came dish after dish: the green-bean casserole with mushroom soup and hidden onion rings; pickles, both sweet and dill; two colors of olives; fat turkeys, one with sage and celery dressing, the other stuffed with sausage and pepper; mashed potatoes so white and stiff-peaked as to make the younger men cry out and look away. It took Cheramie plung-ing a spoon into the mound of potatoes to remind them that their job was to lick and devour that white purity. After reeling through that, heads down, grunting and exclaiming, make way for the pies. Berry with perfect latticework, one carried high in each girl hand. Pumpkin smooth as silk. They got vanilla ice cream, melted just right. Love, wasn't it pure love, safe love, she asked later, that gave her the eight-handed capacity to fix the grand meal? As if she had been frenzied in a lover's arms those twelve steady hours of preparation, she fell asleep all fragrant, with curls on her brow, a tune in her head. Out in the mess, she learned, Johnny and Cheramie took the wishbone and would not wait until it was dry. They broke it, and Johnny got the long half. He won, but deckhands said he had twisted too hard. Later, they said he had wanted it so bad, you had to wonder how it might turn out, the wish that would surely come true.

Now it was goodbye. She went to the nearest shivering, back-slapping man and kissed him. First she kissed on the cheek, then lightly on his lips. As she squeezed his bare shoulder the others crowded in. She kissed them all: wet mustachioed lips, smoke-flavored lips, sour lips, lips that were chapped; men with flut-tering eyes and men whose eyes slung low with hope, hurt, and love. One man's knees helplessly jabbed her thigh. She kissed, and men kissed back.

Marcia gasped. "She'll always outdo me. She can't help but be wild." She hurried her boys away, Father Dan and Cheramie following. One by one, all the kissed men trailed away too, some walking backward, their grins and whole loping lives already fading from, lost to Delana's view. Someone put the baby in her arms.

Opal and Joy closed in on her. "Now it's really goodbye," she told them. "Johnny's leaving."

Joy was merry. "Let him think it. It's important that he thinks so."

"Lord, let him strut." Opal demonstrated, hip jerking.

When they laughed, the women's voices seemed to come slid-ing into Delana's mind like the swing of a hammock posted to oaks, riding on breeze and comfort. Flute sounds of laughter told the firm truth of how it goes on land, which rhythms count. It was easy to believe them in a dumb, quiet way, to believe that Johnny would one day show up on the back step like any hobo come for his plate of eggs. Although she will have been waiting for this, it is not as if every time she steps out the door and catches the smell of blackberry ooze or a snowflake on her tongue she will be part of that tricked doom, waiting for the man. Huh-uh. When he shows, she will ask no questions. She will serve him there, and while he eats she will scrutinize him for signs of change, some new-world ways. Has he after all, she'll discover, been hanging out in small-town taverns down the river, where men drink Skag beer out of buckets? She will watch; be an Opal; command him, "Eat up." In his own time, one day the river will just run dry on him, wash him up to her. *Please, God.*

Two words, a world. Now she had prayed, and her body seemed to hum with some kind of aftereffect. *Please, God* was so simple, who but the most dumb desperate would trust this as high prayer?

Johnny was motioning to her without speaking, pointing up ahead. Cradling Robin, she moved to him on the middle deck, where he would sleep alone tonight. Riverman, he had spotted a dusty cloud way up ahead as something live, and he was lost to his own heart. In a jiffy, it was coming in low along the river, wavering, breaking, and gleaming gold in Johnny's big blue eyes. "Hey, Delana, remember my dream coming upriver? All I knew was black and orange, remember? Well, here we are in it. Here's the living color."

The monarch butterflies were fast in migration, now streaking fire overhead. As they came on flicking color, people shouted and cheered. It was a rare blaze splitting the sky, glistening and blurring in Delana's moist eyes, and she remembered to believe absolutely in the calm order that drives the wild flight: Every year hordes of monarchs choose to fly the exact river path, follow every loop and bend as if enjoying a double shunning of land. And it is not unusual for a great sweep of monarchs to hitch a ride on a southbound tow. Cotillion girls on the river, they flutter on to light in the high hills of Mexico in numbers that torch the sky for miles. Their fire, their intense vibration, makes a song. They would seem to be home to roost for good. They would seem to cherish and need only this massing. But inevitably, in a different season, they make their way north along the river, ravenous for milkweed, which is poison to every other living thing. Pure need drives them back. Now the small creatures are flying south with a vengeance, and Johnny with his upturned, likewise coppery head responds naturally to the call of their flight. And there he is, no matter what, borne on travelers' wind. She must believe that the dream was meant to instruct him in the trueheart ways, that out there on his own journey the deep-down order of passion will seize and guide Johnny right. She thinks to spit fast overhead and—quick—make a wish.